Blood
Ties

Richard Pitman & Joe McNally

By the same authors

Warned Off
Hunted
Running Scared
The Third Degree
For Your Sins
Bet Your Life

Authors' note

This is a work of fiction. Names characters, places and incidents are either a work of the imagination of the authors or are used fictitiously, and any resemblance to actual persons, living or dead, business establishments, events or locales is entirely coincidental.

ONE

In the dying days of the old jump season, after the toughest five months since my comeback, I got a phone call.

'Malloy?'

'Yes.' I didn't recognize him.

'You don't know me, but you'll get to know my voice.'

I hoped not. It had a sniggering, know-it-all tone. I said nothing.

He said, 'You're riding right through the summer?'

'Who's asking?'

'Just listen. You're riding through the summer.' No longer a question.

'Maybe.'

'No maybe. You will be.'

Stern. Commanding. Certain. I felt a nervous ripple in my gut.

He said, 'Over the next few months I'm going to call you a few times - probably on the evening before you ride something fancied. I'll give you riding instructions and you'll stick to them.'

Trainers gave riding instructions, and very occasionally, owners would; complete strangers were a new one on me. But I held my tongue.

'You listening, Malloy?'

'Keep talking.'

'I know something about you. You do what you're told or I give it to Kerman.'

1

Jean Kerman was a ruthless tabloid journalist specializing in dirt digging in sport - she'd ruined at least a dozen careers.

I'd been shamed and scorned enough in my life. There was only one thing left, one secret, and I said a brief intense prayer against his knowing it.

He spoke again.

He didn't know it.

The sudden relief cushioned the shock of what he did say. I stayed silent, trying to gather my thoughts.

He said: 'You've gone all quiet and shy, Malloy.'

'Run it past me again.'

'Don't mess me around! You heard.'

'I just want to be sure I've got everything right.'

There was a pause then he repeated everything in an impatient monotone, like a teacher with a backward kid. 'You and Martin Corish are conning breeders. Town Crier isn't covering the mares you say he is. You're using a cheap ringer and charging the full fee. Now, if that gets out, do I need to tell you how it will affect your little business, not to mention your career?'

A year ago, I'd invested everything I had in becoming equal partner with Martin Corish in the stud he had started. I hadn't a clue what this guy was talking about, but he sounded very convincing. I said, 'I think we'd better meet.'

'I think you'd better get your cheating boots on. I'll be in touch.'

'Listen…'

He hung up.

I rang Martin. His secretary-cum-groom was evasive, defensive. She told me he wasn't around.

'When will he be around?'

'Emmm. I'm not really sure.'

'Where is he?'

'Maybe if you call this evening.'

'*Where is he?*'

'I'm sorry Mister Malloy, I can't say.'

'Look, don't make me drive all the way down there.'

'I'm sorry. I'm just to say he's uncontactable. That's what I was told.'

'Where's Caroline?'

'Mrs Corish isn't well. She's lying down.' The girl was agitated, her voice rising. It was unfair to take out my frustrations on her. There was obviously something wrong at the stud. I told her I'd see her in an hour, clicked the answerphone on, grabbed my jacket and pointed the car toward Wiltshire.

I'd been sucked into enough whirlpools in recent years to sense another one when it was still some way off. I was already feeling the pull of its vortex.

TWO

It was close to nightfall when I reached the farm. As I swung the heavy wooden gate open, insects hummed in the greenery and swarmed around the headlights that illuminated the sign reading: THIS GATE MUST BE KEPT CLOSED AT ALL TIMES. It wasn't unusual for a horse to get loose somewhere on the enclosed three hundred acres. If you could keep them off the roads, you stood a good chance of getting them back unharmed.

Martin Corish and his wife lived in a big farmhouse close to the stable yard. The house was unlit. I pulled in by the low wall and stepped out into the deepening dusk. The outlines of mares and their foals in the nearby paddock merged into single shapes. No dogs barked.

Something was wrong.

I stood, listening. Nothing but the sounds and smells of a warm June night in the country. Insects. Musky flower scents. Quiet whickering from horses. Away across the fields, the eerie cry of a vixen.

I walked into the yard. A phone rang. After half a dozen rings, a light came on inside the office in the corner and glowed yellow through the barred window. Along with the moths and their brethren, I moved quietly toward it.

The top part of the uncurtained window was open. I listened to Corish's secretary. She sounded much more aggressive with this caller than she'd been with me an hour and a half ago.

'*When*? Soon's not good enough. It's been "soon" for the past nine months! Oh, it's different all right! It's worse!'

She was shouting. The other party must have told her to cool down.

'Why should I? I won't wake Caroline! She's out of her head as usual and I can see why she does it! Why should I? Give me one good reason!'

It had to be Corish on the other end and he must have given her a few good reasons, because she shut up and when she spoke again, all the fire had gone out of her.

'But what do I tell Eddie Malloy? But what if he *does* turn up, Martin, what do I tell him?'

Melodramatic by nature, I was tempted to burst in and grab the phone so he could tell me personally, but I'd learn more by staying put.

She said, 'When? Where? What if he asks for your number? Martin! Martin!'

He must have hung up. The girl did the same then worked through every swear word she knew in a steady monotone, as though reciting tables at school.

I went in. She was sprawled in a swivel chair, long red hair unkempt, blue eyes tired and puffy. She gasped and reached toward her groin, pulling frantically at the open zip on her tight beige jodhpurs, trying at the same time to get to her feet and turn her back on me.

In a TV sitcom, it might have looked funny, but I felt an instant pang of regret and shame, almost as though I'd assaulted her. I didn't even manage to redeem myself by catching her as she collapsed in a dead faint. On the way down, her head smacked against a metal filing cabinet.

By the time I was on my knees beside her, she was already bleeding.

The wound was on her scalp and not dangerously deep. Blood trickled across her temple, forming a pool in her ear. Her pulse was steady, her breathing even.

Making a pillow of my jacket, I gently raised her head and eased the makeshift cushion underneath. In the corner of the office was a small sink. As I got up to fetch a wet cloth, I noticed her white swollen belly exposed by the gaping fly of her jodhpurs. Red pubic hair curled over the pink waistband of her pants. Looking around for something to cover her, I scooped a purple fleecy jacket from the swivel chair and laid it on her midriff.

I checked her pulse again, wondering whether I should call an ambulance when her eyes opened and tried to focus on me. I moved aside, not wanting to seem threateningly close. I sat on the chair. Her face remained calm. She reached up to feel her head.

'Fiona, are you all right?' I asked.

She looked at the sticky blood on her fingers.

'Just a flesh wound,' I said.

Puzzled, she stared at me. 'You hit your head on the cabinet,' I explained. 'My fault for barging in like that and scaring you. I'm sorry.'

She made to get up. I was caught between helping her and saving her embarrassment as the jacket covering her bare middle slipped. She grabbed at it. I stood up. 'I've got a first-aid kit in the car - won't be a minute,' I said, and went out into the cool darkness.

When I returned, she was sitting at the desk sipping water from a cracked cup and sobbing quietly. I said, 'Fiona, look, I'm sorry for scaring you like that. I didn't mean to.'

She wiped at her eyes with the bloodstained cloth I'd been using. Opening the first-aid box, I handed her a dry pad. She took it and carried on wiping.

'Got some painkillers here,' I offered.

She raised a hand, pushing them away.

I spent the next fifteen minutes asking questions. Where was Martin Corish? Where was the rest of the staff? Who was tending the horses? I told her I'd overheard her telephone conversation - where had he called her from?

I thought it best not to question her about the stallions, Town Crier especially. Martin Corish was the man with the answers, but if Fiona knew his whereabouts, she wasn't saying. She stayed silent, dabbing at the now dry wound and staring at the desk. Her Snoopy watch read eleven o'clock when I gave up.

Footfalls deliberately heavy on the cobbles, I crossed the moonlit yard, wanting to convince Fiona I wasn't coming back. I started the car, drove a few hundred yards then pulled in, and ran back.

Outside the office once again, I listened for the frantic return call to Corish, but all was silent. Either she'd made it after I'd left or she genuinely didn't know where he was.

I waited twenty minutes. Nothing.

I was tempted to visit Town Crier's box. I knew the horse well, and reckoned it would take a pretty good ringer to fool me. But like a number of stallions, he could be unfriendly toward humans; particularly, I suspected, those who intrude in the hours of darkness. I decided to leave it till next morning.

With no clouds to blanket the day's heat, it was quickly growing cold. I returned to the car, wondering where to spend the night.

The nearest hotel that would let me in this late was about fifteen miles east. But my credit card was swipe-weary and battle scarred. Basic guesthouses would already be locked up and I had no friends in the vicinity.

I sat looking through the windscreen at the stars, knowing the overnight sleeping arrangements were a choice between kipping in the car or seeking a warm corner in Corish's hay barn. The prospect brought a smile to my face as I remembered past conversations with people who envied the glamorous life of a professional jockey.

Last season's glamour for me had included a virus-stricken stable, three periods of suspension for 'irresponsible' riding, and a series of damaging falls, leaving me with a fractured wrist, a broken collarbone and, most recently, four smashed ribs and a punctured lung. Not to mention severely dented confidence and a badly bruised bank account.

Just when I thought it was safe to get back in the saddle, this had to happen. The partnership with Martin Corish was the only investment I'd ever made. No jockey rides forever and the stud was supposed to provide me with some security when I hung up my boots, a notion I'd entertained often lately. I sighed, fighting off self-pity.

I'd find a lay-by and get what sleep I could before returning in the morning. The ignition fired and the buttons on my mobile phone lit up as it beeped into life. Before setting off, I went through the motions of ringing home to my answerphone, though it had been a while since there'd been any worthwhile messages on it.

Tonight there was one and it drew me home at speed.

THREE

I reached the flat at 2 a.m. and stopped barely long enough for tea and a sandwich. I replayed the message again: 'Eddie, Barney Dolan. If you get this in time there's a winner waiting for you tomorrow, er, that's Wednesday. I heard you passed the doctor and thought I'd give you a winner. The bad news is it's up at Perth and it's in the two o'clock. I'll hold off till nine in the morning to hear from you.'

Good old Barney. He was one of a handful of trainers I rode for when it was mutually convenient. My retainer was with Broga Cates, whose flat I was sitting in now. Broga owned a string of twenty-two trained by Charles Tunney, whose Shropshire yard my flat overlooked. Broga paid me a reasonable retainer to ride his horses, and when the stable had no runners, I was free to take rides elsewhere.

Many of our horses had been down with a virus last season and we'd had just eleven winners - a disastrous total that had shaken Charles's confidence. He'd closed the yard for the normal summer break, and buggered off to Alaska for a month's holiday, leaving his secretary to feed the dogs and keep things ticking over.

Until this season, jump racing had always stopped for two months in the summer, but the British Horseracing Board had decided to grant a few fixtures to courses wanting to hold meetings during the summer. Most of the top jockeys had said they wouldn't ride at these meetings; eight weeks was little enough break from the daily grind of driving, dieting and injuries.

I could have done with the holiday - at least my battered body could have - but my bank balance dictated otherwise. So, after an hour's restless sleep, I left rural Shropshire in the early hours of Wednesday morning for the long drive to Perth, a course lying so far north it never risked racing during the winter months.

Every minute on the road took me farther from where I'd planned to be at first light, the Corish Stud.

My thoughts returned to the mystery caller. If my partner was doing what was claimed, how had the guy found out? And how had he discovered my involvement with Martin Corish? We'd kept it quiet. And what was the caller's link with Jean Kerman, the tabloid hack with the poisonous pen?

I'd count myself lucky to have twenty rides through summer, but that would be twenty opportunities for the blackmailer to get at me. And it was unlikely he'd stop at summer's end. What would I do if he asked me to ride a bent race?

I didn't know.

I'd never pulled a horse. Ethics aside, my belief is that as soon as someone gets something on you, you're prisoner for life. Even one guilty little secret will stay fixed to you like a choke-chain - a very long chain maybe, but one that would snap you backward and haul you in to face either justice or another demand.

As dawn lit the hills of the Scottish borders, I was no nearer a solution. The choices were: find Corish and get the truth or track down the blackmailer and deal with him. Even if Corish was guilty, I'd still have to trace the blackmailer. I had to face the fact that this Perth ride might have to be my last until I caught this bastard.

The only way to stay clean was to make sure the blackmailer had no leverage. If I wasn't riding, he couldn't influence my performance.

But how many rides could I refuse before trainers stopped asking me?

It looked like my first decision in the battle, to go north for one ride, was the wrong one. The time would have been better spent trying to find Martin Corish, but I was committed now and at 8.15, I rang Barney Dolan and told him I'd be at Perth by 11.

'Good man, Eddie. You won't regret it.'

I had a very strong feeling that I would.

FOUR

Perth Racecourse lies in the fertile grounds of Scone Palace on the banks of the River Tay. Early mist rose from the water on this hot morning. I was first into the jockeys' room and sat wearily on the varnished bench, dropping my kitbag and saddle at my feet. I hadn't been here in almost eight years.

It was quiet inside the antiquated wood-paneled room. Faint sounds of birdsong came through the open window, and I laid back my head and thought of the days when being in a room like this had brought me only pleasure. Every new changing room, every new course, had been a wondrous adventure to a wide-eyed and breathless teenager, drinking in the history of these old places, sitting on every inch of every bench so I could be sure to have sat where all the champions had sat before me. That teenager was long gone. It seemed a lifetime ago.

The sweet pine-scented air had come from an aerosol. Motes hung in the long sunbeam that warmed my legs. I must have dozed.

I woke feeling stiff. Sitting opposite me, crunching crispbread and sipping black tea, was Keith Allardyce, who'd been born in Stirling, 'two doors down from Willie Carson' as he always said. Cheeks full of soggy crispbread, he still managed a wide smile as I stretched awake.

'Tired?'

'It's all right for you locals. Probably just fell out of bed ten minutes ago. I bet you've even had time for a plate of fried haggis before leaving home.'

'Haggis season doesn't start till August. We're not allowed to shoot them till then.'

'Contact the British Horseracing Board,' I said. 'They'll get it brought forward.'

Keith swallowed. His smile widened and we chatted about what had been happening while I'd been laid up these last five weeks. The northern racing fraternity moved in their own separate world from the rest of the UK, so I picked up some new gossip.

'Have you got a paper?' I asked.

Keith hauled a rolled up copy of *The Sporting Life* from his bag and threw it to me.

'How many in the first?' I asked as I opened it.

'A few, I think. Your old buddy's got a ride, you'll be pleased to know.'

I looked at him.

'Tranter.'

'Oh, Tranter the Ranter, that's all I need!'

Billy Tranter didn't like me. His antics had earned me two suspensions last season just for trying to keep him at a safe distance during races. The animosity stemmed from a successful objection I'd made to a winner he rode at Newbury in November. Nothing personal on my part - Tranter's tiring horse had leant on mine on the run-in; it was arguable whether or not it affected the result, but I owed it to the owner and trainer to try an objection and it was upheld.

Tranter the Ranter lived up to his nickname that day.

Since then he'd had a go at me numerous times during races, using various dirty tricks. I'd responded accordingly in the hope he'd soon tire of it and lose the taste for revenge, but all it did was increase his appetite. My fuse burns slowly these days but eventually, for practical reasons, I'd laid him out flat and stone cold on the weighing-room floor at Bangor.

Next time we rode against each other, he tried to put me through the wing of a fence. Grassing on colleagues isn't done, but after that incident, I told Tranter that if he persisted, I'd make sure he got warned off for a long time. It didn't cool the fire in his eyes. Today would be the first time we'd met since that conversation.

I scanned the race; twelve runners. Dolan's horse, Cliptie, was down to be ridden by his son Rod who, Dolan had told me this morning, had been hospitalized for a few days after a crash with the family tractor yesterday evening. The first that people would hear of the jockey change to E. Malloy would be when it was broadcast to the betting shops shortly before racing.

That suited me. It meant the mystery caller wouldn't have the opportunity to ring me and make suggestions.

I left Keith Allardyce to the remains of his lunch and went out into the sunshine to call the Corish Stud. George, the stud groom, answered the phone but was reluctant to answer questions about Martin Corish. He was hiding something. I resolved to leave after my ride in the first and head back down there to get some answers.

The sun was high as we filed out for the first and my dark colours, black with scarlet crossbelts, held the rays, slowly cooking my upper half. Sweat ran from my armpits over the heavy rib strapping from my last injury. Eager for a cooling breeze, I cantered to the start more quickly than normal. Cliptie, a neat bay gelding, moved nicely beneath me. Well-balanced and alert, he seemed the perfect type for this tight track.

Circling at the start, I watched Billy Tranter with concealed amusement. He'd dismounted and was adjusting his mount's bridle. Tranter's face had been a picture when he walked into the weighing room and saw my head popping through the neck of Cliptie's colours. His smile disappeared as though his facial muscles had been sliced.

Women thought him good-looking, which I suppose he was in a gunslingerish sort of way: high cheekbones, narrow deep-set eyes, strong jaw, and prairie-coloured hair. He could frame a mean look but at five foot five, he was more Alan Ladd than Gary Cooper.

He didn't speak to me, didn't have to. It was obvious that hostilities would be resumed as soon as possible.

Tranter remounted his horse, a big brute, its coat so black the sun glinted blindingly from it at times. It was a long shot in the betting and that made me especially wary. If Tranter felt he wasn't expected to win, he would concentrate on doing me damage. He kept glancing behind as we walked round at the start, both playing a slow game of cat and mouse before lining up.

Dolan was confident we'd win and had told me to lie fifth or sixth and bring him to lead at the last. Tucking Cliptie away in this sort of field shouldn't prove difficult, but if Tranter was determined to be in there scrimmaging with me, he'd have plenty of cover from the eyes of the Stewards.

It was a two-mile hurdle and the starter called us in and snapped the tape up quickly, letting us go to race clockwise for almost two circuits. I jumped Cliptie off smartly and led for the first furlong. He was keen and I had some trouble restraining him. After such a long layoff from riding, I felt my shoulder and back muscles stretch and resist as I gently wrestled Cliptie into submission, playing the bit in his mouth as an angler would play a salmon.

After we jumped the second, he settled and we swung along nicely six from the front with a horse either side. I peeked under my armpit to see Tranter three lengths behind, moving his horse toward the rails. As we turned into the straight for the first time, I heard angry shouts then felt my horse take a heavy bump on the quarters.

I looked round. Tranter had barged up the inside, forcing others to move out quickly. We'd been caught in the domino effect. But Cliptie seemed okay and galloped on. Through clear goggles, Tranter's narrowed eyes were fixed on me. Jaw muscles grimly clenched, he ignored the curses as he continued barreling forward.

Kicking Cliptie through a gap, I moved to the wide outside to keep at least one horse between Tranter and us. It would also give the Stewards a clearer view as we turned to race away from the stands.

But Tranter reined back to come round and move inside as we rounded the bend, at which point he bumped my horse hard, forcing us into the middle of the track.

He followed.

I glared across. 'Tranter, what the…?'

He bumped us again, and then with an exaggerated show of trying to control the big black gelding, he forced him onto mine, leaning and boring diagonally toward the river.

'Straighten up, you bastard!' I yelled, but he was half-standing in the stirrups, pretending to haul at the reins while carrying me off the course. Looking at the bridle, I saw the bit had come right through the horse's mouth. Tranter was without brakes or steering.

We were feet from the white rails and I tried desperately to pull Cliptie up, but Tranter's horse carried us through in a crackling

13

shower of plastic shards as the rails shattered. We were on the downward slope of the riverbank, travelling too fast for an emergency ejection. I made do with getting my feet out of the irons just before Cliptie burst through the glinting surface of the peaceful, slow-flowing Tay.

The sound of half a ton of galloping thoroughbred hitting deep water was like a bomb blast, shaking me almost as much as the shock of the temperature change and the sudden confusion of my senses. Cliptie's momentum carried me under as he overturned in the water.

Temporary panic. Sucked down by the horse. Very cold. Goggles filling through the tiny air holes. Water swilling darkly. On my back now. The sun a watery molten disc above. Terrible memories.

A heavy punch hits my shoulder. Must be Tranter. Mad bastard. I turn, in fear.

No Tranter but Cliptie, kicking out, beginning to swim. The reins move like dark skinny eels. I grab at them and pull myself toward Cliptie's strong neck, which I clasp in a hug, forcing tiny bubbles from his coat. Could use some of them. Not much air left in my lungs. But Cliptie's paddling strongly. Best rely on him.

We break the surface.

Cliptie blows through his nostrils as though applauding himself. I cough and splutter and try to look up. Blinded by the light.

FIVE

The horses were okay. We'd been lucky to miss the rocky shallows and plunge into a deep pool in the river's curve. At the Stewards' Enquiry, Tranter looked suitably shocked and penitent. The patrol film 'showed clearly', according to the Stewards, that the loose bridle had caused Tranter's misfortune and therefore mine. Although he swore the bridle had been correctly fitted, they fined the baffled trainer of Tranter's horse £200.

Now I knew why Tranter had been fiddling with the bridle at the start, a point he quickly raised in his defense, claiming it had felt loose and he'd been worried about it.

I was certain he'd sabotaged the bridle. I'd considered Billy Tranter nothing more than a bad loser, a small-minded guy who harboured grudges. But if he had deliberately loosened that bridle then he'd endangered himself as well as me, not to mention two racehorses.

I wondered what I had to do to stop him. I'd tried being tough on the track, I'd decked him at Bangor, I'd threatened to have him warned off. What next? He was rushing to ride in the second race and I was in a hurry to get back to the stud. I had to settle for tugging his sleeve and speaking quietly. 'When are you going to give up, Billy? When we're both dead?'

He grinned coldly and triumphantly, and I was left unsure as to whether that meant his 'honour' had now been satisfied or if he was already planning the next round.

By the main gate, Cliptie's lad was walking the steaming horse in a circle. Cliptie seemed bright and refreshed for his cool bath. Barney Dolan, his trainer, looked shell-shocked.

He leant against the fence, watching Cliptie with unblinking eyes. He didn't see me until I stopped beside him. The sun filtering through his loose-weave Panama hat cast a tight pattern on his face, making his booze-reddened nose even darker. The knot of his tie hung six inches below his sweat-stained shirt collar and a heavy sports jacket was draped across his forearm. On the grass at his feet lay his battered binoculars case.

'You okay?' I asked.

He pulled his mind to the present and focused on me. 'Mmmm.'

'You don't look it.'

He reached in his jacket for cigarettes and matches, then dropped the jacket beside the binoculars and lit a cigarette. 'He would have won that, Eddie. Pissed up.'

'I'm sorry.' It was pointless telling the Tranter story. I let him believe it was just bad luck.

He nodded again, slowly, not looking at me. He drew deeply and blew smoke into the hot still air. 'We needed that, Eddie.'

Gently I clasped his arm. 'There'll be another time. I'd love to ride him again.'

'Mmmm.'

More smoke. That faraway look again. 'Gimme a call if there's anything,' I said.

He didn't reply.

After an hour's driving, I was yawning at regular intervals. My ribs ached too. After my ducking, the doctor at Perth had restrapped them but the bandages felt tight. And I was hungry. To hell with it. The mystery of Martin Corish could keep until tomorrow. I turned off and headed west toward home.

SIX

I left after breakfast next day and reached the stud just before ten. I parked by the wall of the house as Fiona came out of the yard, leading a mare whose bright chestnut foal followed anxiously, tottering on too-long legs like a child in high heels. Fiona didn't acknowledge me as I got out. 'Good morning,' I called after her.

'Morning,' she said without turning.

'Is Mrs Corish home?'

'Try the garden.'

Following a side path, I came to a gate in a high hedge. The big sandstone house cast a long shadow over the kidney-shaped garden, only the top third of which was in sunshine. Two white patio chairs stood in the centre of the lawn. Another white chair and a matching table had been moved into the sunny spot. On the chair, her back to me, sat Caroline Corish.

She stirred slightly as she heard the metal latch click when the gate swung closed, but didn't look round. I called out, 'Good morning!'

She turned, saw me through her sunglasses but said nothing. I crossed the lawn, lifted a chair and put it down by Caroline's table.

She wore cream-coloured calf-length leggings, which were stained, and what looked like one of her husband's shirts, blue-striped and open-necked, showing a sunburned V of skin. She was shoeless. Her feet were dirty. Cracked dried blood showed on the toes of her right foot.

On the soiled tabletop lay a packet of cigarettes, an expensive lighter, a half-empty bottle of white rum and a litre of cola. She drank from the fat glass in her hand. It wasn't yet 10.30.

Even behind the dark glasses Caroline looked haggard. Fortyish, she was naturally slim but looked gaunt. As she raised the glass, her wedding ring slid an inch along her bony finger. I'd known them for years and had never understood what Martin had seen in her. Most times I'd met her, she'd had something to whine about. Her commitment to drowning sorrows this early told me that Martin was causing plenty trouble.

I kept it light. 'Sunbathing?' I asked, as I sat down.

'Do make yourself comfortable, won't you?' she said sarcastically.

'How are you?'

'Drunk. Cheers.' She emptied the glass in two long swallows and refilled it, the cola frothing and running over the edge.

'What's the celebration?'

She turned petulantly and I was glad I couldn't see her eyes. 'Surviving another night alone in the fucking Ponderosa,' she said, nodding toward the house.

'Where's Martin?'

'Screwing stablegirls, probably.'

'He's been away for a few days?'

'I couldn't give a toss if he never comes back.' She shook a cigarette from the packet and lit it, killing the scent of the flowers with the smoke flaring down her nostrils.

'Caroline, it's important that I speak to Martin soon. Have you any idea where he's gone?'

'Why don't you go and ask that little whore Fiona? Ask her if he plans to be there to hold her hand when she's in labour?'

Oh dear. My thoughts returned to Fiona's open jodhpurs and protruding white belly. And her haranguing of Martin on the phone. I guessed he had more problems than just Town Crier.

In the yard, red-haired Fiona looked almost as rough as Caroline did, though considerably plumper. She was yelling at two lads to get some tack cleaned. They wandered slowly out of the feed-room, chatting as if she didn't exist.

'Glad to hear you've got your voice back,' I said.

She stared at me, flushed from shouting. I asked where Martin was and she continued the silent treatment, which was really beginning to piss me off. I said, 'Fiona, if you want to have a job this time next week then answer me when I talk to you.'

She half-sneered, 'You can't sack me.'

'Martin's disappeared. I'm applying to have the business assigned to me.'

She seemed uncertain. 'You can't. He'll be home to...' She stopped herself.

'When? Tomorrow?'

'I'm not to say.'

'Okay, pick up your things. I'll pay you a month's wages in lieu of notice and send your cards on.'

I turned and went into the office. She yelled after me: 'You can't! You can't!' I brought out a jacket and a shoulder bag. 'These yours?'

She crossed her arms. 'I won't accept them!'

I laid them on the ground. 'Anything else you want to recover from the office?'

She scowled. 'You can't do this!'

I checked my watch. 'It shouldn't take you long to walk to the main gate. Be off the property in half an hour.' I returned to the office. A few minutes later, I was going through the contents of the filing cabinet when the door creaked open. Fiona stood there, the sun haloing her carrot hair. Staring at her feet like a little girl, she said, 'Martin will be here in the morning.'

'What time?'

'First thing.'

'Fine. Come in and start explaining how this place has been running.'

She worked confidently through the paperwork, showing me the accounts. I learned little either way. I was not enough of a financial gourmet to detect the whiff of cooked books and Fiona probably realized this.

Although I knew where Town Crier was stabled, I asked her to take me there to see if that shook her confidence, but she led me to the box without hesitation.

In front of me was a long strong bay horse, well ribbed up with straight hocks and good legs, a fine head with large ears and a bold eye. The only marking on him was a touch of white no bigger than a thumbprint on his forehead. I was sure within a minute this was the genuine Town Crier, and equally certain that physically at least there was not a thing wrong with him.

I asked Fiona when he'd last covered a mare.

'Er. A week ago today, I think. Yes, last Friday.'

'Were you there?'

'What?'

'Did you see him covering?'

'No.' She looked puzzled.

'Who was there?'

'Martin.'

'Who else?'

Her brows knitted. 'A couple of the lads, I think.'

I dropped the subject and told her I was heading into Marlborough to book a room for the evening. I warned her that if she rushed off to ring Martin she'd better tell him that if he wasn't here first thing in the morning, she'd be out of a job and I'd be out looking for him.

SEVEN

I rang home to my answerphone. No messages.

I found a small hotel, removed my rib strapping, had a cool shower and lay wet and naked on the bed, letting the air from the open window dry me. I thought about Martin Corish. He had been my boyhood hero, champion jockey when I was a teenager. It hadn't been just his brilliant riding that had bewitched me: he was interviewed often on TV and always seemed to have a twinkle in his eye and a joke ready, usually told against himself. He was handsome too, but seemed to manage that rare balance of attracting women while not alienating men.

By the time I started riding, Martin's career was winding down, but I'd made no secret of how much I admired him. Admiration which increased when he accepted me immediately as his equal, as a man and as a jockey. He made me feel special and it took me a while to realize that was how he made most people feel. It wasn't contrived on his part; he was simply a charismatic type of guy.

After retiring he'd spent some time working on TV and radio before setting up as a trainer, something I felt he'd put off deliberately till the highs of his riding days were more of a memory. To achieve the same success training would have been a tough enough task without carrying the burden of other people's expectations.

Martin never reached higher than middle rank when he was training, and when that position started slipping he packed up, unwilling to wait for the humiliating slide to obscurity. That's when he set up the stud, which had been going for three years when he'd approached me last summer, offering me a fifty-fifty partnership for £200,000.

In any normal season I'd be lucky to have a twentieth of that in the bank, but I'd come into some money via an insurance company reward. My share had been a hundred and seventy-five grand. I had ten of my own in cash and I'd borrowed another fifteen and gone in with Martin. I guess I'd never really lost that desire to impress him, to win his approval.

It hadn't made me a millionaire but it hadn't proved disastrous either. I'd managed to make the loan repayments quite comfortably and start rebuilding modest savings from the director's salary the stud paid me. But I was a long way from getting my money back.

I lay staring at the ceiling, promising myself I'd resist Martin's charm in the morning, wouldn't be calmed down by layers of bullshit. I'd be as hard with him as I had been with Fiona.

I swung my legs off the bed and stood up in front of the full-length mirror fixed to the open wardrobe door. Fresh bruises added to the colourful display on my ribcage, shellbursts of yellow and blue. On my left shinbone, a familiar old pink scar, legacy of a pin insertion years ago, ran diagonally through the dark hair. My muscle definition was good, but I noticed a thickening round the middle and more flesh on the upper thighs. I'd never had a weight problem but last season a pound or two extra had somehow lodged itself on my frame.

I decided to skip dinner.

After the nine o'clock news, I made a final call to my answerphone. The first message was from Barney Dolan, Cliptie's trainer. He wanted to meet me at Worcester tomorrow to discuss something important.

The second call was from the blackmailer: 'I see from the papers you took a little bath up at Perth yesterday. Most amusing. Don't ever accept a ride again after the overnight stage. I'll be in touch.'

Arrogant bastard.

Jockeys declared at the overnight stage were guaranteed to have their names appear alongside their mount in the morning papers. If this guy didn't know where I was riding, he couldn't ask me to stop one. I was seething as I worked through my diary in search of Barney Dolan's number. He sounded anxious when I explained to him that I had no plans to be at Worcester tomorrow. I had no booked rides and, more importantly, I had pressing business elsewhere.

There was a long pause then Barney said, 'Eddie, I've got to see you. I'm in deep trouble. Fierce trouble. I need to see you tomorrow.'

EIGHT

I was at the stud by 5.30 a.m. in case Martin decided to pay a fleeting morning visit. In the paddocks, mares and foals grazed. Mist rose from the river and dew lay thick on the front lawn of the big house. The yard was empty of people, though equine heads looked inquiringly over box doors, a few whinnying at the prospect of an early breakfast.

The office was locked. I sat on the red-leaded windowsill and watched the sun rise slowly over the pitched roof of the stable block. Just after seven, as the lads arrived on foot and by bike, I heard a car and walked out to see if it was Martin. The car had stopped two hundred yards along the road beside the cottage where Fiona lived. Martin drove a gunmetal grey Rover and the car was the right shape, though the angle of the sunlight made it hard to distinguish colour.

I reversed my car along the drive and blocked the exit road. I'd thought the whine of the fast gear would bring him hurrying to investigate, but he stayed inside for almost ten minutes and didn't look surprised when he came out and saw me.

Many ex-jockeys quickly bloat as they indulge themselves after years of self-deprivation, but Martin had never been more than half a stone over his riding weight. Standing on the steps of the cottage, he looked a stone under it. His five foot ten was stretched and gaunt. With his hunched shoulders, curved spine and drooping head he resembled a jockey off one of the old cigarette cards.

He stood like a prisoner in the dock waiting to be taken down, eyes on the ground as I approached.

I'd spent much of the morning rehearsing angry words, but when I saw his face all I could say was, 'Are you okay?'

He raised a warm but very tired smile, and once again, maddeningly, I felt somehow privileged. It was almost as if he had only three of those smiles left to get him through the rest of his life, and he'd spent one on me. He put a hand on my shoulder. 'Come in and have some breakfast.'

I stopped him. 'I'd rather we spoke alone.'

'It's okay, Fiona's just leaving.'

She must have been standing inside the open door for she appeared on cue, kissed Martin lightly on the cheek and came down the front step where he ruffled her hair affectionately before she walked up the dusty road in the direction of the yard.

The cottage kitchen was untidy. Dirty clothes lay on the floor by the open door of the washing machine and the sink was full of dishes. Old newspapers and office books were strewn on the table, which had a pine bench on either side. Martin cleared a space. 'Sit down, Eddie. Coffee?'

'You sit down. I'll make the coffee.'

He did so without argument, and I found the makings of coffee and toast which he refused. I persuaded him to eat it.

Martin was forty-five. Not only did he still have all his hair but it seemed to be growing wild, out of control, thick and greying and alive. Framing his fine-boned unshaven face, it made him look more like a refugee or half-crazed artist than one of racing's former heroes. But there was none of the usual fire in his blue eyes, which were bloodshot, exhausted-looking, lifeless. If the body had its own hospital, they'd have been in intensive care.

When he'd forced down the last mouthful of toast, he looked at me and said, 'I'm sorry, mate.'

There was no need to start barking questions at him. He went through everything from the beginning, punctuating the story with regular apologies. 'I should have thought more about it, should have called you. I just sort of panicked. It had been building up for weeks and when the guy phoned, I just blanked, panicked.'

The blackmailer had contacted him on Monday, claiming he knew another horse, a ringer, was being used to cover for Town Crier. He suggested Martin approach me to say 'the game was up' and that we'd better co-operate, which meant he would tell me which races not to try in. Martin couldn't pluck up the courage to ring me, and when the blackmailer called on Tuesday and again on Wednesday, only to find Martin was avoiding him, he'd phoned me direct.

I said, 'So he's right in what he says about Town Crier?' Martin nodded slowly, thick tendrils of hair swinging across his eyes.

'What's wrong with him?'

'He's lost it. Just lost it.'

'Lost what?'

'His fertility.'

We looked at each other.

'Completely?' I asked.

He nodded again. 'Went from an eighty-eight percent success rate to zero.'

'What, just like that? Overnight?'

'Almost. Three or four days maybe.'

Stallion fertility is measured in how many mares each horse gets in foal. Town Crier's had always been consistently high. 'You should have called me.'

His shoulders tensed, hunching again as he moved awkwardly in his seat. 'I thought he'd come through it, Eddie. I thought it might be a virus or something.'

I shook my head slowly, rubbing my face as the impact sank home. 'You should have told me, Martin.'

'I'm sorry, Eddie, I didn't know how to tell you! What was it going to sound like less than a year after you put everything you had into the business? After I had persuaded you to invest all that money? What was I supposed to say: "Look, Eddie, sorry but our major asset has collapsed, our top player has just drawn stumps?"'

I was angry and avoided his eyes to hide it, then got mad at myself for being so protective of him. Almost afraid to ask I finally said, 'What about this ringer stuff, that's not true, is it?' I don't know why I asked, because I knew it had to be true or he wouldn't have run away. Like battling on from two fences behind in a steeplechase, you're always hoping for that little miracle, and maybe thought that Martin had scarpered purely because of the pressure of Town Crier's problem being revealed to the public. Maybe that was all it was.

It wasn't. He'd been using a stallion called Acapella to cover the Town Crier mares. Acapella stood at a thousand pounds, half the fee we charged for Town Crier.

That wound up my sympathy and patience to breaking point. 'For God's sake, Martin, they're not even the same colour!'

'Close enough. There's plenty bay in Acapella's family. We'll be okay.'

'He's black!'

He hunched his shoulders again and hung his head. His reasoning was that the colouring wouldn't be a big issue, and maybe we would sort Town Crier out for next season. The fact that Acapella was also less likely to sire a horse of the same ability as Town Crier's offspring didn't matter to Martin at the moment. Most were bred for jumping and it would be five years before they'd see a racecourse. Again, he argued that Town Crier would have overcome his problem long before then so half a dozen or so sub-standard progeny would do little damage to his reputation as a sire.

I said, 'And what do we do when the blood samples from the foals are analyzed for Weatherbys?'

The Jockey Club's administrators, Weatherbys, operated a checking system to prevent the very thing Martin had been doing. As soon as a thoroughbred foal is born, a vet takes a blood sample to send there for testing. The sample proves the mating that is on paper is the one that produced the offspring.

Running nervous fingers through his wild hair, Martin said, 'That won't happen for months. We can sort something out by then.'

'Like what, a miracle?'

'We can say there was a mistake here, or maybe we can get hold of the samples before they get to Weatherbys, or bribe a vet or something.'

I stared at him. 'You're kidding me now, Martin. Tell me you're kidding?'

He clamped his head between his hands and squeezed his eyes shut. 'My head's gone, Eddie. I'm sorry.'

I wondered what he'd told the staff. For each covering there would have to have been at least one other person present. A mare has to be held steady while the stallion is led up and sometimes helped to enter her. Unwilling mares can have hobbles fitted to stop them trying to escape or kicking the stallion, so often there will be three people at a covering.

'What did you tell the staff?' I asked. 'Would they have known who the mares were booked to?'

He shook his head and muttered, 'They thought it was a simple booking to Acapella.'

'And nobody questioned why Town Crier hadn't covered for so long?' He shook his head again.

'What about the insurance? Why don't we just claim on that?' Insurance was available against a stallion's losing fertility and most breeders took sufficient cover.

In a quiet voice he said, 'I didn't take it out.'

'You *what*? We agreed it! It was part of the budget!'

He couldn't look at me. 'Didn't think it was worth it. His fertility rate was so high.'

I sighed. It was pointless getting any angrier. I tried to figure out what we could do to start repairing things.

I asked, 'What are the vets saying?'

Still gripping his head, he said in a tense voice, 'I took a sample of blood and sperm to a vet in Ireland, top bloke. The blood's fine. The sperm is a hundred percent sterile.'

'Temporary or permanent?'

'No way of knowing.'

'What about a second opinion?'

'Who from?' There was an edge in his voice now.

'One of the Newmarket guys.'

'Who'll then know that the Corish Stud has a useless stallion. How long before that gets out to breeders?'

'Martin, how else are we going to solve this? We can't keep it covered up.'

'We've got to keep it covered up, Eddie! Make no mistake about that!' There was some fire in his eyes at last, sparked by desperation. But it was blinding him to logic.

'Martin, we're in a hole, let's stop digging, please?'

He rounded on me, slamming his open hands on the tabletop.

'*You* stop digging! It's all right for you! If the business goes under you've done a few quid. Fine. You go back to riding. You're young. You'll be okay! What have *I* got? Fuck all!'

His fists and jaw muscles clenched and unclenched. 'I'll tell you what I've got, Eddie, I'll tell you what I've got coming at me from all points of the fucking compass! Divorce proceedings. My first child who'll be born just after my forty-sixth birthday. No business. No money. Nowhere to live. And I'll tell you what else I don't have that you don't think about now but by Christ you will when you get to my age, I don't have another ten or fifteen years to pull the whole fucking thing back together again!'

He was reaching across to me, arms extended. If I'd been directly in front of him, he'd have had me by the lapels. His head was low, chin almost touching the table, tears welling. And I was sorry it had taken this much to make me understand why he'd crashed and burned in the past seventy-two hours.

I stayed until noon, comforting him, trying to persuade him we'd come through, that we'd get the blackmailer before he did any damage.

NINE

I drove at speed to Worcester races, where I'd agreed to meet Barney Dolan behind the main stand after the second race. Waiting for him, I watched the boats on the Severn, which flows so close to the track that there has never been a winter when it hasn't flooded the racecourse. Watching the wide muddy river, I was glad Tranter hadn't barged me into this one.

Barney appeared, looking as though he'd just come from our last meeting at Perth; same clothes, tie hanging loose at the same length, identical expression, cigarette freshly lit sending smoke trails up through the weave of his hat rim. We shook hands and when he glanced furtively around the way they do in B-movies, I thought it was all a wind up, though he'd sounded pretty desperate on the phone last night.

'Why all the secrecy?' I asked.

'I don't want us to be seen together. You'll know why in a minute.'

A rowing crew surged past sweating and grunting. Barney and I were the only ones behind the stand. I said, 'Barney, if anybody does see us round here, they'll think we're up to something. Whatever it is you want to talk about, let's do it out front. Okay, people will see us but you're a trainer and I'm a jockey, they're much less likely to be suspicious.'

He didn't say anything, just turned and led me along the single track. Among the crowds once more, we passed a line of glum bookmakers paying out on the second race, and walked on toward the parade ring, which we skirted then came back, travelling the route four or five times while Barney told his tale.

It seemed that my bathing partner at Perth, Cliptie, had been carrying a large amount of cash, carefully placed in betting shops around the country. So large that if the horse had known, he'd probably have sunk without trace. Most of that stake money, thirty grand of it, had belonged to one of Barney's owners, Joe Dimokratia, Joey the Greek. And herein lay the crux: Joey the Greek did not know Barney had used his cash.

Joey was spending the month of June in his home country before returning to collect from Barney the proceeds of the sale of two of his horses, proceeds that Barney no longer had. Barney made it clear that Joey was unlikely to take this news gracefully.

If it hadn't been for the pallor of Barney's complexion and the nervous pitch of his voice, I would have found the whole thing comical. 'So what do you plan to do?' I asked.

'I've got to get the money before he comes back.'

'And what do you plan to use for stakes, if it's any of my business?'

'I've sold another one of Joey's horses.'

'You're kidding. Without him knowing?'

He nodded, shrugged. 'He can't do any more to me if it doesn't come off.'

'Where do I come in?' I asked.

'I want you to be at Market Rasen on Saturday and to leave yourself free for the second race.'

'I'd hardly have thought I was your good luck charm, Barney.'

'You're trustworthy and reliable, Eddie, and you can keep your gob shut. We just got a bad break on Thursday.'

He didn't realize how bad a break and I was tempted to tell him that I thought Tranter had sabotaged the bridle. But I wasn't certain that he had. But supposing Tranter rode against me again when Barney's money was down? I settled for telling him that Tranter held a grudge against me and that while Thursday's incident might have been an accident, Barney shouldn't risk putting me up on Cliptie again if Tranter was in the same race.

'Don't worry about Tranter, I'll sort him out.' He said it in such an offhand manner - almost like, 'forget about the fly, I'll swat it' - that it worried me and made me realize how desperate he was. I'd expected him to blow his top and demand more details about

Tranter and the Perth race, but that faraway gaze was in his eyes again, though this time it looked like single-mindedness rather than despair. He could see the target a week away and wasn't going to be deflected.

Clutching his elbow lightly, I stopped and turned him toward me. 'Barney, if I want him sorting out, I'll do it myself.'

'Leave it to me, Eddie.' He made to walk on again. I held him. 'Barney. I'll sort it out.'

Barney's big red nose made him appear jolly in a music-hall sort of way, but his grey eyes were cold and hard and I wondered how afraid he was of Joey the Greek. He said, 'Eddie, I can't afford another fuck-up.'

'Listen you won't put Tranter off easily, I've been trying to do it all season. Play safe, book somebody else.'

'I want you, Eddie.' He didn't voice it but the look in his eyes said, "You owe me one."

'Fine. Let's say I'll ride. Just make sure you've got a standby in case Tranter turns out to have a mount in the race.'

Barney looked down at me, gripping my shoulders with both hands. 'Eddie, *you're* the standby.'

It turned out that Rod, Barney's jockey son, had suffered no accident on Wednesday. The plan from the start was to declare Rod, an inexperienced claiming jockey, as the rider at Perth to discourage the public from betting on Cliptie so his price would drift. The last-minute substitution of E. Malloy would have gone pretty much unnoticed in the country's betting shops. If I'd been unavailable for the ride on Thursday, Barney said he would have withdrawn the horse and held off until I was free.

Now he planned to try the same ruse at Market Rasen next week. Trouble was the blackmailer had warned me last night never to take another unbooked ride. Barney was staring hard at me, stiff with tension, and I saw in his face a reflection of Martin's haggard features. I couldn't tell which was the devil and which the deep blue sea.

At least it gave us something to work to, a deadline. We had exactly one week to find the blackmailer.

TEN

As arranged, Martin came to see me on Sunday afternoon and we walked to the pub for a late lunch. On the way there, the storm that had been brewing for days broke with a lightning bolt and thunderclap that made you believe in God. We ran but were drenched in seconds by a deluge that left us gasping for breath, then laughing stupidly, and finally splashing like children through the water overflowing the road drains.

By the time we reached the pub, it had rained itself out. We sat at a white table in the beer garden, steaming gently in the sun.

Martin drank beer. I sipped mineral water as we waited for sandwiches. We had agreed yesterday that Town Crier had to be officially taken off the market so that we weren't compromised further. Martin was to phone the two breeders with mares booked in and tell them the horse was carrying a slight injury, nothing permanent, but the vet thought he'd be off for a few weeks. It was close enough to the end of the breeding season for them to be unlikely to request a new date.

'How did they take it?' I asked.

'Mrs Sansome was annoyed and moaned like hell but she's a bit of a cow at the best of times. Parsons was okay. I got the impression he might even have been a bit relieved.'

I nodded, watching him. He looked much more positive, alive again. I'd persuaded him that things would come good if we worked through them. First priority was identifying the blackmailer and persuading him he'd been misinformed. The second was to find out what was wrong with Town Crier and fix it. And the third was to offer the owners who'd had a 'fraudulent' covering by Acapella a free nomination to Town Crier next year.

This was the one Martin was most nervous about. 'Eddie, can't we avoid that, somehow?'

'How?'

'I don't know.' He squirmed uncomfortably, shaking water drops from his hair. 'I just don't think we can tell them it was a mistake. How incompetent are we going to look when that gets out?'

'As incompetent as you can get, but our honesty in admitting it will go a long way in mitigation. And we'll be better off admitting it before the blood tests from the foals force our hand.'

'It's not going to be as easy as you think.'

'Listen, it's the least of our worries. We made it bottom of our list yesterday. Let's keep it there until we've sorted out the others. Now who else knew about Town Crier's fertility problem?'

'Nobody.'

'Nobody? You didn't tell a soul?'

He avoided my eyes.

'I told Caroline.'

'Right. When?'

'End of March.'

'Did she know about Fiona at the time?'

He shook his head. More droplets. It turned out Caroline had found them in bed together a few weeks later, though Martin said it did nothing more than confirm what she'd been accusing him of for years. 'She almost enjoyed it. Finding the evidence which would save all the cross-examination in the future.'

'Who else knows?'

'Fiona.' He lowered his gaze.

I sighed. 'Why didn't you just take out an ad in the local paper?'

'Fiona wouldn't breathe a word. I'd bet my life on it.'

'So it must have been Caroline.'

'Couldn't have been.'

I leaned across the table. 'It must have been, Martin! You can't have it both ways!'

He threw his hands wide and the waitress bringing the sandwiches had to jig quickly sideways. He apologized and turned on his most charming smile, but she'd been looking curiously at us dripping oddities all the way down the path and seemed keen to get back indoors. Martin paid and she hurried off.

I lifted a thin ham sandwich. Martin continued gesturing. 'Carrie would have absolutely no motive for giving the game away.'

Between bites I said, 'Never heard of "hell hath no fury" and all that?'

'Look, all she cares about is screwing me for as much as she can in the divorce settlement. Why should she risk.' he sought the word 'devaluing my only asset? *Our* only asset?'

He had a point. 'Have you asked her?'

'What, if she's told anyone?'

I nodded.

'That's the last thing I need - for her to know I'm being blackmailed!'

'*We* are being blackmailed.'

'We, I know. It's the only reason she's still there. She knows we won't be able to sell the business until Town Crier's back on song, so she'll have to sit and suffer till it's sorted out. Or rather I'll have to suffer the constant bloody nagging.'

'I thought you were in the cottage with Fiona?'

'I am but she summons me every day for a bloody progress report.'

He bit fiercely into a sandwich. I said, 'You're going to have to ask her.'

'What do I say?'

'Just ask if she's mentioned it to anybody.'

'And if she has, do you think she's going to tell me?'

'I don't know, but if you don't ask, we won't find out.'

He sipped beer and sulked. I was learning more about him all the time. I said, 'Martin, it's the only card we've got at the moment. You have to play it.'

'I'll speak to her tonight,' he said quietly.

'Don't accept the first thing she says,' I warned.

'Unless it's yes.'

I smiled. 'If it's yes, make sure you get the name of the guy she told.'

'That'll probably cost me another ten grand on the settlement.'

We moved on to priority two - could Town Crier be cured? Any vet we used would have to be discreet and totally trustworthy. If

35

word got out about the stallion, I doubted we'd ever restore breeders' faith in him.

Town Crier had been three or four pounds short of top class when racing over a mile and a half on the flat. When breeders are trying to get jumping stock, there aren't many reliable stallions. As most 'practicing' jump horses are geldings, there is no stud career waiting after retirement. No matter how talented they've been on the racecourse, the chance to pass on genes had disappeared, commonly in their formative days, along with their testicles.

So for ex-flat stallions to establish themselves as good sires of jumping stock normally takes years, as their early crops are usually tried on the flat for a couple of seasons at least. If they don't prove successful, they're often put over jumps where it might take three or four seasons for them to shine. Even then, breeders will be cautious and wait a few seasons more to check if the rest of that stallion's progeny also show talent over hurdles or fences. By the time a jumping stallion does make a name for himself, he can be sixteen or seventeen - or, more likely, dead.

Town Crier was twelve and could easily have another decade at stud, covering approximately a hundred mares a season. Multiply that by his fee, which would rise in accordance with the success of his stock, and you could see what a blow it would be to the stud if his infertility proved permanent. It was this simplified breakdown of figures and prospects that drained the colour from Martin's face.

I'd called an old friend and fellow jockey who also happened to be an excellent vet. His name was Brian Kincaid, and I'd arranged to meet him while he was at work in Gloucester next day. Martin was very anxious about it. 'Can't you just give him the samples? He doesn't have to know what stallion they've come from, or even the stud.'

'And what's the likelihood of his learning anything more from the samples than your man in Ireland did?'

He had no answer for that.

'He's going to have to examine Town Crier, Martin.'

He clasped his head, fingers pushing out thick wings of almost dry hair, and stared at his feet.

'Martin, I trust this guy. I've known him for years. He's one of the old school.'

He nodded, head still in his hands. 'Okay, okay, Eddie.'

'I'll ring you as soon as I've spoken to him.'

He finished his beer and stood up, soggy trousers sucking noisily at the chair. 'I'd better get cracking.'

As we returned to my flat, he had one more go. 'Couldn't we bring Town Crier to him, tell him it was something else?'

'Then expect him to give us one hundred percent trust?'

He hunched his shoulders again and stuffed his hands moodily in his pockets. We walked the last half-mile in silence.

ELEVEN

Next morning I found Brian Kincaid in a stall at a Gloucester stud, with his arm so far up a mare's backside his right cheek rested on her buttock. He winked and smiled at me. I nodded. He was watching a small monitor, pointing with his free hand to what looked like a white UFO on the black screen.

'Cyst, I'm afraid,' he said to the man holding up the mare's tail. 'It may look like an embryo but it's another cyst.'

The man swore. 'Bad luck,' said Kincaid, withdrawing his arm and a thin cable. The cable was attached at one end to the computer and at the other to an egg-sized rubber ball. He placed the ball in a white bowl on the table, peeled off the long dirty rubber glove, dropped it in the bin and reached over to shake my hand. I took his rather gingerly. The smell of fresh horseshit rose from a brown plastic bin beside him, and the apron he wore was heavily soiled with shit and blood and membraney type stuff. 'How're you doing, Eddie? Nice to see you.'

'And you.'

He introduced me to the disgruntled tail-holder, the stud manager, who was anxious to get the next mare in. Kincaid said, 'Just one more to do and we'll have a cup of tea.'

I nodded. 'Sure. No hurry.'

The mare with the cyst was led out and the rear doors slid open to reveal another mare waiting in the yard with her foal. A lad half-pushed, half-carried the foal in and placed it in the stall beside its mother, who walked quietly after them. Kincaid swung the half-doors closed to stop her kicking and a groom held her halter while the stud man pulled her tail aside.

Kincaid bent low, plucking a fresh blue glove from a box of disposables and pulling it onto his right arm, which he then eased inside the mare. A few seconds later, he drew out eighteen inches of shit that seemed moulded beautifully to the shape of his arm all the way to the crook of his elbow. A deft flick saw the load dumped in the bin. Two more excavations, carried out while chatting congenially to the tail-holder, and he was happy enough to pick up the scanning bulb and go back in.

His eyes turned in my direction. 'You'll have seen this before, Eddie?'

'Once or twice.' I'd been raised on a stud farm, but had never quite come to terms with how casually vets took this part of their job.

Kincaid passed the scanner over the top of the uterus, and watched the ultrasound waves paint a picture on the screen, which seemed clear to Kincaid and the stud man but looked like it always did to me - abstract.

'Twins,' Kincaid said.

The stud man swore again. Thoroughbred mares showed a high incidence of twins, which might at first seem like good news for the breeder. But mares rarely carried healthy twins successfully; if they went their full term, they tended to be born weaker than single foals, which made them poor investments.

This meant that in almost every case the vet would decide which embryo should be killed in the womb to allow the other to develop. The vet simply 'popped' one embryo, squeezed it between his fingers, but a wrong decision by him could prove the most expensive pop in the history of the turf. What if that squashed embryo held the genes to be a Triple Crown winner?

The vets were in the happy position that nobody would ever know how that embryo would have turned out. They based decisions on whatever evidence was available from a fourteen-to twenty-day-old blob. Inevitably, the smallest or most misshapen one would be popped and then everyone just hoped for the best.

Kincaid withdrew his arm and put on another fresh glove before gently pushing his way along the vaginal tract. No scanner to help now, everything done by feel. The mare shifted uneasily and the lad at her head cooed and comforted her. Her ears and eyes were back, almost as if she sensed what Kincaid was trying to do in there. He spoke quietly to her. 'It's for your own good, old girl.'

He eased out his arm and said to the stud man, 'I'll have another look at her on Thursday.' Using clean cotton wool and soapy water, he spent a minute thoroughly cleaning the mare's vagina and the surrounding area before she was led out through the sliding doors at the front.

The stud man didn't look too happy. Kincaid put an arm across his shoulders. 'Good days and bad, Stan, good days and bad.'

Stan nodded.

Kincaid said, 'Any chance of a pot of tea?'

Stan wandered off to fetch it. Kincaid smiled and stretched, yawning. 'How goes it, Mister Malloy? What's the big mystery this weather?'

Kincaid was a six-footer and strong looking. He had to waste hard to ride at ten and a half stone. His natural weight would be over twelve. He only rode as an amateur with maybe forty or so mounts a season, but was one of the best amateurs I'd ever seen and well respected in the weighing room.

In his early-thirties, he was fair-haired and threw quite a distinctive profile with his hooked nose and prominent, slightly upturned chin. The lads called him Mr Punch, often in a puppet-show voice, and he took it with good humour - but what a ribbing he'd got last year when he married a girl called Judy. He had smiling blue eyes and was very even-tempered. I don't think I'd ever heard him complain, but he always had a sympathetic ear for others who wanted a moan.

And like most vets I'd known, Kincaid was a true animal lover. One of the things he'd always claimed had stopped him becoming a professional jockey was the expectation of a number of owners and trainers that the whip be used to maximum effect on their horses. 'No way do I want my living to depend on that,' he'd told me once.

He stood now, hands on hips, smiling at me as smelly steam rose from the bin between us. 'You look well,' I said.

'Bloody tired.' And he yawned again then took a couple of steps into a gloomy corner and reached out. On a shelf was a shiny platter of sandwiches. Kincaid swung it toward me, resting the edge against his soiled apron. 'Sandwich?'

'No, thanks.'

He started munching happily, enjoying my expression. 'God, you'll catch beriberi or something.'

Smiling, he shook his head. 'Beriberi's caused by a thiamine deficiency. Plenty of thiamine in blood and shit.' He waved the platter and I turned away in disgust. Kincaid laughed.

The stud man brought a tray with tea on it and I took it from him. We headed across the yard to sit on a low wall in the sunshine. Kincaid brought his sandwiches and as I laid down the tea tray, he reached for the pot and said, 'Will I be mother?'

I grabbed at it. 'Will you hell! Poison yourself if you like; I prefer tea minus the germs!'

He laughed again.

We spent quite a while on that wall; our shadows had shifted noticeably by the time we got up. I outlined the problem, missing out the ruse Martin had pulled on some breeders. Kincaid talked me through the reproductive system of the stallion in detail but the bottom line was that never before had he heard of such a sudden loss of fertility, not without an obvious physiological cause.

He agreed to come and see Town Crier on Wednesday afternoon.

Back at the flat, I checked my answerphone - nothing of consequence. I called Martin and told him when Kincaid was coming. 'Did you get anything out of Caroline?' I asked.

'Dog's abuse.'

'She hasn't told anyone?'

'Definitely not.'

'Do you believe her?'

'I'm inclined to. She went ballistic when I even suggested it.'

'Guilty conscience, maybe?'

'Well. I don't think so.'

He questioned me on everything Kincaid had said and I dressed things up a bit.

I asked how serious Caroline's drink problem was.

'She never drinks while she's asleep.'

'So it's pretty bad?'

'Morning till night, most days. Very steady though, can shift a couple of bottles before blacking out.'

'Is there any way she could have told someone about Town Crier while she was drunk?' 'Like who?'

'I haven't a clue. It was just a thought. That might be the reason she doesn't remember saying anything.'

He was silent for a few seconds. 'Could be,' he said. 'But how do we find out?'

'Who does she see? Does she drink with any of her friends?'

'Friends? Eddie, all of Caroline's friends are forty proof and don't talk back.'

'There must be somebody she sees outside of the stud. What about a hairdresser, a local shopkeeper or something?'

'On the odd days she goes out she manages to be relatively sober, which means she'd most probably remember what she'd said. Anyway, she wouldn't discuss stud business outside. Shit, she doesn't know much stud business to discuss!'

Except that Town Crier's a dud, I almost said. I left it at that and told Martin I'd see him next day, and we could go through the list of breeders whose mares were carrying what they thought were Town Crier foals.

I spent the rest of the evening hoping the blackmailer would call. Finding him was top of our priority list, and I had nothing to go on. I'd copied his last message from the answerphone on to a normal audio tape, and played it repeatedly in the hope that something would trigger my memory.

London accent, voice pitch on the high side, suggesting he was fairly young. I had to assume he was quite deeply involved in racing; he knew the implications of using a ringer at stud and he seemed to have the know-how to set up whatever betting coups he was planning. I resolved to start the process of elimination tomorrow, involving Caroline if necessary.

TWELVE

'I'll say one thing, Martin, you don't mess about.' I was examining the list of 'conned' breeders. On it were two prominent Jockey Club members and the wife of the High Sheriff of Wiltshire.

He shrugged, half-smiled.

'You'd better start thinking up a convincing story for when you have to go back and tell them a mistake was made,' I said.

'No problem. So long as Town Crier's okay, that's the main thing. I'll come up with something.'

Martin brewed tea while I got my portable radio-cassette from the car. We sat at the kitchen table in the cottage playing the blackmailer's tape. Martin concentrated, brow furrowed, right ear inclined toward the sound. He said, 'There's something familiar about the voice.'

Pressing the play button again, I watched him. He looked frustrated. 'I can't say I know it.' He gestured with his hands. It's not somebody I know, if that doesn't sound daft, but it's familiar, I've definitely heard it.'

'Recently?'

He shook his head, listening again. 'It's like someone I've heard but I don't know the person. Like somebody on TV, a newsreader or something, know what I mean?'

'Sort of.'

His frustration was almost painful to watch and the tip-of-the-tongue element was getting to me too as I silently urged him on. I said, 'You're lucky I don't have my whip with me. I'd be sorely

43

tempted to give you a smack to make you go through with your effort.'

He laughed, easing the tension.

We played that tape until it squeaked, drew up lists of people Martin had met recently, tried to plot Caroline's movements, but came up with nothing. I wanted to confront her, but Martin asked for one more day to try to pin down the voice.

Brian Kincaid was due down next day and Martin offered me the spare room. I refused as politely as I could. The presence of the sour-faced Fiona (boy, could Martin pick 'em) and the thought of spending the night in that dismal cottage held no appeal. Maybe I was getting too used to my own company. Anyway, I went back to the small hotel in Marlborough where I'd stayed last week.

Skimming through the *Racing Post* I checked the entries for Market Rasen on Saturday. Cliptie, my synchronized swimming partner from Perth, was entered in the second race. Sure enough, the jockey's name was given as R. Dolan, Barney's son, and I wondered how the poor kid felt about being used as a stooge in betting coups.

If Barney was to pull this off and the Corish Stud was to stay out of the weekend scandal sheets, then we had four days to find the blackmailer.

On Wednesday, Kincaid spent more than an hour with Town Crier, giving him as full an examination as was possible without anaesthetic. Martin anxiously followed him, asking questions which Kincaid handled good-naturedly. He took away more samples and left in an ill-concealed state of excitement, which raised Martin's hopes till I told him Kincaid was simply thrilled at being involved in such an unusual case. 'It's the scientist in him coming out. If he finds the cure he'll want it named the Kincaid Serum or something.'

Watching the vet's car disappear along the drive, Martin said, 'He can call it the Kincaid Master Triumph Total Genius Cocktail if he wants, so long as he cracks it.'

We returned to the yard. The phone in the office was ringing. Martin hurried over but it stopped as he opened the door. 'Damn!'

He picked up the receiver and dialed a short number, listened and noted something down. He dialed again. 'Tom, you rang me...Uhuh. Yeah, Friday's fine.' He hung up and said to me, 'Blacksmith.'

'Makes a change from blackmail. What did you just do? How did you know it was him that called?'

'Just dialed one four seven one, that tells you the last person who called you.'

'When did that system start? Do you have to apply to have it installed?'

'Don't think so. We didn't. It was Fiona who showed me how to do it. You don't need it anyway, your answerphone's always on.'

'Answerphones don't tell you the number of the last blackmailer to call.'

THIRTEEN

On Thursday morning, Barney Dolan rang, sounding nervous. I assured him I was okay for Saturday. If we hadn't nailed the blackmailer by Friday night, I'd been prepared to tell Barney I couldn't take the ride. It wouldn't have been worth exposing the stud just to do Barney a favour. But now that we had an ideal opportunity to get the guy's number, I was happy to ride, knowing I'd get an angry call from him after Cliptie ran.

Priorities one and two were coming along nicely, and if over the weekend I could bail Barney out of trouble with Joey the Greek, it could yet turn out to be a productive week.

The rest of Thursday and Friday proved quiet, frustrating and boring. In the blackmailer's hall of fame, our guy must hold the record for the smallest phone bill. I began wondering if something had happened to him. Maybe blackmail was his stock in trade and another 'client' had sorted him out.

At noon on Friday, I checked the next day's declarations and I cursed when I saw Tranter's name against a runner in Cliptie's race.

I was about to call Barney Dolan to warn him when the phone rang. The pause before the caller spoke increased my heart rate and stopped my breath for a second.

'Eddie?'

It was Martin. I almost swore at him. He said, 'I think I've got our man.'

'The blackmailer?'

'Yep.'

'He called you?'

'Nope.'

'Come on, Martin!'

'I'm looking at a picture of him.'

Martin arrived that evening and produced a cutting from a monthly racing magazine called *Bloodstalk*. It was a full-page story about the Corish Stud and what a fine establishment it was. The writer's name was Simon Spindari. There was a head and shoulders picture of him at the top of the page - young, dark-eyed, olive-skinned, smiling. Your original Latin lover.

Martin explained that the feature was commissioned as 'Advertorial': the magazine had been paid £1,250 and had written the piece in a very positive light.

Martin said, 'I twigged when I noticed the cutting on the office wall. That's where I'd heard the voice before. He came twice to interview me and I found out this morning he came once when I wasn't there and spent the afternoon with Caroline, boozing.'

'Who told you?'

'Fiona.'

'Why didn't she tell you before this?'

'She said she didn't want me to think she was telling tales on Caroline, trying to turn me against her.'

'Telling tales? A journalist having a few drinks and a chat?'

Martin looked uncomfortable. 'Well, Fiona thinks it was maybe more than just a few drinks. Which is fair enough, Caroline's got her own life to lead now.'

But I could see that in his mind it wasn't fair enough. The thought of Caroline with someone else hurt him, and perhaps he now saw why she might have betrayed him and told Spindari about Town Crier and what a bastard her husband was. She could have been drunk or simply vengeful. 'Have you asked Caroline about it?'

'Thought it best not to in case she warned the guy.'

I nodded, thinking. 'Are you sure it's him?'

'Positive.'

'Okay.'

Martin watched me. 'What do we do now?' he asked.

'I don't know. It'll take a bit of thinking out.'

'Why don't we just ring him up, tell him we know who he is?'

'Where does that leave us though? He's still got damaging information.'

'He's always going to have that, isn't he? Doesn't matter what we do.'

'Unless we can make him believe Caroline was lying to him,' I said.

'How do we do that?'

I told him what I thought we should do, and when he called me a genius, my thoughts went back to the days when he was my idol. His praise always made me ridiculously proud.

Before Martin had sussed the identity of the blackmailer, the plan had been for him to come to my flat and wait for the call while I was at Market Rasen. Now he had to make a quick return trip to the stud to put plan B into action.

Before leaving, he begged me to ring Kincaid to ask about progress on the Town Crier samples. The vet had a ride at Market Rasen and we'd agreed to meet after racing. I promised Martin that if Kincaid got a breakthrough, he'd be on the phone quicker than you could say 'sperm count'.

I spent most of the journey to Market Rasen trying to figure out how I was going to cope with Billy Tranter in the second race, which was tailor-made for more of his villainy.

Cliptie had fourteen opponents and was a twelve to one chance in the betting forecast. If he won, Barney would recover Joey the Greek's cash and more besides. But such a big field on this tight undulating track would have Tranter slavering with anticipation.

The best way of staying safe and getting a clear run would be to jump him off in front and try and hold on to the lead, but horses are individuals and need riding in different ways. Dolan had told me Cliptie did best when covered up and delivered very late. A tricky horse, and, in Tranter, a tricky rival.

FOURTEEN

The past few days had been cooler, and it was grey and overcast with dark clouds rolling in from the west as I headed for the weighing room. We could have done with some rain earlier in the week to soften the going, though the management had been watering and claimed to have produced perfect ground. Against Tranter, I feared I'd be hitting that ground hard at some point between 2.45 and 2.50, and had my doubts about how 'perfect' it would feel then.

But trainers seemed convinced as there were more than ten runners entered in each race, a rare thing these days. This meant the weighing room would be busier than normal. There were the usual calls of welcome and jocular abuse as I worked my way through valets and jockeys in various stages of undress till I reached my peg.

In the changing room, there is an unofficial pecking order based on success and experience and everyone observes it. The top jocks always got the positions closest to heaters, toilets, saunas, etc., then the scale slides to the bottom, the dingy corners where you find the humble conditional jockeys, their eye as firmly fixed on that number one peg as it is on a Grand National victory.

The place smelled of leather and sweat and tobacco smoke, liniment, saddle soap, boot polish and hope. And we treasured it as the sanctuary it was. No trainers or owners allowed, no matter how rich or how well connected. Valets, jockeys, racecourse officials only. It was our own little Wendy House where the baddies couldn't get us and where most of us hoped we'd never have to grow up.

I knew Barney Dolan liked a drink, but I hadn't seen him drunk. Not until I walked into the paddock. Sweat beaded his forehead and each cheekbone, as though his red nose was radiating heat. His eyes were bloodshot, his pupils the size of confetti. He stank of gin and slurred his speech as he gave me instructions. I squeezed his arm. 'Cool it. We'll be okay.'

He just nodded stupidly and tears welled but didn't fall, as his face seemed to freeze with the terror of losing. You could have transferred the picture straight into a Gamblers Anonymous leaflet and captioned it 'Addict at the end of his tether'.

I'd been pretty tense myself for the past hour. Tranter hadn't turned up. I'd sat in the changing room, waiting to see his face as he came through the door. I would know by his first look if he intended to try and do me again today, but he didn't arrive and minutes before the deadline a substitute jockey was declared.

I knew now I could ride the race without constantly watching my back. I'd been looking forward to giving that good news to Barney Dolan in the paddock but his mind was no longer open for business, closed down for the afternoon by that well-known racecourse firm, Fear & Booze.

The mounting bell sounded. Barney stood rooted. I went over to Cliptie and the lad legged me up. Cliptie flicked an ear and rolled an eye toward me, probably wondering which little adventure I had in store for him today. I clapped his neck as we walked round. 'Relax, I forgot to bring my swimming trunks.' The blond lad looked up at me and smiled.

As we left the paddock, I looked toward the car park to see Billy Tranter running for the weighing room as furiously as his saddle and kitbag would allow. I whistled loudly through my teeth, which wasn't the smartest thing to do as Cliptie jibbed in surprise and jumped sideways, but I caught Tranter's eye and gave him a wide smile and a high wave. I saw his mouth form a curse as he slammed the saddle to the ground and kicked it.

We cantered to the start.

My stupid antics had stirred Cliptie up, and he wouldn't settle to walk round. He jogged and skittered and generally worked himself into lather, and I was glad that Dolan wasn't capable of holding up a pair of binoculars. By the time the tape rose, Cliptie was in such a sweat, I could hear my boots squeak against his sides as I fought to settle him. He fought, throwing his head about, pulling hard, so determined that he barely took off at the first hurdle then almost tied himself in knots as he hurried to overcome the stumble and resume his headlong gallop.

I hadn't managed to rein him back an ounce as we approached the second and I stopped wrestling and just concentrated on getting him over safely. He jumped it cleanly, eager to return to fighting me.

If trainers give riding orders, most jockeys try to stick to them, even if they think they are wrong. It's better to lose a race you could have won than to disobey orders. If the horse gets stuffed then at least the blame can't be laid on you. The reverse side of this is the fact that a large number of races are decided by decisions taken during running, and I was about to make one for good or bad.

Cliptie needed holding up in the pack then brought with a late surge to give his best. If he tried to lead all the way, he'd run out of puff or enthusiasm and pack it in before the finish. On the other hand, he was using so much energy fighting my efforts to settle him he'd have nothing left at the finish anyway. So I stopped pulling against him, sat as still as I could and talked softly, sending messages down the reins to say, 'Okay, you win, no more battles, I promise. Take it easy now, do your own thing.'

And he understood. The frantic attitude disappeared. The pace didn't ease much, if any, but the gallop became rhythmical, smoother, not so taxing. The less I moved, the more his excellent balance was apparent. We jumped the third. I glanced round. We were twenty lengths clear. Five to jump.

How was Dolan coping with this?

Cliptie held together beautifully over the next two. Unfaltering. Three to jump.

Attempting to lead all the way is different from any other race-riding tactic. Normally you'll have a calm, settled horse who's a proven stayer, who enjoys being out there on his own, who relishes the battle when challengers come at him late in the race. But even on those types there's always a little spider of doubt waiting to unravel its web, anticipating that blip in the stride or breathing that tells you it will be a miracle if you last home.

And it's not only getting home, returning in one piece, puttering into the petrol station on your final whiff of vapour. On a thoroughbred, there is a pack after you. A pack of animals. And you have a fierce desire to win. Not just for you, often for the horse, for your partner, the one who's done everything he can to stay ahead of that pack. Sometimes you can almost feel the primal fear from him as he falters and tries to keep going, to keep living.

The worst feeling of all is the helplessness. That was the sensation I dreaded most and that was what I found myself expecting as I went to the second last on this horse who was trying to lead throughout for probably the first time in his life.

I forced myself to look round again.

They were coming.

The dark pack closed like some snaking eraser deleting the distance between us.

Ten lengths behind. Two to jump. Three furlongs to go. Six hundred and sixty yards. How much was each worth in pounds to Barney Dolan?

But Cliptie was holding together. Then, a hundred yards off the hurdle, he went... faltered. The tiniest of tremors but one that I knew signified the beginning of the earthquake.

He cleared the jump but failed to get away cleanly, lost his stride. I gathered the reins, sat lower, gently tried to bring him onto an even keel. His breath rasped, ears came back. I talked to him. 'Come on! Stay with it! Not far. One more jump.'

I daren't look behind. The simple turning action could easily throw him off balance again. I didn't know how near they were.

Then I heard the hoofbeats.

Approaching the last, he was almost exhausted and hit the top, stumbled, but somehow got his legs out in front and stayed upright. I was now a passenger. Dead freight. I was convinced that if I started riding a finish Cliptie would go to pieces.

Hoofbeats right and left. Loud panting. Then in the periphery of my vision a dark stretching nose each side of Cliptie's quarters, both gaining, reeling us in, foot by foot, reaching our breast girth, jockeys like dervishes, every instinct in me screaming to kick and scrub and push but my brain overruling, forcing me to sit still and stay balanced, letting Cliptie do everything for both of us. Ninety nine percent of onlookers would think I was throwing the race.

The winning post seemed eerily fixed, never coming nearer, the only movement from those other two snorting, sweating, whip-marked animals, their heads at Cliptie's shoulder now, at his throat, his jaw, his nose.

Then past him.

And the post.

'Photograph,' the PA blared.

'Photograph.'

In most tight finishes, you know if you've won or not. Normally you'll glance across as you hit the line, but I'd been so afraid to move for fear of unbalancing Cliptie that I'd kept staring straight ahead. He pulled himself up very quickly, exhausted. I jumped off and led him toward the unsaddling enclosure.

A few punters by the horsewalk asked me if I'd held on and that made me more hopeful; others cursed me for not riding out the finish. Dolan waited in the enclosure. The colour had gone from his face though his nose stayed stubbornly red, making the surrounding skin look even paler. He swayed gently as though just holding on for the result before keeling over.

He lumbered across, almost blocking my way as I led the horse in, and tried to ask silently but the intended quizzical expression resulted in one slightly tilted eyebrow and crossed eyes. At least if we'd lost he'd feel no pain till he sobered up. I looked at him and shrugged. It was as though we had a pact of silence. The lad took Cliptie and I clapped the horse's lathered neck. Cliptie's sides heaved and his head hung.

I watched the two other jockeys involved ride in; neither entered the winner's spot.

The PA crackled slightly and breaths were held. 'Ladies and gentlemen, the judge has called for a print before deciding the outcome of the second race.'

Unless it was desperately tight, the judge could usually nominate the winner from the negative. We'd now have to wait a few minutes more for a full print to be produced. I went to weigh in then hurried back out. Beside me, Barney stared straight ahead and kept swaying, rhythmical as a metronome.

After five minutes without an announcement, there were murmurs of 'dead heat'. Finally, the PA crackled again. 'Ladies and gentlemen, the result of the photo finish… the judge has called a dead heat between number three, Cranston Hall, and number seven, Cliptie.' I grabbed Barney's arm. 'Will that do?' Bets on dead heats are settled to half the stake. Cliptie's Starting Price was twelve to one. I wondered how much Barney had bet. But he smiled stupidly and nodded then said, 'Fixed Tranter, too. Fixed Tranter.'

I smiled. 'What did you do?'

Comically, he bent over and swung his arm, releasing a phantom bowling ball. 'Old spud up the arse trick!' he bellowed. I later found out he'd got someone to block Tranter's car exhaust with a raw potato. Barney bowled again in a demented action replay then fell over and lay on his back, cackling at the sky.

FIFTEEN

Brian Kincaid turned up half an hour later, and we took Styrofoam cups of black coffee outside and stood by the empty parade ring during the running of the next race. Kincaid's hooked nose touched the edge of the narrow cup and he had to tilt his head back as he drank. He had no news of any breakthrough on the Town Crier samples, and told me that progress would be quicker if we would allow him to contact the Equine Fertility Unit in Newmarket.

The lab had some ultra-sophisticated equipment but much of their work came via the Jockey Club, and I was as nervous as Martin about any involvement with them. From the beginning, Kincaid had taken the view that if he asked no questions he'd hear no lies, so when I confirmed we wanted the EFU guys left out he didn't push it, just told me we'd have to be patient.

I watched Kincaid ride in the last, admiring how stylish he looked for such a tall man. He rode a brilliant race to catch Tranter's horse close home, and that made victory all the sweeter for me. Although Kincaid had never given up hope on his horse, Tranter's had been well clear on the run in then started idling so badly that Kincaid caught him in the shadow of the post and won by a neck.

I went to applaud Brian Kincaid as he came in. Riding toward the winner's enclosure Kincaid wasn't smiling, he was grim-faced and obviously very angry. Jumping from the saddle, he forced a smile for the winning connections and managed a few terse words with the trainer before hurrying inside the weighing room. I followed him.

He got up from the scales and strode into the changing room, dumped his saddle and whip on the bare wooden table and wrenched open the buckle of his helmet strap. The way he tore the helmet off must have hurt his ears and as he turned to face me, his fury made him almost unrecognizable. Kincaid was the most relaxed guy you could meet, and if anyone had offered to bet me I'd one day see him in such a rage, I'd have lost a lot of money.

I'd been anxious to ask what had happened, but as I stopped a few yards from him he moved forward, eyes burning through me, and pushed me firmly aside with both hands. I turned to see who his target was, and as a scowling Tranter appeared carrying his gear, Kincaid took two more steps, drew back his right arm and unleashed a punch Tyson would have been proud of.

The only sound that came from Tranter was the crunching grind of gristle giving way to a hammerhead of knuckle. His mouth opened half in surprise, half in protest, but before a word could form, he was hurtling backward, scattering tack and dropping his own gear as he fell. A dozen men, jockeys and valets, stood still. Through the doorway, an official moved forward inquiringly. Kincaid stepped over Tranter and slammed the door.

No outside observers now.

Grabbing the dazed Tranter, Kincaid hoisted him up and tore at his colours until much of Tranter's flesh was exposed. Grunting, he lifted him off his feet and half-laid, half-threw him down on a long trestle table. Kincaid picked up Tranter's own whip and started thrashing him, high hard strokes across his pale skin. Weals rose in instant red ridges as Tranter, still semi-conscious from the punch, groaned and tried to turn.

We all looked at each other, nobody sure what to do. From time to time, scores were settled in the privacy of the changing room. It was usually short and sharp and soon forgotten about but Kincaid was out of control. He started shouting: 'If you ever do anything like that again I'll kill you, you fucking despicable little turd!' He was grunting with the effort of beating Tranter.

'Brian, enough!' I said, grabbing at his elbow. He wrenched free and raised the whip again. I seized the collar of his silks from behind and jerked him back, off balance. 'You'll kill him!'

He stared down at me. He was red-eyed with rage. I took the chance of reaching up to grip his shoulders. 'Brian, for God's sake, calm down! Calm down!'

He stared at me and I thought he'd gone permanently mad. He was panting, and blobs of spittle had appeared at the edges of his mouth.

With a mixture of gentleness and firmness, I led him slowly away from a prostrate Tranter as the others watched. They moved aside to let us through. Quietly I said to Colin Blake, 'Get the doctor.'

Blakey moved quickly toward the door as I sat Kincaid on the bench. He stared straight ahead but his breathing eased and the rigidity seeped from his body until he was half-slumped, elbows on knees, head drooping, gazing at the floor.

Two hours later, Kincaid's demeanour had changed to one of deep depression. We were in a small country pub, looking at glasses of whisky that neither of us had any real appetite for. His all-out assault had been triggered by Tranter's abuse of his horse after being caught on the post. As they'd pulled up Tranter had steered himself behind Kincaid's mount so that he couldn't be seen from the stands and thrashed his own exhausted horse savagely with his whip around the head and neck. Brian described it graphically. Tranter lashed across the velvety muzzle and, more painfully, down the horse's last rib so the leather flap wrapped under the soft part of the belly to bite into the fleshy purse that held his penis. Kincaid said Tranter gave the poor beast a welter of vicious strokes before he'd managed to reach him and almost wrench him from the saddle.

But the vet was disgusted by his own behaviour and lack of self-control, and no matter how much I tried to reassure him it was justified, his mood grew blacker. I told him Tranter had never lost consciousness and that the bewildered doctor had said he didn't think there would be any permanent damage.

Nor was there any danger of Kincaid being disciplined. No witness would snitch and, spiteful as he was, it was highly doubtful that Tranter would either. 'You'll have to watch yourself though,' I warned Kincaid, 'the little bastard won't forget it easily.'

Kincaid and I left the drinks unfinished and went our separate ways.

Back at my flat, Martin confirmed that the first part of our plan to beat the blackmailer had been carried out. As agreed, he persuaded Fiona to call Spindari and warn him that he was being set up.

Spindari had denied he knew anything about the blackmail attempt, but Fiona told him that Caroline, with Martin's knowledge, had deliberately fed him false information on Town Crier in the hope that Jean Kerman would print the story and leave her newspaper open to a huge libel suit from the Corish Stud.

When Spindari asked what Fiona's interest in it was, she'd said she was pregnant by Martin who had reneged on his promise to marry her and gone back to his wife. The simplest of motives: revenge.

Martin had spent the evening waiting to see if our plan had worked. The blackmailer would be aware by now that I'd ridden a winner at Market Rasen, having accepted exactly the type of ride he'd warned me against. But he hadn't called. It looked like he'd swallowed Fiona's story.

SIXTEEN

Martin stayed overnight and next day we travelled to Worcester to visit Kincaid to try to cheer him up. The vet's mood had improved greatly since the previous evening; Judy, his wife, had told him he'd done exactly the right thing and that she'd have thought less of him if he hadn't given Tranter a beating.

As we drank tea, Judy moved around the big kitchen preparing lunch and joining in the general conversation. Martin was growing increasingly impatient to ask questions about Town Crier. Kincaid noticed and suggested that we might like a conducted tour of the facilities.

As soon as we were outside, Martin pressed for news of progress on the samples. Kincaid explained he was still waiting for some results on the blood and sperm specimens.

'Results from where?' Martin asked nervously.

Kincaid smiled. 'Don't worry; they don't know which stallion the sperm is from or why I've asked for the analysis.'

'Who are *they*?' Martin asked.

'Specialists, Casper and Denbourne, a big lab. Lots of vets use them for analysis.'

'Thoroughbred specialists?'

'Specialist analysts, all animals. Look, the samples should be here by Tuesday at the latest. I'm as anxious as you guys to crack this. I don't like mysteries.'

Martin nodded and ran his fingers through his grey mop, pushing it away to reveal that telltale gauntness, as though all the worries in his head were sucking at the skin, stretching it tighter over the fine bone structure.

Kincaid reached out and squeezed his shoulder gently. 'I'll ring you as soon as the results come through.'

The best that could be said about the next three days was that Spindari failed to resurface. It looked like we'd beaten the blackmail threat.

Kincaid called me just after nine on Tuesday morning: the lab could find nothing in the sperm to offer a clue as to the cause of the sterility.

'Where next?' I asked.

'Can you give me till the end of the week?' He sounded serious, thoughtful.

'Sure. What're you thinking?'

'Ask no questions, Eddie.'

'Brian…'

'Eddie, listen, I won't drop you in it, I promise.'

'Okay. Can I make one stipulation?'

'Shoot.'

'No Horseracing Forensic Lab.' The Horseracing Forensic Lab dealt mostly with security issues - the last thing we needed.

'Fine. I'll call you. Oh, are you at Stratford on Friday?' He asked.

'I've got nothing booked, but I'll probably be there mooching around. Better than sitting here in this heat looking down on a one-horse yard.'

'Dust in the mouth? Tumbleweeds outside the saloon?'

I smiled. 'Something like that.'

'See you on Friday.'

I had to ring Martin with the bad news, but I decided to dress up the facts a little. I told him the samples had highlighted something that required more investigation, further tests, and that Kincaid had asked us to hold on till the end of the week.

Martin took it well and quizzed me for details. I told him Kincaid had been talking medical terms and I hadn't really taken it all in.

When I saw Kincaid at Stratford on Friday, he seemed very positive. He told me he expected to have some results by Monday at the latest. I'd agreed to ask no questions and I held to the deal, content to wait a few days more. Kincaid had been very upbeat and wasn't the type to raise false hopes.

He was at Stratford for a ride in the last. We stood talking just inside the changing-room door. I suggested we have dinner somewhere before driving home. He smiled ruefully. 'Afraid not, Eddie. I haven't eaten since yesterday morning. Got to do ten eight in the second at Southwell tomorrow.'

'On what?'

'Tubalcain.'

'They must fancy it.'

He nodded, smiling.

'Excuse me!' A voice from behind us. It was Tranter. We'd been half-blocking the doorway. We moved aside and there was a sudden yelp. We turned to see Ken Rossington, a valet, clutching his right foot and hopping about in apparent anguish. Kincaid had stood on his toe, and although he was most apologetic, Rossington made his usual show of it. One of the changing room's jokers, he'd milk any potential laugh for all it was worth.

Tranter looked in poor shape; bruised eyes, nose still swollen and misshapen. He sat on the bench. Kincaid followed him and it seemed for a few seconds he was going to approach him; there was an air of conciliation about the vet. Kincaid took a couple of steps inside the room, hesitated, then turned and strode out, a trace of anger back in his face.

Tranter didn't watch him leave. Unpacking his kitbag, he showed no emotion.

I rode in the second race and the fourth, both unplaced, and loitered till after the fifth on the chance some poor bugger might crock himself and let me in for a ride in the last, but they all returned safe and I headed for the exits to beat the crowds. Driving home, I speculated on the chances of Kincaid's coming up with something by the time I saw him at Southwell next day, but Kincaid didn't make it to Southwell. He never left Stratford alive.

SEVENTEEN

I heard about it next morning driving to Southwell. It was an item tagged on to the end of the news on Radio 5: 'An amateur jockey and prominent vet has been found dead in what is believed to have been an horrific accident at Stratford Racecourse. Mister Brian Kincaid, who was married with a baby daughter, apparently collapsed in a sauna and died of severe hyperthermia. Mister Kincaid's body was not found until early this morning. Racecourse officials say there will be a full inquiry.

'And now the weather. '

And now the weather.

I must have imagined it. Nobody could report the death of a friend of mine and simply say 'And now the weather'. Impossible. A hoax or something. It had to be. I pulled over, mounting the grass verge. I was vaguely aware of a lorry thundering past, horn blaring, shaking the car. I sat gripping the wheel, staring straight ahead, replaying the news clip over and over in my mind.

I don't know how much time passed before I reached for my phone and found the number of Stratford Racecourse in my diary. I asked for the clerk of the course. Unavailable. Could they confirm the news report? Not prepared to comment. Where could I get confirmation? Sorry, couldn't help.

I had a friend in Jockey Club Security, Peter McCarthy. We'd helped each other over the years. I knew he tried to avoid working Saturdays, so I rang his home number and held for ten rings before he answered.

'Mac, Eddie Malloy. I just heard a news item that said Brian Kincaid is dead. Is it right?'

'Eddie, yes, I'm sorry. Only heard myself about half an hour ago. You knew Brian quite well, didn't you?'

'What happened?'

'The theory is, apparently, that he went into the sauna for a half-hour session after the last race and collapsed in there, by which time everyone had gone home.'

'Collapsed?'

'It seems he'd been wasting quite hard to make the weight at Southwell today. Tragic, isn't it?'

My mind overloaded temporarily with doubts, questions, and images of how Brian would have looked after lying in a sauna for hours.

Mac said, 'Eddie, are you all right?'

'Mmmm. Surely the sauna cabin has some sort of safety cut off?'

'I don't know, Eddie. There will be a full inquiry.' I simply couldn't think straight. Had to get off the phone. I told McCarthy I'd call him later.

I got out of the car and wandered over to a stone wall hemming black and white cattle into a big field. Resting my hands on the wall, I stared across the field into dark woods, trying to pull my thoughts together.

Brian Kincaid was dead. An accident in a sauna.

No way.

Not Brian. He was a highly intelligent man with considerable medical experience. Light-headed from fasting maybe, but he would have been more aware than most of the dangers of losing consciousness in a sauna. At the first sign of dizziness, he would have got out, I was certain of it. But he didn't get out, so either somebody knocked him unconscious in the box or prevented him from escaping.

Logical progression: who?

Logical answer: Billy Tranter.

I leaned against the wall, trying to close down my emotions and think objectively. After the chances he took at Perth and the persistence he'd shown in persecuting me, it had occurred to me that Tranter might have the germ of a psychotic disorder. Whether it could have mutated into psychopathic was another matter. I needed to know more.

I got back on the road to Southwell. The last thing I felt like doing was riding horses, but Tranter would be there and I wanted to see him. Watch him. Study his behaviour. Analyze it. That's what the logical side of me wanted to do. What the rest of me wanted to do was find him guilty without trial and beat him until he died.

The news at noon ran the same item on Brian's death; no further details. Two minutes later, my phone rang. It was Martin. 'I just heard on the news, about Kincaid.'

'Uhuh.'

'Tell me it's not true, Eddie?'

'It's true.'

'Ohhh. Jesus Christ! What are we, jinxed or something?'

'What are you worried about? The samples? Town Crier?' I was just in the mood for an argument. Ready to take my anger out on somebody.

'Eddie, what are we going to do?'

'What are *we* going to do? What the hell's Judy Kincaid going to do? She has a three-month-old kid with no father! We've got a mangy fucking stallion firing blanks! Whose shoes would you rather be in?'

There was a long pause, and then Martin said quietly that he would call me later. I told him to be more bloody respectful to Brian Kincaid's memory when he did. Memory. God, you'd think he'd been dead years. Yesterday I'd spoken to him. Yesterday. In the corridor in the weighing room. He'd been telling me he was wasting hard for this ride.

And who was behind us when he said it? Who was listening? Who could have made a reasonable assumption that Brian might use the sauna yesterday afternoon?

Billy Tranter.

I pressed the accelerator to the floor, speeding dangerously, stupidly, toward Southwell.

EIGHTEEN

My temper had cooled by the time I reached the course. The guys in the weighing room weren't as subdued as I'd expected and it made me angry, made me want to preach a sermon telling them they ought to be grieving for Brian Kincaid. But the fact that he was an amateur meant that he was never really part of the 'brotherhood'. It wasn't a matter of not being accepted, simply that most professional jockeys see each other almost every day in the same way as soldiers in a small elite unit do.

We know each other's characters and weaknesses and share the same dangers daily. Amateur jockeys are tolerated and grudgingly respected if they are good. Brian had been respected but there seemed little emotion at his death, only shock at the manner of it. There was a lot of speculation about how terrible it must have been, and some juvenile nominations of the ways of dying some of them would prefer.

Bill Keating came in and told everyone he'd spoken to the caretaker at Stratford, the bloke who'd found Brian's body

'He said it was like a potato crisp.' That silenced everybody. Tranter was in the corner. I watched his face but saw no emotion. I was sorely tempted to approach him and ask him to account for his movements every minute of yesterday, but had to settle for watching him whenever I could: observing, looking for some flicker of satisfaction when Brian's name was mentioned. But I saw none. And paranoia crept in. I imagined him congratulating himself

65

as he cantered to the start, pictured him locking himself in the toilet so he could gloat and have a good laugh.

I resolved to wait in my car after racing and follow Tranter, but as the afternoon wore on realized that would be a foolish thing to do. Pointless.

Where did I expect him to head for, the scene of the crime? Or did I think he'd go home and erect a banner saying 'I killed Brian Kincaid'?

Half-disgusted, wholly frustrated, I left after my ride in the fourth and drove to Worcester to see Judy Kincaid. The dread of facing her grew mile by mile but I felt I had to go there, pay my respects, and trot out the standard, 'If there's anything I can do'.

She was in bed under sedation; the baby was sleeping in the arms of her sister, who slowly paced the kitchen floor as her husband made coffee. All three of us sat for half an hour in that collective daze that descends on the newly bereaved and suspends social conversation, excuses long silences.

They promised to tell Judy I'd called in. As we said goodbye, I had the strongest of urges to stroke the baby's forehead. I reached out and rested my hand softly on the warm pink skin. A tiny smile flickered on the round sleeping face, and I thanked God she wasn't old enough to understand how much she had just lost.

NINETEEN

I slept on my suspicions, and they were stronger when I woke. Once again, I rang Peter McCarthy, the Jockey Club Security man.

'Eddie, how come I don't hear from you for months then the only time you can find to call me is at weekends?'

It was warm-hearted banter. In the humour market, Mac and I usually traded at about the same exchange rate, but this morning it was the last thing I felt like and I steered him straight on to Brian's death.

'I know very little about it, Eddie.'

'Well, do yourself a favour and get some sniffing around done.'

'You mean, do you a favour?'

'Mac, there's no way that was an accident.'

'How do you know?'

I argued my case for Brian's medical expertise, which Mac accepted as a reasonable foundation, then told him everything that had happened with Tranter.

'You ought to be very careful who you mention this to, Eddie. That's a pretty serious allegation.'

'That's a fact, Mac! I'm not alleging anything. I'm telling you what happened between Tranter and Brian, and I'm telling you that Tranter heard us talking on Friday and could have made a reasonable assumption that Brian was going to be in that sauna.'

'Ah, but—'

'Ah, but nothing! You came to the same conclusion I did just then when I laid out the facts.'

'It's obvious the slant you're taking.'

'Because it's the logical bloody slant to take!'

There was a pause and I pictured him shaking his head slowly.

He said, 'I think you'd best wait and see what the inquiry comes up with.'

'Which will be when? Weeks? Months?'

'I don't know. Let's see what the police have to say. The coroner's report might throw up something.'

'Like what? What evidence is going to be left in a desiccated corpse?'

'That's not for us to say, Eddie.'

'Come on, Mac, don't go all superior. The cops have to be persuaded, as from now, to treat this as suspicious.'

'I wish you luck in your persuading.'

'It would be easier with your help and you damn well know it. And you know that's what I'm asking for.'

He sighed, long and deliberate, straight into the mouthpiece.

'Okay, after the beating last week, did Tranter say he was going to take revenge on Kincaid?'

'Well, I didn't hear him say that.'

'Did anyone?'

'I don't know.'

'Can you find out?'

I can ask around, sure, but—'

'Perhaps you could also ask if anyone knows what time Tranter left Stratford on Friday, and were there any witnesses to his leaving, and did anyone know where he was going, and can anyone at his ultimate destination give him a credible alibi?'

That cooled my ire. Mac was being sensible and logical, while chiding me gently for not being the same. He'd just set off a train of simple deduction, a straightforward elimination process that I should have gone through before even picking up the phone to him.

Chastened, I told him I'd press on with it and get back to him soon. I paced the flat trying to concentrate, to clear my mind so I could start again using calm logic rather than anger and emotion.

The flat was uncomfortably hot. The heat wave persisted. I went outside, scrambled over the big five-bar gate and walked up onto the gallops. The sun threw long shadows across the grassy slope. I spent more than an hour roaming the open spaces, spooked a couple of hares, heard skylarks above and steadily ordered my thoughts.

Back in the flat, I sat down with my diary and began making calls. The first was to Bill Keating, the jockey who'd spoken to the caretaker at Stratford. The caretaker was a friend, and Bill said he thought he'd speak to me quite freely if I called. His name was Charlie Kenton and he answered at the first ring.

'That was quick,' I said.

'I was just about to make a call myself! My hand was on the bloody phone! Didn't half give me a fright. Who is it?'

I introduced myself as a close friend of Brian's. Kenton was happy to talk, with the performing instinct of an accomplished gossip. I let him warm up with a gruesome rendition of how he found the body and what he'd told the police. When I got the chance, I asked questions.

'How come he wasn't found till next morning?'

Kenton blustered about not being able to be everywhere at once, that his duties were different on racedays, and that generally it was nothing to do with him that Brian's body had lain in that sauna all night.

'Did nobody see his car left in the car park?'

'Ah, there, you see! He didn't bring his car. He got a lift with a mate.'

'Who? Which mate?'

'Scotty Fraser, so they tell me.'

'And wasn't he travelling with Scotty?'

'Apparently not.'

'How did he plan to get home?'

That stumped him. 'Er, I'm not sure on that one.'

I pressed him on whether he himself had been around the weighing room after racing. I was hoping to find out if Tranter had been among the last to leave. But Kenton admitted that he'd been on 'traffic duty', which amounted to directing cars out of the public car park. He gave me no further useful information.

I called Scotty Fraser and was glad, in a sad way, to find him as depressed about Brian's death as I was. Scotty felt guilty about not giving Brian the promised lift back.

'What happened, did you forget about him?'

'No, I was heading to the weighing room after the last to meet him and I was told he'd already left.'

'Who told you that?'

'Billy Tranter.'

My second call of the day to McCarthy interrupted a late Sunday lunch. He wasn't pleased.

Scotty Fraser had gone on to explain that he'd called Tranter yesterday, demanding to know why he had said Brian had left Stratford. Tranter told him he'd done it to get back at Brian after the beating. He'd overheard Brian mention he was getting a lift home and thought it would be a nice little touch to leave him stranded. I told Mac all this.

'Well, there you are then,' he said smugly.

'Mac, come on! Tranter would say that, wouldn't he? He's hardly going to admit killing him.'

'Equally, if he intended to kill Kincaid, he'd have to be pretty bloody stupid to drop himself in it now the way you're suggesting.'

'Why not? He had to make sure that Fraser didn't go looking for Brian.'

'Perhaps, but he could have done that just as easily by forging a note or something.'

'And who'd have delivered it to Fraser?'

'Wouldn't have been a big problem.'

'Mac, why are you being so negative? How come you can't see the obvious?'

'How come you've got tunnel vision? Tunnel vision trained on Tranter?'

'Because he's the only one I know with motive. And he's crazy.'

'Motive for what? You're seeing demons round every corner, Eddie. At the moment, we have nothing more than a very unfortunate accident which, with hindsight, some might say was waiting to happen. We have a jockey who's probably malnourished to some extent, already riding more than a stone below his natural weight; he's ridden that day having taken no sustenance at all in the previous twenty-four hours. It's quite probable he's drained and light-headed then he goes and bakes in a sauna. What price a collapse? You wouldn't get big odds.'

We fenced for another ten minutes and Mac said he'd speak to the police officer in charge and raise the possibility of 'foul play'. I urged him to tell them to have a word with Scotty Fraser.

Then I rang Kenton, the caretaker back at Stratford, and he said he'd be happy to show me around. We agreed to meet early next morning.

TWENTY

I was at Stratford before 8 a.m. Kenton was holding the main gate open as I came up the drive. The sauna was situated at the end of a row of showers. Kenton told me it was less than two years old. I went inside the box while he chirped on, pointing to where he'd found Brian and how he'd looked like 'some little alien'. I wanted to yell at him to shut up and get out. Not once had he mentioned Brian's family or expressed sympathy for my loss of a friend. I needed time to look around. I asked him if he'd mind returning to the car and bringing me my mobile phone. He took the keys and hurried off.

Trying to block out the image of Brian's corpse, I examined the sauna box: standard, nothing unusual, two benches either side, one above the other, the coals corralled in the corner, water bucket on the floor nearby. I pulled the door closed from the inside, feeling an unexpected wave of trepidation as it clicked shut on the ballbearing catch.

I pushed it. It needed a little weight behind it but gave quite easily. I repeated the action then went outside and did the same; opened and closed it half a dozen times. The handle was of wood, shaped like a bow, about a foot long. Crouching, I looked closely at it, ran my hands down the soft pine. Relatively new, it had its share of dents and grazes though it gave slightly even under the pressure of a fingernail.

Where the bottom of the handle met the door, just on the underside of the curve, a ridge ran across. I traced it with my finger; no deeper than a millimeter, it had smooth edges. Facing the door, maybe six feet away, was a solid wall tiled in white glaze. I knelt and looked up at the ridge, but the light wasn't good.

'May I ask what you are doing?'

I turned slowly to see a well-dressed, white-haired man - the clerk of the course, Gilbert Grimond.

'Saying a prayer for Brian Kincaid.' On my knees, it was the first thing that came into my head and it was enough to throw Mr Grimond temporarily. 'Oh,' he said. I didn't think it was the right time to tell him that what I was really doing was trying to figure what had been wedged against that handle to keep Brian Kincaid from escaping. What had been used to cover the end of the instrument so that the ridge it left was soft, barely perceptible.

I decided the real reason could wait until I'd spoken to McCarthy, told him what I'd found. Bad decision.

McCarthy was in meetings all day Monday. I left several messages for him but it was late evening before he called me at home. He sounded weary at first, giving the impression that I was the final one on his 'to do' list and all he wanted was to tick off my name and get a decent night's sleep. When I told him about the door handle, he wakened up a bit. 'I'd better go up there in the morning and have a look,' he said.

'I'll meet you there.'

'No, that's a bad idea. You're much too close to this without having any real reason to be so. Not to the outside world, at least.'

'Mac—'

'Eddie! If there is a case to be investigated here, the police are going to be touchy enough about me bringing it to their attention. If they think you're the one behind it all, driving things along, they'll make life difficult.'

'But—'

'Also, what they will see is a vendetta against Tranter. Leave it to me. I've got no axe to grind, and apart from anything else it *is* my job.'

'So you say, but how come you always clock on when the rest of the shift have done the donkey work?'

'The craftsmen always come in after the labourers, Eddie. Like the stallion that finishes the job after the teaser's done the dirty work. '

I smiled. 'The stallion? Getting a bit above yourself, aren't you?' But he was probably spot on. I'd been involved with various police forces in the last few years and if there was a right way to rub them up I'd yet to find it. I contented myself with the thought that evidence was beginning to build - circumstantial maybe, but it was early days and the outlook was promising.

In a more positive mood, I made a sandwich and sat down to listen to the radio news, half-hoping for some breakthrough by the cops. But there was nothing at all on Brian's death – a stale story, filed away and forgotten. I wondered how Judy was bearing up, whether she was still under sedation.

The phone rang. Martin, sounding strung out. 'Eddie, I'm sorry about your friend, but we've got to do something about this horse!'

'What's the big hurry? The stud season's almost over.'

We got into a long argument about the urgency of solving Town Crier's problem. I got the impression that Martin was feeling neglected because Town Crier was no longer my priority. I told him if he felt so strongly about the problem, he should solve it himself. He said that was just what he would do and slammed the phone down.

Ten minutes later, I called him back and arranged to meet next day. He promised to be at my flat early and was true to his word, getting me out of bed.

Even allowing that I was unshaven and bleary-eyed, I still looked better than he did. That terrible concentration-camp gauntness and desperation were in his face. I made coffee. Martin paced, unwilling to sit down.

'What's wrong, Martin?'

'We can't let this slip, Eddie. We've got to sort Town Crier out.'

'I know but there's no big hurry any more, is there? We've got seven months before the start of the new season.'

'We've got nothing like seven months! If the story gets out and we have to submit to tests on him, we're fucked!'

I couldn't understand the sudden desperation. 'Martin, what's happened? Has Spindari been back in touch?'

'No, but—'

'So how is the story going to get out?'

He marched up to me, shoving his face in mine, shades of madness in his bloodshot eyes. 'It could! It just could! And you don't care anymore! You don't give a monkey's fuck! What am I supposed to do, eh? Tell me!' Then he broke down in tears, deep racking sobs. He sank to the floor, crying uncontrollably.

An hour later, with a pint of coffee inside him, he was calmer. He admitted he'd been drinking far too much and that Caroline and Fiona were putting 'unbearable' pressure on him. The bills were mounting, Kincaid was dead, and my attention was elsewhere. He said he just felt everything was slipping away from him and that if he could only be sure Town Crier would recover, that would give him strength.

I looked at this hero of mine, slumped at my table, beaten by his own doubts and fears. This hero, this man, this child. And I promised I'd make everything better for him.

He suggested we visit Brian Kincaid's partners and try to find out what had happened to the samples Brian had sent off. He seemed in no fit state to meet anyone but he promised he'd be okay. Foolishly, I believed him and set up a meeting that afternoon with John Brogan, the senior partner in Kincaid's surgery.

I found a clean shirt for Martin and persuaded him to have a shower and a shave. Just as he closed the bathroom door, the phone rang. It was McCarthy. I looked at my watch: 10.25. I'd assumed he'd be travelling to Stratford as promised but the call was on a clear line, no mobile. I said, 'I thought you were going to Stratford?'

'I'm at Stratford.'

'So what do you think?'

'I think we've got problems.'

'The cops might have problems,' I said with some satisfaction, 'not us.'

'We've got problems, Eddie.' A serious tone I should have recognized sooner.

'What's wrong?'

'The sauna's gone.'

'What?'

'Somebody burned it down in the early hours of this morning. And the weighing room with it.'

TWENTY-ONE

I was driving as fast as my brain was working which wasn't sensible on these country roads and the tyres screeched complaints at each bend. Martin stared straight ahead. He'd just lost the argument about concentrating on Town Crier rather than Brian's death, which I was now almost certain was murder. He paid me back by not responding to the questions I threw out as we headed south. Few needed answering. But I could have used some murmurs of encouragement now and then.

'I mean, if Tranter's done this where does he stop? He kills Brian, burns down the weighing room to get rid of the evidence, the whole weighing room, mind you... I wonder if it was anything to do with McCarthy going there this morning. How could he have found that out?'

I asked Martin to get Mac's number from my diary and dial for me. Silently he did it and handed me the phone. Mac's mobile was switched off. Martin tried the racecourse number. It rang out unanswered. I cursed and returned to one-sided speculation about Tranter and his psychological history, motivation, private life, etc.

Finally, as we sped down the slip road onto the M5, Martin spoke. 'What if it wasn't Tranter?'

'Well, if it wasn't, I wouldn't want to be the cop who's got to solve it. I never knew anybody else who disliked Brian. Who could have a motive besides Tranter?'

'You talk like you and Kincaid were blood brothers or something. I mean, how close were you? He might have been up to all sorts of stuff?'

'Like what?'

'I don't know. Could be anything!'

I was angry with Martin. But he and McCarthy had now said I should be more objective about possible suspects, so I kept quiet for the next few heat-hazed miles and concentrated on trying to come up with alternatives. I failed, but it set me wondering if Brian's partners had an opinion on it.

The practice was located on the Worcester/Hereford border, and we got there twenty minutes early and waited in a small hot yellow room where an oscillating fan riffled the dog-eared pages of old Sunday supplements.

The meeting was disastrous. Brogan knew nothing of Kincaid's work for us and hadn't the faintest idea where any samples might have been sent to. Martin quickly lost the place completely and started berating Brogan, accusing him of being incompetent, of being in collusion with some unknown enemy. In the end, I had to apologize and almost drag Martin out. We had a serious argument in the car. Serious but pointless. His sole focus was Town Crier's fertility problem and he was obviously willing to batter and bludgeon his way through all obstacles in his attempt to find a solution. He saw no reason to make allowances for others.

'You simply can't go around behaving like you did in there!' I said. 'Brogan owes us nothing. He'd've been well within his rights to have slung you out of there...bodily!'

'Eddie, what you can't seem to understand is we don't have the time for anything else! Hear that? We! You're in this with me but you're too fucking busy being nice to people! You're only interested in everyone thinking you're a nice guy! We're bleeding to death, man!'

We travelled in silence for the last hour, and as soon as we reached my place, Martin got straight into his car and roared off without saying a word. Back in the flat, I wondered what to do next.

What a bloody mess.

I grabbed the whisky bottle and sloshed some into two inches of water. Sipping methodically at the scotch, I waited for it to seep under the door marked 'Inspiration' in my brain and open it from the inside. Come evening, I was on my second drink, watching the moonrise. I'd spoken to McCarthy. He'd told no one why he was going to Stratford, so unless the caretaker had twigged that I suspected foul play, and he'd blabbed to someone, then either the timing of the burning was coincidental or it lent even more credence to the murder theory.

Mac had told me the police were waiting for the Fire Department's forensic report so he'd reserve his opinion until that came through.

I tried to figure out how I could learn more about Tranter's movements on Friday evening, but the only people likely to know were his friends, if he had any. If he did, then they'd probably know exactly what he thought of me.

Another hour of pondering brought no ideas, though Martin's mind had obviously been at work on the drive home. Just as I was falling into bed, he called me with a ruse of his own.

TWENTY-TWO

By noon next day, Martin had compiled a list of the labs equipped to carry out the analysis required on the Town Crier samples. We'd agreed to split it and ring them posing as a partner from Brian's practice - further deception. I took three numbers and left Martin with four and a warning not to lose his temper.

Forty minutes later, I had scored a blue line through all of mine: negative. Martin was waiting for one to return his call, which they did within the hour: zilch. None had received samples from Brian or his practice. Martin got edgy again and started slagging Brian off, saying he'd done nothing with the samples, claiming he'd been stringing us along. I knew Martin was under severe pressure, but couldn't listen to another tirade. I hung up on him and left the phone off the hook.

It was hot and I was hungry. I had little to eat but plenty to chew on. I wasn't too depressed. The death of a friend tends to balance your perspective. The stud was important to me financially but otherwise, if it went under, I could live with it. I'd had my share of hardship in the past and always got through.

Martin would probably crack up, but he'd drained me dry of sympathy. Even if we came out okay in the end, I knew our partnership would never be the same. Idols with feet of clay, indeed.

I found some salad in the fridge and boiled a piece of fish. Less than 300 calories and it would keep me going till evening. I had to do ten stone at Uttoxeter tomorrow, which meant losing at least three pounds. A five-mile run this afternoon would help and a sauna tomorrow morning. The thought shook me, and I knew I wouldn't sit in a sauna again without thinking of Brian Kincaid through every sweating minute.

After lunch, I cleaned up around the flat then changed into my running gear, pulling on two extra sweaters. As I laced my shoes, the phone rang.

'Eddie, still want me to tell the police about Tranter?' It was McCarthy. He was notorious for trying to tease, for not coming to the point.

'What do you know, Mac?'

'I know Tranter left Stratford soon after racing finished on Friday.'

'Maybe he did but what was to stop him turning round and coming back.'

'Well, for one thing, he didn't have a car.'

I waited. Mac said, 'About five miles from the course, a Mercedes 600 ran into Tranter's Volkswagen at traffic lights. His car had to be towed away and the Merc driver took him home.'

'Who told you all this, Tranter?'

'No, one of the Stewards who was acting at Stratford, for 'twas he who was driving said Merc.'

'So how come we haven't heard this juicy piece of gossip on the grapevine?'

'Because our rather embarrassed Steward asked Tranter to keep it quiet, and Tranter, knowing which side his bread is low-calorie-spreaded, has done exactly that.'

'So who told you?'

'The crasher. The Steward.'

'Who is.?'

'Not for publication, Eddie.'

'Fine.' I was miffed and not yet convinced. Tranter could have hit Brian on the head before leaving, I supposed, but could he have wedged that door closed, confident nobody would have discovered it?

'Also,' Mac said, 'to put the proverbial tin lid on your theory, Tranter was in Ireland when the weighing room at Stratford burned down. If you still think Brian Kincaid was murdered, Eddie, you'd better find yourself another suspect.'

A blue haze hung over the vast parklands as I ran along an old cart track. The sweating had started before I'd broken into a jog and now, beneath the layers of clothing, under the tight-cuffed plastic body suit, I could feel and hear the sponginess under my arms as they pumped out a steady rhythm. I was thinking more clearly and had spent the first two miles wondering who could tell me more about Brian Kincaid. I was certain he hadn't lied about sending the samples to a lab. Before leaving the flat I'd even taken the chance of checking with the Equine Fertility Unit at Newmarket, the one I'd made Brian promise he wouldn't use. They had nothing.

That was the first piece of the puzzle. The second was that Brian had been murdered, I was sure of that. And the third was that Tranter no longer seemed a suspect.

So what had Brian Kincaid done to make somebody kill him?

It was pointless returning to his professional partners. Martin had blown any potential trust there. But who else had Brian associated with?

The best bet would be to speak to Judy again. I owed her a call anyway but visiting after bereavement was never easy, least of all when your motive was selfish.

I took a cool shower, fighting the temptation to lay my head back and drink from the gushing jets. Any intake of liquid would counteract the sweating. I gargled a strong mouthwash, dressed, and dialed Judy's number. Her sister Amanda answered and told me Judy was with the police in Worcester.

'Couldn't they have come to her?'

'They did, yesterday. She wants to know more so she's gone to Worcester Police Station to see the chap from Warwick.'

Brian died in the county of Warwickshire so the cops there would be in charge of the investigation. Her sister said Judy had found strength when she learned that Brian's death was being treated as suspicious. 'She badly needs someone to blame for taking him away. Now she's got the bit between her teeth, she's determined to do all she can to discover who was responsible.' I told Amanda I'd like to help if I could and she said Judy would be in that evening, and she was sure she'd appreciate a visit.

When I got there, Judy, in pressed tan slacks and a cream blouse, welcomed me. Slim, with cropped fair hair, she was tall, almost gangly, and wore no make-up. Her cheeks always carried a reddish bloom; a true country girl. Her blue eyes were defiant despite signs of weeping.

She led me through the house to a big garden where Amanda was rocking the baby in a shaded cradle. Amanda's husband Dave was barbecuing meat that sizzled temptingly and smelt delicious, making me regret I was wasting hard for Uttoxeter tomorrow.

I asked about plans for the funeral. Judy didn't flinch. She said, 'The police said that if evidence of suspicious circumstances might come to light, it would be better to delay the funeral until after the coroner's inquest.'

'When will the inquest be?' I asked.

She shrugged, 'They said, weeks, maybe months…but it's for the best…for justice for Brian.'

I nodded. I had no way of knowing if the police had simply been paying lip-service to Judy's concerns, but I was glad Brian wouldn't be buried until someone had investigated, even if that someone was me.

We sat until dusk, when marauding insects made things uncomfortable. What I'd expected to be an ordeal turned out to be enjoyable and uplifting. We talked about Brian, recounting stories, remembering funny episodes, laughing freely; even Judy, whose eyes sparkled at times with memories. If anyone had happened upon us, they'd have assumed we were discussing a dear friend long dead but it had been less than a week since his murder - a word, understandably, still forbidden.

I worked the conversation around to Brian's friends and associates, and by the time I left I had the names of three people who'd been fairly close to him. Judy told me he'd probably thought highly enough of them to confide, talk about any worries.

Judy said, 'I'd try Alex Dunn first. Brian loved Alex. He was Brian's mentor. "The best vet in the world", Brian called him. Used to call him it to his face, too, and Alex always blushed.' She smiled again then the smile disappeared and concern took its place. She said, 'God, I wonder if Alex knows. He and Brian had spoken half a dozen times in the week before, but Alex hasn't called since.'

I tried to show only a casual interest. 'Have they always stayed in close touch?'

Judy, distracted, shook her head slowly. 'I don't think so. It must have been Christmas when they last spoke. Until lately, that is.' She turned toward me. 'Brian said Alex was helping him out with what he called a "fascinating little problem."'

TWENTY-THREE

Alex Dunn's practice was in Newmarket and although I'd heard his name, we'd never met. When I got home, I rang a friend down there on the pretext of looking for a good vet I could recommend to someone.

Without prompting, he mentioned Dunn. 'Got a reputation as a bit of a nutty professor, likes experimenting, does some homeopathic horse stuff if you can believe that, but he gets results. Works on his own in a little place at Six Mile Bottom. Lives alone, doesn't smoke or drink, but bets like a lunatic.'

He gave me a couple more names. We hung up, and I called Martin and told him I had an idea where the samples might be, though I didn't elaborate. He wanted more info, but the last thing I needed was him racing off to Newmarket to grab Alex Dunn by the lapels.

He said, 'So what are you going to do?'

'I'm going to try and see this guy as soon as possible but it'll have to be Thursday at the earliest. I'm riding at Uttoxeter tomorrow.'

'Give me his name, I'll go and see him.'

'No, Martin, leave it to me. I'll call you as soon as I know something.'

He argued his case, temper flaring again. He slammed the phone down on me.

I saw Tranter at Uttoxeter next day. He ignored me, even during the race we contested and which I won. My other two rides

84

were unplaced, but with earnings for the evening of almost £700, I wasn't too unhappy, and drove home eagerly anticipating tomorrow's trip to Newmarket.

They were racing there, and I learned from the racecourse office that Alex Dunn was attending in an official capacity. There was no break in the weather and as I steered along the drive approaching the racecourse, heat haze distorted the images of cars and pedestrians ahead.

After the first race, I spotted McCarthy. He was walking toward the stables at right angles to me, his chubby face trying to sweat itself cool. I hadn't seen Mac for a while. Looked like he'd put most of his weight back on. His wife tried to keep him on a sensible diet, and when he'd been pitching for promotion last year he'd followed it, but when he was pipped for the big job he'd let himself slip again. Pushing seventeen stones now by the look of him.

He didn't see me till I was almost by his shoulder, and when he did his scowl deepened.

'Hi,' I said. 'Hot, eh?'

'What are you doing here?'

'Nice to be made welcome at the headquarters of racing.'

He stopped and turned, mopping his brow with a handkerchief. From the front, I could see a tinge of grey in the dark hair at his temples. He said, 'You don't like flat racing, Eddie, what are you up to?'

'Same as I was last time we spoke. I'm trying to find out who killed Brian Kincaid.'

'Leave it to the proper authorities.'

'What exactly are the proper authorities doing about it?'

Mac glanced around. At six foot two, his vision covered a wide sweep. He didn't care to be seen talking to me. We'd been in a few scrapes together, though he'd always come out of it well enough. He said, 'Look, I need to speak to one of the stable security staff. Can we meet somewhere quiet during the next race?'

The bars would be quiet while a race was on, but flat races seldom lasted longer than a few minutes. I suggested meeting at the stables. He agreed. I asked him where I'd find Alex Dunn.

'Why do you want him?'

'I'll tell you in ten minutes.'

Mac said if Dunn wasn't out on the course, he usually watched the racing from the owners and trainers stand. He told me I couldn't miss him - six foot six and very thin with white hair.

I recognized Dunn immediately from the description. He was in the stand. On the steps behind him was a noticeable gap; few would have a decent view over his head topped by a Panama hat. I watched him throughout the mile race that was in progress: a rolled up newspaper in his left fist, fixed like a pathfinder to the binoculars, which moved slowly as the commentary built, the crowd murmur grew to a rumble, the approaching hoofbeats drummed louder.

Then they were past the post.

The noise died. Dunn's binoculars came down but he stared gloomily into the distance, as though watching a large wager disappear over the horizon.

He gripped the crush barrier with both hands and almost slumped forward. My inclination was to let him compose himself, but my instinct told me to move in while his defenses were low. He stood like a skinny breakwater as the crowd moved around him and the stand emptied. Within a couple of minutes, he was alone.

I approached him head on up the steps, smiling. 'Mister Dunn?'

He nodded, wondering if he should know me, frowning as he searched for a name. 'Eddie Malloy.' I said, holding out my hand. 'I am a friend. I mean I was a friend of Brian Kincaid.'

There was an immediate change in his brown eyes. He swallowed dryly then held out his hand. He looked to be in his late-fifties, though the hat hid most of his hair, which was Aspirin white and would, I guessed, make him appear considerably older.

'You knew Brian?' I said.

He nodded, struggling for normality but showing no surprise at my change of tense. I decided to go for it, but the PA system drowned out my next words. I repeated them. 'The samples you were helping Brian with, they were from one of my horses.'

He was already quite pale but that spooked him, driving what remained of the colour from his bony face. At the same time, his whole body recoiled a few inches as though I'd raised a hand to hit him. A poker player he wasn't.

Taking off his hat, he ran skeletal fingers through his thin hair, put the hat back on and said, 'Which samples?'

He was trying.

I stared at him. 'The samples from my stallion. The semen, blood, biopsies.'

He checked his watch, hand shaking slightly, and said, 'I'm very sorry but I'm actually on duty today.'

'I can wait. We can meet after racing.'

'I have quite a few appointments.'

'We need to talk, Mister Dunn. I'm sure you know why.'

He looked at me as though I was a bailiff. I thought for a few seconds he was going to start crying. He said, 'Perhaps you could come and see me at home?'

'Fine. This evening? Six-thirty?'

He nodded slowly, watching me like I was the snake, he the rabbit. He gave me his address and phone number when I pressed him. I left and went to meet McCarthy.

He was still inside the racecourse stables. I waited, pacing the perimeter. I was pretty keyed up. Dunn had behaved as though he'd murdered Brian himself. Surely his demeanour couldn't simply be down to his involvement with the samples analysis? I smiled. Maybe there'd be a bonus in this yet. Maybe Dunn could crack Town Crier's problem. Maybe he'd already cracked it.

McCarthy waddled toward me and we walked into the shade of the stable buildings. He told me the autopsy on Brian had shown up a long thin bruise on the scalp above the right temple which could have been caused by a 'blow from a third party' or from a fall. The fire that destroyed the weighing room had started, they reckoned, as a grass fire outside after the weeks without rain. What they couldn't say was whether it had been arson.

'Come on, Mac, at three in the morning? It's hardly going to be spontaneous combustion.'

'They're still looking at it, Eddie. I'll keep you in touch. Now why did you want to see Alex Dunn?'

'Why do you ask? You interested in him too?'

'Should I be?'

'Are we going to spend the rest of the afternoon swapping questions?'

'Would you like to?'

We smiled. Mac said he wasn't particularly interested in Dunn, and since I was nervous about the Town Crier samples, I played it as cool as I could and told him that Brian and Alex Dunn had been close friends and I'd wondered if Dunn could give me a lead.

'And did he?'

I tried to look disappointed. 'Nah, nothing. He's still in shock too from Brian's death.'

'I didn't know they were good friends.'

'Well, old friends. Judy Kincaid told me they didn't see much of each other but they were in touch recently. Just a shot in the dark.' I was keen to move McCarthy off the subject in case he sent the police to talk to Dunn. The vet would probably drop dead at the sight of a warrant card.

Mac said, 'So, what next?'

I sighed. 'I don't know. Any suggestions?'

He put a hand on my shoulder. 'Yes, go home and hang up your pipe and deerstalker. Let the police handle it. You're getting too old for all this amateur sleuthing stuff.'

I smiled. 'And what does that make you?' Mac was at least ten years older than I was.

'I'm a professional sleuth.'

I raised a mischievous eyebrow but resisted saying, 'Oh, yeah?' He promised to keep me informed of police progress, and I wandered off trying to convey an air of resignation though it was important not to overplay it. Mac knew I wasn't a quitter.

I had a sandwich in a pub then rang Martin to tell him I'd set up a meeting and was hopeful of having something more solid soon. He grunted… moody bastard.

Alex Dunn's place wasn't easy to find. I asked directions of a garage attendant and got there at 6.25. An old bungalow with flaked cream masonry and mustard-coloured door and sills, it lay down a narrow road facing acres of deep woods. There was no car in the drive, and if Dunn was at home, he wasn't coming out. I went around the back along paths bordered by colourful but neglected plants and shrubs.

The house looked much bigger from this side. I tried the door of the long porch. It was open. I knocked on the half-glassed door inside. Silence. I returned to the car and waited. An hour later Dunn hadn't showed, and I was angry with myself for so easily accepting his suggestion of meeting here.

If he had no intention of keeping the date, I had little intention of breaking it. Starting the engine, I cruised along and found a track into the woods. I turned in and drove till I could no longer see the bungalow.

I got out, taking with me the waterproof I always carried, and headed through the woods for the house, stopping twenty yards in and settling on the ground where I could see without, I hoped, being seen.

Come darkness, no vehicles had passed. The only sounds were from nocturnal creatures on the prowl. I decided to do some prowling myself and just after eleven, I returned to Dunn's place and broke in.

TWENTY-FOUR

The biggest room had been converted into a lab, which, unlike the rest of the property, was clean and tidy to the point of obsession, to the point where I replaced each phial, each box, in its exact spot. I spent more than an hour checking cupboards and shelves, searching for anything marked with Brian Kincaid's name.

I tried a door in the corner of the lab. It was locked. I rooted in drawers for keys and found one that fitted. It was a big cupboard piled high with cardboard boxes marked with huge letters: Guterson's Gloves. Hauling the top box down, I eased aside the already open flaps. Nothing but blue arm-length gloves for use in veterinary examinations. Why lock up a stock of rubber gloves?

I went to the office and raked through filing cabinets, drawers, and a Rolodex telephone list where I found Brian's office number, and, in fresher ink, his mobile number.

Beneath the big wooden desk, I discovered a box file of copy invoices. Under the bright lamp, I worked through them until I saw a name I recognized, a name that halted my finger on the page and brought me to a breath-holding stop, as the man himself would have done had he appeared in front of me - Edward F. Malloy: my father.

I felt faint as his figure loomed huge in my mind. I'd spent years trying to erase his memory, succeeding only after psychiatric help, and now he was back, unintentionally, uninvited, but with almost the same shattering impact of the worst days of my life. I had to get out of the room.

I stood outside, leaning against the corner of the house, the dry old paint flaking under my hand. Staring at the full moon, I recalled the disciplines of old and made myself breathe deeply, hearing the breaths, focusing on them, using them to clean my mind again, to erase that picture before the well-remembered anxiety attack set in.

But I was out of practice, and the face of my father stayed stubbornly where it was. I resigned myself to the anxiety attack but it didn't come. And I stood there for God knows how long, wondering if finally, at the age of thirty, I was capable of coping with thoughts of the past.

I went inside, sat down and looked again at his name, which seemed to take up the whole page. I stayed there till the impact lessened, until the name diminished and took its proper place on the page above the address: a stud in Newmarket. Someone had told me years ago that they'd moved here. And then I thought of my mother too, and the dread drained from me and sadness seeped in.

I pulled myself together enough to start wondering how long my father had been a client of Alex Dunn's. The invoice was marked 'Quarterly as agreed' and was for £1,050. It was dated 30 March. I skipped through and found one other issued at the end of December. Both, unusually, were headed 'Professional Services'. Most invoices in Dunn's file carried details of the work, like scanning, cyst removal, etc.

What was Dunn doing for my father that had already taken six months and looked to be ongoing? Why were the details not shown? I noted the address and phone number of my father's stud then checked the remaining rooms and left.

I'd brought no overnight bag but I was confident I'd pin Dunn down next day at Newmarket races, so I drove into town and found a hotel.

Next morning, Saturday, I called the number Dunn had given me as his home telephone. No answer. I tried several times without success.

Faced with a few hours to kill before racing started, I asked the hotel porter for directions to my father's place. It was a short trip. I drove fifty yards beyond the entrance and parked. Turning in my seat, I watched the gate. Trees and bushes shielded the house from the road. I just kept staring at the gate, hoping for I don't know what. This was the home of my parents, a home I had never known.

We'd come to England from Ireland when I was seven and I'd spent the next nine years on a farm in Cumbria. My father kept horses and had dabbled in breeding. It had always been his ambition to own a proper stud farm. Now he did, though it looked to be a small operation. Now I watched, wondering what I would do if he suddenly appeared, or my mother. And my first thought was that I would duck out of sight. Would they recognize me now? I looked in the rear-view mirror. Had I changed much in the fourteen years since I'd left home?

In looks, maybe not; inside me, immense changes. Forty years was what it felt like in my head, not fourteen. I started the car again and pulled slowly away.

Dunn failed to turn up at Newmarket races. I drove to the bungalow. It was deserted, the broken glass still on the floor in the porch.

Where the hell had he gone and why had he panicked? I went in and spent more than an hour going through the copy invoices again, making notes of all his clients then getting their phone numbers from his Rolodex.

On the long drive home, I tried to figure out what it was I'd said that had scared Alex Dunn so badly. I'd only raised two issues: Brian's death and the samples from Town Crier. Which one had set him off? And what exactly was Dunn working on for my father?

A possible link came to mind. Tenuous but worth exploring.

At the flat, I skimmed through the stallion ads in the *Directory of the Turf,* checking the stud names below the glossy colour pictures. The Keelkerry Stud, named after my father's hometown, had a quarter-page ad dominated by the picture of a bay stallion called Heraklion whose career highlights, and those of his offspring, were listed in bold type.

I rang Martin and told him what had happened in the past twenty-four hours. Dunn's sudden disappearance cheered him immensely; he was convinced the vet must know something about the Town Crier samples and equally sure that we'd soon find Dunn. I asked Martin to call the Keelkerry Stud posing as a breeder who wanted to send a mare for a very late covering.

'Why don't you call?'

'We don't get on. I haven't spoken to my father in years.'

Martin said, 'They'll think I'm mad calling this late, the season's virtually over.'

'Act a bit eccentric then. Tell them you made a last-minute decision.'

I explained how I wanted him to go about it: to ask advice on which stallion to use then name two or three from the ad and see what the reaction was.

Ten minutes later Martin called, excitement in his voice. 'No Heraklion!'

'Who did you speak to?'

'I think it must have been your mother.'

'What did she say?'

'She didn't question me at first, seemed anxious to have the chance of some unexpected revenue. She did a bloody good selling job on every stallion but Heraklion. When I suggested him she said he'd been retired for the season and I said, "Oh, still hasn't recovered from his problem then?" which threw her. I told her some friends of mine had tried to book mares to him a couple of months ago and the horse had been on the easy list. She rallied then, I'll say that for her, said he'd been suffering from a complex fracture of the off hind after being kicked by a mare. "An accident," she said, "inherently sound, you know, and we're sure he'll be back to his best next season."'

So, two smallish studs who'd lost their best stallion. Perhaps Heraklion had been kicked, but the stud's link with Alex Dunn made it too much for coincidence. Martin told me my mother had almost desperately tried to sell him a covering from one of the other stallions. Business must be pretty bad. I felt a pang of remorse having deceived her.

Martin was set on finding Dunn, determined to stake out his place if necessary, and I knew by his tone he wouldn't be argued out of it this time. I could have used some help but Martin was too fiery. He promised to stay calm and be guided by me, so I gave in and told him Dunn's address, warning him that he mustn't pounce.

'If he turns up, try and follow him. We'll learn more that way.'

'Sure,' he said. 'Don't worry.'

'Stay in touch with me on my mobile. I'll probably be in Newmarket tomorrow anyway so let's meet.'

When Martin hung up, I resisted the urge to replace the handset because I knew I'd find it hard to pick it up again to call my mother. I dialed and tried to steel myself for the voice I'd last heard when little more than a child.

It rang seven times then, 'Keelkerry Stud.' It was my father. The voice had changed; less volume, weaker, as though the edges had worn away. I couldn't bring myself to speak. 'Hello!' he said. 'Hello!' And that impatience, that pent up anger I remembered so vividly, was still there. My top lip filmed with sweat. My mouth dried up. I replaced the receiver quietly, irrationally afraid he might be able to tell it was me and call me to account for it. I lowered myself slowly onto the chair by the window and sat gazing out, seeing nothing. My throat tightened and I swallowed repeatedly, pumping out silent tears.

TWENTY-FIVE

The following day I packed an overnight bag and headed to Newmarket, determined to speak to my parents. I was no longer a child and I wasn't going to let my father return me to that state. I was a grown man with a legitimate interest in his association with Alex Dunn, and I was damned well going to ask some questions.

That was the theory at least, but much as I disciplined my brain, my emotions mutinied. A few times I checked the speedo and found it registering way below my normal speed from subconscious dread of reaching my destination.

Martin called me at nine o'clock. He complained of being cold and stiff after sitting in the woods for half the night waiting fruitlessly for Dunn. I offered to meet him for lunch in town, but he told me to come to Dunn's place, said he wouldn't move till the vet appeared.

I was in Newmarket before ten and on the approach to the Keelkerry Stud, my stomach tightened, causing me to shift in my seat. I pulled into the verge about a hundred yards before the gate, steeling myself not to drive past this time. I'd get out here and walk across, go through the gate and straight to the front door. No hesitation. No stopping.

I checked my face in the mirror. As I reached for the door handle, a light blue Vauxhall Estate coming toward me slowed and indicated then turned and nosed up to the gate. The driver was so tall he had trouble getting out of the car. It was Alex Dunn. He opened the gate and drove through, then closed it behind him. The driveway was screened by a high hedge.

I ran across the road, making my way along the hedge line. The stud stood alone on open land. I heard Dunn switch off the engine. A car door slammed. I hoped my father might be there to meet him. Perhaps they'd start talking in the yard. No. Just faint footsteps on gravel then another door closing. No knock. No greeting. It sounded as if Dunn had simply walked right into the house.

I looked across at my car on the verge and the sunlight glinted on a side window, almost blinding me. I couldn't leave it there much longer. If anyone in the stud saw it, they might become suspicious.

I'd have to drive about half a mile round a long steady bend before the car could be parked out of sight. I hurried to the car, did a U-turn and sped down the road. On foot again, I came at the stud from a different angle, cutting across meadows to see how far back the trees and hedges ran. They seemed to border the rear and sides of the property in a looping semi-circle. A couple of furlongs down from the house and stables, they thinned enough for me to peer through at eight fenced-off paddocks with maybe a dozen horses grazing quietly in the sunshine. All were in view of the buildings. Once through the trees and onto the property there was no decent cover.

I'd hoped to get inside, close to whatever horse Dunn was visiting and eavesdrop on his conversation with my father or the groom or whoever. But unless I could get through the thick hedges beside the stables, then it would mean crossing open ground, which would leave me exposed. If I was to face my parents again, it wouldn't be as an intruder.

I circled the perimeter, but couldn't find a safe way in. I returned to the hedge close to where Dunn's car was parked. Perhaps I'd hear something as he left.

But he didn't leave. At dusk his car hadn't been moved. I'd had my phone switched off in case someone rang as Dunn came out. As darkness fell, I walked what I considered to be a safe distance away and called Martin. He was still outside Dunn's place, hungry and frustrated, and when I told him where I was and why, he said, 'Why the fuck didn't you call me? You knew Dunn was there, you could have saved me hanging around this shithole any longer!'

'I thought he'd leave at any time and maybe head your way.'

'Well, he didn't, did he?'

We were silent for a long moment then Martin said, 'Did you say he's been there since this morning?'

'Around ten he arrived.'

'Fuck me! That's one long consultation. I wouldn't like your old man's vet's bill.'

'I think he could be paying in kind.'

'Huh?'

'Dunn might be living there. He's been doing some unspecified work for my father for the past six months or so.' I told him about the invoices I'd found, mysteriously short on detail. Martin arrived within twenty minutes and we watched together until the last light went out in the house just after 11. So Dunn was a guest.

We were tired and hungry and I suspected I also looked as scruffy as Martin with his heavy stubble and soiled clothes. We returned to the hotel I'd stayed in the night before and persuaded a bored young girl to fix some sandwiches. We downed a large scotch each and trudged wearily to bed after arranging a 6 a.m. alarm call.

In the morning, Martin was going in to collar Alex Dunn.

TWENTY-SIX

We were outside the Keelkerry Stud just after dawn. Alex Dunn's car was still in the drive. We'd travelled in separate cars and we met around the bend, half a mile from the stud. Martin joined me on watch, on foot in the chill of morning. We dissected what we'd learned, theorized, argued quietly then finally agreed a plan.

At 8.40, Martin pulled away toward the stud and parked outside the gate. From a distance, I watched him go in.

Twenty-five minutes later, he reappeared and drove off, as agreed, in the opposite direction from where I was stationed. I hurried to my car and cruised past the stud and out of sight again, where I turned quickly and came past once more. As I slowed to turn again, Dunn's blue estate overtook me at speed and I accelerated smoothly, following him.

I stayed well behind until approaching the edge of Newmarket town, where I had to close up for fear of losing him. He slowed going down the Bury Road as strings of racehorses crossed at regular points on their way to and from the gallops. Near the bottom close to the town centre, Dunn took a right, and as I turned off, I saw his tailgate disappear in another right turn through the gates of a famous racing yard.

I parked and phoned Martin. 'How did it go?' I asked.

'He's rattled all right! He knows something. I told him if he didn't come up with the samples and the results by this time tomorrow, I'd bring the police in.'

'Did you speak to him alone? Was my father there?'

'Just Dunn. He was coming down the drive as I was walking up. He kept trying to get away, said he had an important appointment, and tried the same thing with me that he did with you: "Come and see me at home this evening."' Martin put on a whingeing voice.

I said, 'Well, he's reached his important appointment. I'm outside one of the big yards in the town. Think it's worth keeping a tail on him?'

'No, no way. He's too scared to do anything now. He said he'll definitely meet us at his house tomorrow morning. Ten o'clock.'

'Do you believe him?'

'Eddie, he'll be there.'

He wasn't. Next day we were there before 9.30 and waited till 11. Dunn had been home. The broken pane had been replaced, the shards swept up. I broke the new one and we went inside. The house had been cleared, very effectively, not a thermometer left in the lab, a pen in the office or a sock in a bedroom drawer. Each empty room seemed to deal Martin a physical blow. By the time we'd finished the tour he looked stunned, defeated, and sounded that way too when he spoke. 'What do we do now, Eddie?'

'We find out where he's gone.'

'How?'

I looked at him, the tired eyes, the hangdog look, and I realized how much he was pissing me off. Martin was fine if things were going well; otherwise, he either blew his top or whined and moaned, expecting somebody else to solve his problems. 'We'll find him,' I said coldly, and walked out and along the path to the front gate.

Martin followed. 'But, Eddie, I can't spend any more time here. I've got stuff to do; we've got a business to run.'

'Go home and run it then.'

'Just for a few days, then I'll come back and help you.'

Yeah, when I've found Dunn, you'll ride in and play the tough guy.

'Fine,' I said.

I watched him drive off and wondered how he could so quickly become disheartened. My resolve had been strengthened by Dunn's disappearance. You didn't flee your home and workplace over a few stallion samples. Dunn was involved in something serious. And how close was he to the Keelkerry Stud? To my parents? Could they be implicated?

I headed for their stud, a cold determination in me suppressing the emotions of the past few days. I parked at the gate and marched up the drive. The house was of yellow stone, big deep windows, climbing plants around the door where my gaze was fixed. The white door, coming closer as though a movie camera lens was tightening on it. I was conscious of the sounds of gravel crunching, but seemed somehow removed from the notion that it could be my feet making the noise. All I was aware of was my unblinking focus on that door.

I reached it.

Pressed the bell.

Waited.

It opened slowly. My father stood there. Still taller than me but age showing: thinning grey hair, hollow cheeks, loose skin on his face, his throat. Shoulders drooping, hair growing from his ears, eyebrows getting bushy - and hatred in his eyes. No, not hatred, scorn. His jaw muscles clenched and he slammed the door shut so hard I felt a mild shockwave on my face.

I didn't move. Stayed there, chest out, head high, and was proud of myself for it. And I reached for the bell again and I pressed it and I held it and I could hear it inside hammering like a fire alarm. The ringing went on for more than a minute before the door opened again. My mother. Older, smaller, softer, kinder-looking, the way I remembered her from my infant days. Her hair shorter but shining rich auburn as I remembered it, a small vanity from a bottle which looked so out of place framing the pale skin, the pale, pale skin.

No hint of shame on her face as she looked at me. I'd never known her speak a word against my father for his treatment of me, but there had never been any hatred in her either. Sadness, yes. Despair, maybe, but at least she'd never hated me for what had happened.

'Eddie,' she said quietly, and stepped aside, pulling the door fully open. Not trusting myself to handle the emotion of saying the word 'Mum', I just accepted the silent invitation to go inside.

She led me along the hall, her slightly splayfooted walk exactly as I remembered it, to a small cluttered office with one swivel chair. No cozy sitting rooms; this was to be a short formal discussion as far as my mother was concerned. She said she'd bring another chair for herself and politely offered me tea. I declined, unwilling to accept the little gestures that moved me into the same bracket as any trade caller at the stud, that helped her forget she'd carried me inside her, nursed me, and loved me once, her first-born.

She returned with a light pine chair, closed the door and sat opposite me, open-faced, pleasant, receptive. And, setting my emotions aside for the first time when thinking of her, I wondered what kind of woman this was. How could she not be moved enough to show some feelings? How could she stand so rigidly by her man to the exclusion of everything else on the planet? Had she never questioned that loyalty? Still closely involved in racing, she must have known about my troubles over the past eight or nine years. Had there never been a twinge of regret, an ounce of longing to come and comfort me?

Here she sat waiting for me to state my business. No 'How have you been, son?' No 'Good to see you after all these years.'

She said, 'Edward's out in the yard.' A cue to start talking, reassurance we wouldn't be disturbed by the man she could no longer even bring herself to refer to as my father.

I said, 'How have you been, Mum?'

'We're all right.'

We. The Siamese marriage.

'My father looks very strained.'

She blinked at the word 'father'.

'Edward has... this has come as a bit of a shock to him.'

'It would after fourteen years.'

She nodded, blinked again. Some emotion there at last. I said, 'Aren't you going to ask how I've been?'

'You look fine.'

'I'm well practiced in looking fine, Mum, at making it look like I'm solid and sane.'

She looked at me, determined not to be drawn in. 'Why did you come here, Eddie?'

'After all this time, you mean? You forgot to tag that on to the end of your question, Mum.'

She stiffened slightly in her chair. 'If you've come to open old wounds.'

I leaned toward her, elbows on my knees, hands clasped in what I realized was close to anguish. I'd willed myself not to react like this but I couldn't help it. I said, 'Open old wounds? Mine never

101

closed, Mum! They bleed and weep every day of my life. They keep people away from me! They fester. Don't talk to me about closing.'

Her pale face flushed. She wasn't coping any more, not with this adult, this son who was no longer a child.

I said, 'Was there no remorse? Ever? Even in the early days?'

She stood up, held on to the chairback, tears rising. 'Please go,' she said.

I shook my head. 'No, I'm not going.' And I felt filled with power, with knowledge that I could stay if I wanted, that neither of my parents was a threat any longer. I could stay and take revenge, dish out some torment.

Then just as suddenly, the notion seemed vile, abhorrent, shameful. I stood, calmed myself, and in a quiet voice said, 'I'm not going until I know what Alex Dunn's been doing for the Keelkerry Stud.'

TWENTY-SEVEN

When I left, my mother saw me out and watched till I was through the gate. Driving into Newmarket town, I tried to come to terms with my feelings; a strange mixture of personal achievement, self-renewal, a growth in stature that felt almost physical, and a wish that I had come years ago and said my piece.

But there was also a feeling of being used. When she'd sussed that I could actually help my father, my mother had become quite enthusiastic. She'd admitted that Heraklion, their top stallion, had suffered a similar loss of fertility to Town Crier and at around the same time. Faced with a ruined investment, my father had asked Alex Dunn to do what he could. It seemed Dunn was an old friend and had offered his services for the comparatively small retainer of £350 a month.

She said Dunn had been sworn to secrecy and that was why he'd panicked when I had confronted him at the races. I told her it had to be more than that but she said she had no reason to doubt him. Yet Dunn had so far failed to find a cure for Heraklion.

If my father knew I was involved, he'd reject my help. My mother accepted it on his behalf on the condition that he mustn't be told. Whether or not the stud was saved, my father must never be allowed to believe I'd done anything for him. My mother's side of the bargain was that she would try to discover Dunn's whereabouts. He and my father were friends, and my mother thought she should be able to get information without arousing suspicion. She had my home and mobile numbers though I departed the house under no illusions. As soon as this was over, the phone numbers would be burned, and I would once again become the invisible member of the Malloy family.

That prospect bothered me little now. For a few days, I'd harboured a fantasy that I would appear on my white steed after fourteen years and save the Malloy business, drag my parents back from the brink, finally winning the approval I'd craved. But the last couple of hours had brought home to me that although there would always be an instinctive, emotional link to them, a vague longing, they were people in their own right - and as people rather than parents, I cared little for either of them.

Dunn's story of being rattled by my questions didn't stand up. Vacating his house overnight, lock, stock and stethoscope, smacked of abject fear. Was he linked to Brian Kincaid's death? How many other small studs were harbouring infertile stallions? How many of these cases had Dunn been working on? Well, I was in the best place to find out. Newmarket was nothing but a racing community and redolent with jealousy and bitchiness. A few days spent in the pubs and hotels should prove productive.

I couldn't afford to go on staying at the hotel I'd been using, so I found a bed and breakfast for two nights, got my phone out and booked a place on the gossip train, first stop Francis Loss, racing manager to Sheikh Ahmad Saad.

F. Loss was an old friend, known since his riding days as Candy. Sharp and well educated, he'd landed himself a top position with one of the most prominent Arab racehorse owners and breeders in the world. His job was to offer advice to the Sheikh on every aspect of his thoroughbred operation, from buying foals to setting fees at the two major studs he owned. If there was anything afoot with local stallions, Candy would know about it.

Candy agreed to meet me for half an hour. He was flying to the Middle East that night. We met at seven in a hotel in town and I felt distinctly underdressed as Candy approached in about a grand's worth of clothes and footwear. Five foot eight, late-thirties, Candy had kept the slim athletic shape he'd had when riding. He smiled as he shook my hand. Good teeth and tan, dark brown eyes and shiny chestnut hair, which, most of the time, successfully hid, his only physical blemish: a port wine stain below his right ear, the shape of Italy on a map.

I bought him a mineral water and we did the long-time-no-see routine for a few minutes. Candy had never got above himself. People always found him the same way, open and friendly, but I thought I detected an air of wariness. I knew I'd have to be careful. Gossip conduits are two-way and I needed to get what I could without Candy picking up any link with Brian Kincaid.

I said, 'Listen, you know I do a little bit of amateurish nosing around from time to time?'

He smiled. 'Not quite so amateurish over the last year or two from what I hear.'

I returned his smile. 'I've got a guy who's offered me a few quid to try and help him out. He owns a smallish stud which ain't gonna be a stud much longer unless he discovers what's gone wrong with his best stallion.'

I thought I saw a sudden spark in Candy's eyes but it lasted a millisecond. He sipped his drink and looked interested. I said, 'The horse completely lost its fertility at the start of the season. The vets have tested everything except its IQ but they're stumped. If it's not sorted out before next season he's finished.'

'Which stallion?'

'Sorry, Candy, I can't say. The guy's managed to keep it a secret from most breeders, or at least he thinks he has. I know you'll think I've got a cheek asking you for information and not offering much from my side, but I'm trying to do my best for him.'

'So what are you asking me, Eddie?'

I shrugged. 'Just if you've heard anything on the grapevine about anyone else who's got the same problem?' I was taking the chance Candy was unaware of my involvement in the Corish Stud, far from Newmarket, and a partnership I'd never publicized.

'Stallions have fluctuations in fertility.'

'We're talking more decimation than fluctuation here. From eighty-eight percent to zilch as quick as you could say, "No foal no fee".'

He fingered the port wine stain under his hair and looked thoughtful. 'So why did he bring you in? Does he think the horse has been got at?'

'As I said, he's desperate.'

'Do you think the horse was got at?'

'I don't know. What would the motive be? How would you do it so the vets couldn't detect it?'

He shook his head slowly, fingered his tanned chin. I said, 'So you haven't heard of any other stallions in the same boat?'

He continued thoughtful, staring at the tabletop, and said, 'No.'

I sighed and sipped some scotch. He said, 'Sorry, Eddie.'

'Not your fault.'

'What's your next move?'

I almost started shooting off about Alex Dunn disappearing but something in my brain slipped the safety catch on and I settled for saying I'd heard Dunn specialized in fertility and I was hoping to track him down. 'Any idea where I could find him?'

'Sorry, Eddie, I've heard the guy's name but I don't know much about him except that he's a bit of a quack. I wouldn't set too much store by this "specialist" stuff.' Candy seemed anxious to finish the conversation. He said, 'It's an interesting one. I'll sniff around a bit myself over the next week or so, see if I can find anything out.'

'Good. That'd be great, Candy.'

'No problem. Maybe you could keep me in touch with progress from your end?'

'Sure. Sure I will.'

'Fine. Give me a ring any time.'

I smiled. 'They've got phones in Lear jets now, have they?' He stood up, smiling, and finished his drink. 'It's not all a bowl of cherries, Eddie, as the saying goes.'

'Strawberries and cream, more like.'

He laughed. 'See you. Keep in touch on this.'

'Will do.'

He turned and left. I waited a few seconds then followed quietly and watched him cross the car park. He got into a Range Rover and immediately made a call. I had a hunch Candy knew more than he was saying.

I rang Martin, gave him some work to do to take his mind off things. 'I want you to ring round as many studs as you can and give them that story about a late booking. Make a list of who's willing and any stallions they try to steer you away from.'

'What about my phone bill?'

'Our phone bill,' I reminded him. 'Come on, Martin, twenty-four hours ago it was death or glory to get to the bottom of this. Now you can't even be bothered making a few calls?'

He grunted something and hung up. I called McCarthy.

'Mac, did you know Alex Dunn's moved out of his house?'

'It's not the sort of thing I get wildly curious about, Eddie.'

'I know, but if you could find me his new address you'd be doing me a favour.'

'Why? I thought you'd spoken to him and he said he didn't know anything about Brian Kincaid's death?'

'That's right, but as I said to you he was in pretty deep shock at the time and I just wondered if maybe, once he'd had time to think, something might have come to him.'

'Like what?'

'I don't know, Mac, but I want to speak to him again.'

'Eddie, tell me what this is really about?'

'I've told you, it's a quiet time for me. I'll be lucky to get ten rides in the next month and I don't mind filling my days in trying to make sense of Brian's death.'

'And I've told you, leave it to the coroner, let him try and make some sense of it!'

'Mac, come on! I don't like doing this but you owe me one. More than one.'

'You don't like doing it? You're always doing it! I should have kept notes! Traded bloody IOUs!'

I smiled. 'Your hysterics are coming on again, Mac, careful!'

'I'll ring you back.'

'When?'

'As soon as I know something.'

'Soon, Mac, please! On my mobile. I'm in Newmarket for a few days.' That brought him up short. 'Newmarket? What for?'

'I've just told you, I want to speak to Alex Dunn.'

'Eddie, you'd better not be working for Compton Breslin.' He sounded genuinely annoyed. Breslin was a rich bookmaker.

'What would I be doing for Breslin?'

'Don't be so bloody disingenuous.'

'Me? I don't know the meaning of the word!' Which was the truth but I didn't need to ask anything else. Dunn was obviously a serious gambler. I wondered how much he owed Breslin.

Mac said, 'I'll tell you this now, Eddie, if you're working for Breslin I want nothing more to do with you.'

'Mac, you've got my word on it. When did I ever break my word?'

'Okay. Fine. Goodnight.'

He hung up. The smile was still on my face. I loved these little jousts with McCarthy.

It wasn't yet 8.30 and I knew there were two evening racemeetings on. Breslin's credit office would be open. I'd never met the guy but I'd seen him on the racecourse. He was renowned as a proper bookie of the old school, one who'd back his own opinion and lay large bets. He paid promptly and expected the same from his clients. I rang his office. He answered the phone personally. I said that we might have a common interest in Alex Dunn and he agreed to meet me in a local Chinese restaurant at 9.45.

TWENTY-EIGHT

Breslin was your stereotypical big fat bookmaker: jewellery, checked suit, torpedo cigar, slick hair, and Chaplin moustache. He looked like he'd just stepped off a Blackpool postcard. He was watching my face as he lumbered toward me, and sat down in a jingle of watch chains and bracelets. He smiled at me. 'Bet you thought this was my showman's gear, strictly for the racecourse?'

'Well, I did, actually.'

His smile grew wider, moustache spreading. 'You're always on show in my business,' he said, looking down at the checked waistcoat. 'The more prosperous you look, the more people want to take money off you. And the more they try, the more I get to keep.'

I nodded, smiling. He glanced around and beckoned a waiter. 'Anyway,' he said, 'that's my excuse for prancing about dressed like one of the Marx Brothers. At night, alone in my room, I slip on my Versace, which has seen nothing but lamplight and a long wardrobe mirror. Sad, isn't it?'

I smiled. I liked Breslin. He ordered the best wine and half a dozen courses as though listing runners in a race. The waiter didn't seem at all surprised, and I guessed this was a regular haunt. He said, 'Need to keep the waistline up to Industry Standards. Dirty work but some bugger's got to do it.'

We got talking about Dunn. 'You're looking for him?' Breslin asked.

'I'd quite like to speak to him.'

'Been a bad boy, has he?'

'Not that I know of. I just think he might be able to help me out.'

'Got a veterinary problem?'

'More of a personal one, really. Well, on behalf of a friend.' I mentioned Brian Kincaid and gave him the same spiel I'd given McCarthy.

'I can give you his address,' Breslin said.

'The bungalow out at Six Mile Bottom?'

'You know it?'

I nodded. 'But it's no good.' I told him about the moonlight flit.

He laughed. 'Well, bugger me; I wonder if he'll welch this time?'

'Does he owe much?'

He shrugged his big shoulders. 'About seven grand. It's not the end of the world.'

He wasn't showing off. He didn't seem that concerned about it though he said sure, he'd like to know where Dunn turned up if I managed to find him. In exchange, he told me a few details about Dunn's gambling habits. One tidbit was to prove very useful.

Thankfully, Breslin brushed aside my offer to pay the bill and we parted on good terms. Always a better audience than a performer, I'd enjoyed his company. He gave me his card and we made mutual promises to stay in touch.

My first stop next morning was a newsagent's shop where I picked up a little tourist booklet about Newmarket, Headquarters of British Racing. Inside was a map listing the names of all the training yards, along with the trainers currently inhabiting them. Breslin had told me that a significant number of Alex Dunn's bets in the last eighteen months to two years had been on horses trained by William Capshaw, a highly successful Newmarket trainer.

I found Capshaw's yard location on the map, and just to double check, I walked down the Bury Road past the yard. It was the same one Dunn had gone to after Martin had confronted him. I thought it unwise to pass the yard gates again and took a different route to the High Street.

So Dunn was getting information from Capshaw's yard. In exchange for what? Veterinary services? I couldn't recall seeing Capshaw's name among Dunn's copy invoices, though that might be the deal, no cash.

In a small cafe, I ordered coffee and got out Dunn's client list: no sign of Capshaw's name.

Perhaps Dunn was holed up at Capshaw's place. If so, would he be careless and park his car close by? It was worth risking another walk past, more slowly this time. My mobile rang, shattering the peace in the sunny little cafe and bringing sour looks from three elderly ladies. It was Martin. I went outside. He'd phoned thirty-nine studs. Eight had given him reasons for suspicion.

I didn't want him with me and managed to persuade him to look more closely at the studs involved. I asked him to plot their locations on a map, find out their histories: who was running them, their background, if they'd had the same employee through their hands, etc. - enough work to keep him in Wiltshire for a few days and out of my hair.

On the off chance I'd been spotted around Capshaw's yard, it would be best to delay another stroll in that direction until this afternoon. If I watched the yard from a safe distance around lunchtime, maybe I'd see some of Capshaw's lads heading for the pub. It would be easy to strike up a conversation over a drink and try to find out if the vet was a temporary lodger, but some of the lads might recognize me and start spreading the wrong kind of stories.

I decided to stick to lone observation, at least until late afternoon, and found a car park close enough to Capshaw's place to let me watch the main exit road from the yard. I had no view of the yard itself, and if Dunn came out of it and turned right, I'd miss him completely, but better to cover half the options in relative safety than all of them in an exposed position.

In the car, with the windows rolled down, I settled back with a copy of *The Sporting Life* which would offer extra camouflage if necessary.

I wondered how Dunn was running his business. Would he be having his calls automatically transferred to wherever he now was? I called his number. Answerphone. That meant he would have to play it back, although he could do that remotely.

As the 11.30 radio news began, my phone rang. 'Alex Dunn is at his house at Six Mile Bottom.' The caller immediately hung up. I started the car and headed for Dunn's place, wondering who my informant was. Perhaps Breslin had put the word out. Quick work if he had.

I pulled up, blocking Dunn's driveway in case he made a run for it, but his car wasn't there. Either I'd been hoaxed or I'd just missed him. I went through the green iron gates to the rear of the bungalow. As I turned at the end of the wall, I stopped short. Two men were sitting on an old garden bench. They wore expensive summer suits and lounged lazily, faces, in very dark glasses, tilted to the sun.

The man closest to me stood up and came forward, smiling, welcoming. 'Mister Malloy, how kind of you to drop in.' Bewildered, I shook his hand, waiting for him to introduce himself. He didn't. His friend was standing now, smoothing out imaginary wrinkles on the front of his trousers. They were mid-twenties, fit and hard looking, tall as University oarsmen.

I said to the one who'd greeted me, 'You called me?'

'That's right. I understand you're seeking advice.'

'Information. I've got all the advice I need at the moment.'

He was still smiling. It annoyed me that his eyes were hidden, the high sun glinting off his gold framed dark glasses. He said, 'The wrong kind of advice, Mister Malloy. It's good reliable advice you want, and luckily that is our specialist business. Come and sit down.' He put a hand lightly on my elbow. I eased it away. 'No, thanks.'

'Fine. I give the same high-calibre advice standing up.'

'Which is?'

'Drop what you're involved in and go home. Stick to riding horses.'

'Who do you work for?'

'We're a charitable organization dedicated to keeping people out of hospitals.'

'You're threatening me?'

The smile faded. Stern-mouthed he said, 'I'm offering you genuine professional advice. You won't realize how valuable it is unless you don't take it, then you'll reflect on this conversation with a bit more circumspection.'

An educated hit man. He took off his sunglasses, exposing blue eyes, which looked very sincere. He said, 'It is very important to me that you leave Newmarket within the hour and that you stay away from the town and the people who live here. It is vitally important to me that you stop asking questions.'

112

He was serious. I didn't know what to say or how to take it. 'Do you understand how important it is to me?' he pressed.

'If you tell me why, it might just drive the message home.'

A flicker of anger in his cold eyes and what seemed a conscious effort to regain the calm expression, and that was when I knew how potentially dangerous he could be. I thought it best to call it quits for the time being.

They came out onto the road and watched me till my car was out of sight. Curiouser and curiouser. No heavy stuff but they'd looked the part all right, and I was in no doubt the gloves would be off next time. Where had Dunn got these two from? The guy spent all his money gambling, how was he paying them?

And why had things accelerated so quickly?

By the time I reached Newmarket, I'd decided to pack up and leave immediately. Dunn would have his spies out and would think I'd fled. Maybe he'd return home then, and it would be a nice surprise for him when I turned up there in a couple of days. At my digs, I made a show of throwing my things in my bag, leaving it unzipped as I hurried to the car and scooted along the High Street and out of town at a pace that would have drawn attention. Hamming it up, but if it helped tempt Dunn to the surface I could forgive myself.

I returned to my flat for a change of clothes. It was late afternoon. The yard was still as quiet as it had been since the end of May. It would be another month before the horses were back. A racing yard without thoroughbreds is a melancholy place.

I thought about Charles Tunney, the trainer. The man who'd buggered off to Alaska for a month after watching some TV series about a town there. Impulsive man, Charles. I smiled, thinking about him.

Charles and the stable lads were my only regular contacts, a big bantering family without emotional obligations. I missed them all.

I'd planned to avoid Newmarket for a few days in the hope Dunn would think I'd given up, but I couldn't face another day in the flat. I packed enough clothes for a week and headed east again, stopping only to fill up and buy groceries.

I pulled up in front of Dunn's bungalow, blocking the drive again. I went down the path, heels clicking loudly on the flagstones, and round the back.

Nobody on the garden bench. Nobody in the house. The second glass pane I'd broken hadn't been repaired nor the mess cleaned up. On the trip across, I'd decided on a plan of attack. Anxious to get started, I returned to the car and drove to the clearing in the woods I'd used last week. I took my kitbag and walked to Dunn's, where I unpacked the bag then cleared away the broken glass.

I listened to the messages on Dunn's answerphone; all were from customers and had been left that morning so he was emptying his machine regularly. Next time he did, I'd try Martin's trick of dialing the recall code to see where Dunn had called from. I used the phone to call McCarthy on his mobile. He didn't sound delighted when he heard my voice. 'Did you find Alex Dunn?' he asked.

'Nope, that's why I'm calling. I need to see you, Mac.'

'That means you want a favour.'

'Have any of the "favours" you've done me in the past worked against you? You've always come up smelling of roses.'

'Mostly because you dropped me in deep shit to begin with.'

'Ha! Where have you been sharpening your wit?'

'On the horns of all the dilemmas you've left me in.'

'Touché, Mac. First two rounds to you.'

I could almost feel his smug smile down the phone. I said, 'Where are you going today?'

'Got a meeting in London. A long one.'

'Want to come here afterwards for dinner?'

'Where's "here"?'

'Newmarket.'

'No, thanks. I promised Jean I'd take her out.'

'Where are you tomorrow?'

'Sandown.'

'Can you spare me half an hour there?'

'I suppose so.'

'I'll get there before racing. Want to meet by the parade ring?'

'No. Meet me in the car park an hour before the first. I get nervous talking to you on course.'

'Okay. I'll see you in the car park.'

'Eddie, I'll stay in my car. Come and find me.'

'Sure.'

I didn't want to leave Dunn's bungalow in case he came back, but I thought it was time to start building up a few alternatives. I'd have to tell Mac more than I'd originally planned to, but not enough to compromise his position in Jockey Club Security.

I rang Martin, who was barely halfway through the task of analyzing all the information on the suspect studs. The staff histories were proving the toughest, as I'd known they would. I left him to it.

I found three tea bags lying on an otherwise bare shelf in Dunn's kitchen and made a mug of strong black tea, which I sipped as I dialed Compton Breslin's office. A girl told me he was betting at Yarmouth. I called his mobile. His cheery voice brought an immediate picture of him in his loud suit. I asked him for a list of all Dunn's bets this season. He promised it would be ready for me to collect in twenty-four hours.

I sat by the silent phone for a while then paced the living room. Looking out of the front window I saw the glint of the sun reflected from deep in the woods and realized I hadn't driven the car far enough into the trees. I was reluctant to leave in case Dunn called to empty the answerphone then someone else called immediately after him, wiping out his recall number.

I'd need to be desperately unlucky for that to happen. Deciding to chance it, I hurried out into the woods and ran toward the car. I couldn't have been gone more than ten minutes, but when I returned the flashing light on the answerphone had stopped.

It had been emptied. I grabbed the handset from the cradle before another call could come through and dialed 1471. I jotted down the number given by the recorded voice, even said thank you to the lady. Dunn must still be in Newmarket; that was the STD code.

My impulse was to dial it immediately but that might prove counter-productive. If Dunn realized I'd tracked him down, he'd probably take off again, sending me rapidly back to square one. It would be much better if I could find out the address the number belonged to. Mac should be able to get that. I rang his mobile again: switched off. I tried him every fifteen minutes until six then gave up. Tomorrow would have to do.

TWENTY-NINE

I wandered through Sandown's car park looking for Mac, and then I saw his silver Rover come in off the road. He bypassed the turn into the officials' entrance and backed into a space against the fence. I walked over and opened the passenger door to see Mac's belly touching the steering wheel.

He was red, flustered, and trying not to look it. 'Sorry I'm a bit late, Eddie. The traffic's deplorable.'

'No hurry. Not on my side anyway.'

'Well, I don't exactly have all day. What was it you wanted to talk about?'

'Alex Dunn.'

'Again?'

I told him about Dunn's disappearance, about the two hard men I'd run into at his house, about how anxious Dunn was to discourage me from finding him. I was still playing it around Brian Kincaid's death, not mentioning anything about the stallions.

Mac said, 'So you think Dunn's involved in Kincaid's death?'

'I don't know. But I do know that a simple question from me sent him into a panic that was bad enough for him to up stakes and leave his home and business.'

'What makes you so sure you were the catalyst?'

This was where things got tricky. I didn't want to bring Martin's name into it at all, let alone tell Mac it was the confrontation with him that had been the real cue for Dunn's vanishing act. I busked along, trying to convince Mac that the pure shock on Dunn's face

116

when I'd first approached him at the races told me that he had to be deeply worried.

I chose my words carefully, but Mac assumed I was trying to implicate Dunn in Brian's death. He shifted heavily in his seat so he was looking straight at me. 'You'd best be very careful, Eddie. You can't make accusations on hunches.'

'Come on, Mac, it's more than a hunch, you've known me long enough to realize that.'

'The same as your first suspect in Kincaid's death was more than a hunch? Tranter, he of the cast-iron alibi?'

'Okay, fair enough. That was a mistake.'

He sighed. 'So what do you want me to do?'

I looked at him. 'Mac, don't make it sound like it's all for me. You guys should be investigating Dunn's disappearance.'

'What disappearance? He's told the racecourses that normally use him he's unavailable until further notice. If we "investigated" every vet, doctor or starter who decided to take a few weeks off work, we'd never get anything done.'

'It's more than that, Mac. He's up to something. I'm tipping you off, trying to make sure you're not left with large helpings of egg on your face.'

'Very philanthropic of you.'

A frown I knew well gathered on Mac's face. This was the poker hand where he had to decide whether to fold and leave me to it or draw some cards. He'd be worried about coming in too late if this blew up. Not much point in the Jockey Club Security Department having their finger on the pulse of a dead case. He said, 'Okay. Let me see what I can find out.'

'Maybe you could start with this?' I said, giving him the recall number used by Dunn to clear his answerphone. Mac promised to ring me when he had something then asked me to leave the car 'as unobtrusively as possible'.

I did and he drove away to take up his customary spot in the car park. I'd considered going into the racecourse for an hour to see if I could pick anything up, but decided against it. Until I'd nailed Dunn, it was important to make him believe I'd been scared off.

I'd just settled and turned the ignition key when I noticed a familiar figure step out of a black Mercedes parked about six rows in front of me. It was old Iron Fist in a Velvet Glove himself, the guy who'd warned me off at Dunn's bungalow. He set off toward the stands.

I let him get up the steps and through the main doors before I started to get out to follow him. As I did so, the driver's door of the black Merc opened and out stepped another man I knew, another man I'd seen recently: Sheik Ahmad Saad's racing manager, Mr F. Loss. Candy.

I stayed in my car, waiting to see if anyone else would come out of the Merc, but Candy locked it and headed for the stands, striding out boldly in his perfectly cut pinstripe suit.

I relaxed in the seat, drumming on the steering wheel, trying like hell not to jump to conclusions. What was Candy's connection with the hit man? Were they associated 'professionally' or had Candy simply, and perfectly innocently, offered him a lift to the races? If so, why had they sat so long in the Merc? Why had they entered the racecourse separately?

What should I do next?

Before I could make any connection, I had to find out who this guy was. Maybe Mac would know him by sight. It was simply a matter of getting Mac within safe viewing distance of Iron Fist, which might not be too difficult. Today's crowd wouldn't be that big and it was still half an hour before the first race.

I locked the car and headed for the entrance.

THIRTY

Wending my way through the parked cars, I came upon an old friend, Charlie Harris, a racecourse photographer. Charlie was unloading his gear. I had an idea and asked him to lend me one of his cameras with a zoom lens, promising to return it by first race time. He told me it was a spare and that I could keep it all day if I needed to.

I soon found Iron Fist. He was by the parade-ring rail with his equally tall friend from Dunn's place. Two for the price of one. I climbed the steps to the balcony. Three horses were being led round and as each of them approached the pair, who were deep in conversation, I raised the camera and took a few shots; more than I'd intended with the first burst as the rapid motordrive reacted to my heavy finger and fired off a salvo. I shot the whole film, then found Charlie Harris by the unsaddling enclosure and returned the camera.

Esher High Street is a short walk from Sandown Racecourse. I doubted I'd find a one-hour-development place but not only did I find one, the girl offered to produce standard size prints within ten minutes. My intention had been to order eight by sixes to give Mac a clearer picture, but I could get those done later.

My luck had been good and I didn't want to push it by going back into the racecourse. I couldn't be sure that the hard men, or maybe Candy if he was involved with them, hadn't already seen me. I sat in my car and dialed Mac's number.

'Mac, can you spare a few minutes to come to the car park?'

'When?'

'Now. It's important. I won't keep you long.' Shortly afterwards I watched his grey-suited bulk amble toward me.

Mac, grunting as he stooped, settled into the passenger seat, his dark wavy hair brushing the roof. I showed him the pictures, told him I'd just taken them. 'Recognize them?'

He stared, brushed his finger over a slight flaw on one of the prints. 'No.'

He didn't convince me. 'You've never seen them before?' I asked.

'Can't be certain I've never seen them before but I definitely don't know them.'

'Think you could find anything out?'

He nodded thoughtfully. 'Maybe.'

I turned to face him. 'Mac,' he looked at me, 'can you still make the telephone number top priority? This was a bonus today, and I'm glad for it, but what I really need is the address that call was made from.'

'I'll do my best.'

'Good. Thanks. Can you call me when you get it?'

'Okay.'

He left. I was glad he hadn't drawn it all out with the usual whys and wherefores. I drove to Dunn's place, stopping off at Compton Breslin's office to pick up a Private & Confidential envelope and the last three seasons' formbooks as promised. Heavy skies hung over Six Mile Bottom, particularly dark and sombre above the woods opposite Dunn's bungalow.

No lights flashing on the answerphone. I dialed 1471 again to reassure myself and found it was the same number as this morning. In the dim kitchen, I shifted the table and a chair close to the window. I couldn't risk switching the light on. I plugged in the charger for my mobile and left the phone slotted into it. Armed with a cup of coffee, pens and a thick notepad, I settled down to try to find some strategy in Alex Dunn's betting habits.

The computer printout listed 2,418 bets in the space of 123 weeks with total stakes of £482,115. Almost half a million.

It worked out at an average of just under £200 per bet. Dunn's losses in the period were £98,777.

Breslin's customer monitoring was very efficient. He'd put a note in telling me that his profit margin on Dunn's bets, 20 percent, was slightly worse than average for Breslin since he normally expected a margin, on all business, of around 22 percent. Breslin also apologized for being unable to provide a more detailed analysis of Dunn's bets. The printout showed every horse he had backed but there was no trainer or jockey information, something Breslin said was being built into his new computer programme.

Almost all the bets had been struck on course, which meant betting tax wouldn't be deducted. Comparatively few had been placed by phone. I stared at the list of horses' names feeling like a commentator studying for the Charge of the Light Brigade. I'd sat down to this with considerable optimism but now it looked as if it would take days.

I sighed, sipped tepid coffee and set up list headings on my pad: Owner, Trainer, Jockey, Date and Racecourse. Then, starting with Dunn's very first bet, I opened the relevant formbook.

By the time McCarthy rang, I was working by a flashlight lodged between books.

'Any news, Mac?'

'Yes, though I'm not sure it's what you want to hear. The telephone number you gave me is from a public callbox in Newmarket.'

'Public or in a pub or something?'

'In the street, the High Street.'

'Where exactly?'

'Well, I don't know exactly but there can't be many, it's hardly Sunset Boulevard down there.'

'Can you find out exactly where it is?'

He sighed. 'It'll have to be tomorrow.'

'Morning?'

'I'll do my best.'

'What about Butch Cassidy and the Sundance Kid?'

'Nothing, I'm afraid. I've showed the pictures to my own people. Nobody can put a name to either though some mentioned seeing them around recently.'

'How recently?'

'The last three or four months is the best guess.'

'Mac, could you put a man on one of them for a few days?' That sigh again, louder this time. 'Eddie, it's very difficult.'

'I know it is but I need a favour. I'm sure it'll be worth your while finding out who these guys are.'

'Leave it with me.'

'Till when?'

'Please don't push me, Eddie.'

'I'm in a pushy mood.'

'Are you ever any other way?'

I smiled. 'Where are you tomorrow?' I asked.

'Back at Sandown. Aren't you riding at Market Rasen?'

'Not unless there's a message on my answerphone, promising me a winner. I'll still be here in Newmarket. Will you call me in the morning?'

'I will.'

'And Mac, look out for those guys again tomorrow. I'll be interested to know if they turn up and more interested to know if either of them is seen in the company of Francis Loss.'

'Why?'

'I saw one of them getting out of Loss's car at Sandown today.'

'So?'

'Just a thought. No big deal but if either of them is seen with Loss again, I'd like to know.'

'Leave it with me.'

'Okay. Call me tomorrow.'

At 9 p.m., my mobile rang.

'Hello?'

'Mister Malloy, it's Alex Dunn.'

The last person I'd expected. Odd, too, to feel I was sitting in his house.

I stayed silent. He said, 'Do you still want information about your stallion?'

'I want to know what's wrong with him.'

'I can tell you that. Meet me tomorrow at noon at your father's place.'

'Are you there now?'

'No, but I'll be there at noon tomorrow, I promise.'

'You've promised before.'

'I know. I'm sorry.'

There was something wrong. Dunn's heart didn't quite seem to be in what he was saying.

'Why this time?' I asked. 'What's changed your mind?'

'Today I... look, I'll tell you tomorrow.'

I still had doubts but there was little to lose. 'Okay. I'll be there.'

'I'll see you then.'

I considered ringing my mother, hesitated, put down the receiver and picked it up again. Dialed. The answerphone at the stud clicked on, my mother sounding all proper. I hung up.

I decided it was best not to let Martin know I was meeting Dunn next day. He might go blundering in, scaring him. There was also a strong chance Dunn wouldn't turn up and I didn't want another scene with my partner if that happened.

Best if I went alone.

I was there at 11.45. Dunn's blue estate was in the drive. There was no sign of any other vehicle. I wondered where my father's car was. I went to the house first and rang the bell. No answer. I waited a minute then pushed through the creaky gate into the stable yard.

Something wasn't right.

A row of empty boxes. Last time I'd been here all six had been occupied. Now the doors stood open.

I resisted calling Dunn's name and moved forward slowly, quietly.

I thought I heard a groan coming from the box in the corner and something moving in the straw. I glanced behind me as a car passed on the road, the sound fading quickly into the distance. I walked toward the open box, stopped outside and listened. Silence.

I looked round again then took a step inside. The half-doors were unevenly opened, the gap throwing an oddly shaped wedge of sunlight against the wall of the box, highlighting the dust motes, tiny stars above the straw landscape.

A sudden noise made me turn, but someone pushed a wide hood over my head, light cloth, the sun still bright through the material as I was spun round, as a pad was clamped across my nose and mouth, sweet-smelling but sharp, recognizable even as consciousness left me. Ether.

THIRTY-ONE

When I woke up the sun still shone. Blue sky. No clouds. I was staring at the sky without having to tilt my chin. Couldn't understand it. Blinking wildly, screwing my eyes up against it as consciousness returned, senses revived. And I could feel something familiar beneath me, feel it and smell it. A horse. Warm, reassuring.

But skittish. Whinnying lightly. Shuffling.

Couldn't see the horse. Wasn't astride it. But fixed there. Uncomfortably. Tied on spine to spine. Wrists bound under the neck, ankles roped underneath, as though girthed. Thought it must be a dream, an after effect of the ether. I tried to get up, almost wrenching my wrists out of their sockets. Tried my legs: the same. They'd been splayed across the animal's ribcage, fastened under her belly, fixing me like a hog on a spit except that nothing had been shoved in one end and out of the other. Not yet.

The sun was hot on my body. I raised my head. I was naked.

Nearly laughed.

Tied to a horse. Naked.

I'd heard of King Midas in reverse. Now Lady Godiva in reverse.

No blonde hair to cover my modesty. Nothing. Funny. I might have laughed if I hadn't been so uncomfortable.

What was happening? What the hell was Dunn doing to me?

As my mind began to clear of ether, there came a sound that blew away all my comical notions: the unmistakable snort of a stallion. Off to my left, not underneath me.

He neighed excitedly and tramped the ground and I realized that I was tied securely to a mare in season.

I turned as far as the bindings allowed, trying to see exactly where he was. The first pass reminded me of the shark in 'Jaws'. His head glided past, mouth open, big stained teeth, eyes wide, ears pricked. Black he was.

I swallowed, prayed for my brain to clear properly.

The mare moved nervously beneath me. I could hear her ears flick. I realized her spine was noticeably dipped. An old hand, her back curved with age and the strain of bearing foals. God only knew what was going through her mind.

The black stallion came alongside, rubbed himself against her, jamming my right leg. The mare shied. Somebody said, 'Whoah!' quietly and held her steady.

'Dunn!' I called out. 'Dunn! Is that you?'

No answer.

'You crazy bastard! Get me off this!'

The stallion came in again, nipped my bare calf, snorted, rubbed again. I could feel no bridle. I raised my head. No one was holding him.

I pulled with hands and feet but the rope bit tight and the mare whinnied and reared, giving me a brief rollercoaster view of the big black stallion as he prepared to mount her. They held her steady then suddenly he was up, his huge dark head and wild mane blotting out the sun. I yelped in fear as his front legs clasped mine hard to the side of the mare, and his big open brown-toothed mouth bore down on me.

But he slipped off.

Then he was up again, more anxious now, eyes wide and white, staring madly at this strange intruder, this naked helpless chaperone. Then he was in her and on me, grunting, slobbering and biting at her neck, catching my left arm, biting me. I wanted to cry out in pain and fear but didn't want to enrage him so I lay there, eyes closed in terror, feeling the rhythmical pump of his loins, thinking of the times I'd sat astride others of his breed beating just as rhythmically with my whip.

I curved my spine desperately downwards, trying to follow the line of the mare's, trying to get some of the weight of the stallion off me as his belly spread on my pelvis. Sweat lubricated our backbones, allowing me to slip that vital few inches lower as the stallion's sweat rubbed into a froth covering my genitals and thighs. His huge lolling tongue painted saliva on me as his head rose and fell, and I heard his teeth grate against the hair on her neck and I prayed he wouldn't take my arm in his mouth.

Suddenly the mare neighed and moved as voices urged her forward. The stallion raised his head and almost screamed as he tottered after her, struggling to keep his penis inside. I saw what I thought was a pitchfork arcing upwards, the tines hitting the stallion in the mouth. He squealed and backed off, and I lost sight of him as the mare trotted off, bouncing and bending my spine. She went in a straight line and I realized she was still being led. Raising my head again, I saw us approach the gate in the corner of the sandy quadrangle we'd been locked into. The gate was open. The escape route was there. I sighed long and loud.

But the mare was pulled up short and my bonds quickly cut. I was dragged to the ground, landing hard on a sharp stone that bit into my buttock.

Then the mare was away through the gate.

And the gate swung closed.

And I rolled over to find myself alone with a half a ton of dark wrathful thoroughbred. He stood foursquare by the gate staring after the departing mare, his neighing almost a roar, his huge penis pulsing and swinging, pushing through the bars of the gate as he reared.

I began moving sideways at a crouch, anxious to stay below his line of vision. All around me was a high paneled fence, sheer and unscalable. The stallion blocked the only exit route.

He reared again, pawing the air then catching the top bars of the wooden gate with his hooves as he plunged down. I'd crept into the far corner. The fading sound of the mare's hooves finally went out of human earshot, and a few seconds later, he turned and came toward me as if he'd known exactly where I was all the time.

Big black head down, thick neck stretched, eyes rolling wildly, ears laid flat, his shoulder muscles bunched and flexed as he came at me in a determined swinging trot. I sprang to my feet, painfully aware of my nakedness, blood running down my bitten forearm as my hands automatically covered my genitals. His open mouth twisted sideways, dripping red where the pitchfork had pierced him, and the sun caught silver strands of saliva spanning those teeth.

I looked around for a weapon: nothing. Nothing but loose dirt. The dirt.

I bent and scooped a double handful as, teeth snapping, he came at me. I threw it at his eyes and saw most go in his mouth, but it slowed him long enough for me to race past him, deliberately brushing his shoulder so he would have to make a full turn to come after me.

I heard him splutter and cough as I sprinted for the gate about thirty yards away. Then his hooves grinding as he spun, and his angry snort. My bare feet pounded the small stones but I wasn't aware of any pain as the strongest surge of adrenalin I'd known for years carried me to that gate, hoping and praying that whoever had put me in here wasn't lurking, ready to cut off my escape.

I could hear the stallion's hoofbeats, swore I could feel his breath on my neck, but I was within springing distance of the gate and my outstretched hands caught the top bar with perfect timing, helping me vault over to land on my back and roll in the dirt, praying once again that the bastard wouldn't try to follow me.

He didn't. And I lay laughing with relief and saying, 'Jesus! Jesus!' giggling nervously and uncontrollably at the craziness of it all. I thought how ridiculous I must look.

Only his head was over the gate and he stared at me, snorting in rage and frustration. Smiling I said to him, 'It wasn't me that put her off. Maybe it's your technique.' I rose, very relieved, still smiling but feeling some sympathy for the stallion. 'You need to treat them better. Bottle of bubbly. Some nice flowers. Try that next time.'

Then the elation ebbed quickly as I realized my attacker was probably still around. I stood and listened but could hear only the stallion breathing loud and pawing.

Where were my clothes?

Moving stealthily outdoors on bare feet isn't easy, but I made a reasonable attempt at it, nursing my injured arm as I went in the direction the mare had been led. I found her, unperturbed and alone in a box. I rubbed her nose and she shied away, staring at me.

I said, 'I didn't mean to break up the party, honestly.'

I skirted the buildings, checking the other boxes, the feed room and the barn where I picked up a shining hand scythe.

Nobody. No more horses. Working my way to where I'd started, I returned to the open box where I'd been grabbed. I remembered thinking there'd been someone in there.

Holding the scythe loosely in my right hand, I pushed the bottom door of the box fully open and saw the straw behind it. Then I pushed the top door. It was gloomy inside, but I couldn't hear so much as a breath. Cautiously I went in.

My clothes were on the floor beside the thin white-headed corpse of Alex Dunn. His body held some warmth but no pulse. He lay on his side in the foetal position, his face frozen in a painful grimace. There was nothing I could do for him, and I felt a powerful urge to get dressed and get my wound attended to. The last thing I reached for was my shirt. Lying on the straw beneath it was a large brown envelope.

My name was written on the front in broad black letters. Opening it carefully, I moved toward the light as I drew out a handful of typewritten notes. I stood in the sunshine but had never felt colder as I read those pages. They listed the most painful, shameful episode of my life, baring and freezing my soul in a few hundred words of harsh detail. I closed my eyes, raised my face to the sun, tried to find some hope, some miracle that would let me look again at the papers and find something different.

There was no accompanying note, no blackmail threat. None was needed. What I held were photocopies.

Someone somewhere had the originals.

THIRTY-TWO

In four separate interviews with the police over the next forty-eight hours, it became obvious they were highly skeptical about my story, especially with regard to the stallion and mare. If it had happened, they said, then Dunn had been trying to take some crazy revenge on me before killing himself. The vet had left a typewritten suicide note claiming I'd been hounding him over gambling debts. Still unable to disclose the real reason, I insisted that all I'd been seeking from him had been information on Brian Kincaid.

When the news of Dunn's death broke, my parents reappeared to be grilled by the CID. Dunn had offered them a two-day break in a Welsh holiday cottage he owned. He'd volunteered to move in and look after the horses while they were away.

In the days after Dunn's death, I frequently found myself swamped by anger. Rage at my mother and father and the police and Dunn; anger at him more for dying than anything else, dying and removing my only solid lead to this whole bloody complicated mess. What the hell was going on? Who was behind all this? What was behind it? Much more than the gambling problems of a racecourse vet, I was certain.

Then there was the dire prospect of the blackmail call when it finally came, the task of convincing these people who held the originals of the photocopied documents that I'd do whatever they wanted to keep this quiet. And all the time the fury of old was building in me, bolstering the determination to find them and deal with them, pay them back. I thought I'd mellowed in the past couple of years, God knows I'd worked at it, but it must simply be part of my character to react badly to threats. Well, not badly; foolishly. My fear threshold is always overcome by cold anger and pig-headedness - a poor survival mechanism.

It had been three days since Dunn died, and I'd left the flat only briefly to buy fresh dressings for my bitten arm though the wound wasn't deep and would heal quickly. The papers I'd found in the stable were locked away in a small metal filing box. I'd expected a call from the blackmailers. None had come. They were making me sweat.

I'd like to have established a link between Dunn and Capshaw the trainer, but I simply hadn't had the time to cross-reference all Dunn's betting records with the formbook to check Breslin's suspicion that an unusually high percentage of bets had been on Capshaw-trained horses.

Now I had all the time it took for the blackmailers to get in touch. Hours, days, weeks. I'd best get to work on the printouts. I sat long into the night, stopping occasionally to look at the silent phone, never expecting there to be a cut-off point when they might not call.

They didn't. I woke, stiff and uncomfortable, to sunshine through my window, my head on one of the thick printouts, the heat from the desk lamp warm on my right cheek. I filled the kettle then dragged the phone as close to the bathroom door as possible, and stepped in the shower.

Wet-haired and chewing toast, I returned to the desk to review the previous evening's work. A high percentage of Dunn's bets had indeed been on Capshaw's horses. The first place Dunn had gone that morning when we'd given him a fright at my father's stud had been Capshaw's. There had to be a link.

One person who'd seemed close to Dunn was my father, and only he or my mother could have told the vet what had happened all those years ago. And Dunn had told the blackmailers and they had killed him. I'd yet to learn how he'd died. The cops refused to release the cause of death, pending further enquiries. I needed to talk to my father.

I called the stud. Mother answered, sounding very strained, still shocked.

'Mother, it's Eddie. Are you all right? You sound quite—'

'I'm fine.' Tension now too on hearing my voice.

'I need to see you both.'

'Edward is ill, he's not seeing anybody.'

'I think he'll be seeing me all right.'

'He's not at all well.'

'I'm afraid he'll feel even worse when he sees what I've got. Please prepare him for a shock - another shock, I suppose I should say. And you too.'

'Wait until things are better, Eddie.'

The first time since childhood that I'd heard her say my name. A strange feeling, like a drowning man staring hopelessly up at the deck of a liner only to see a hand stretching down toward him. I was silent for a moment. Then, more softly, I said, 'Things aren't going to get better, Mum, I'm sorry. Not until we sort this out.'

'Please.'

Her voice, cracking, almost brought me to tears. 'You'll understand when you see this, Mum, you will. I'll be there this evening. I'll try for around seven.'

I heard the shortest of sobs before she hung up.

When I arrived, my mother stood at the window, arms folded, eyes cast down, not looking at me as I came along the path. Then she moved away and I heard her footsteps in the hall. She opened the door, her weary, unsmiling face, tired and old but not yet defeated. That touch of iron in her eyes, a look she'd always had.

'Hello,' she said quietly and stepped aside to let me in.

'Hello, Mum.'

Still no smile.

This time she led me into a large drawing room, tastefully furnished but sadly unlived in. A lonely old table and two easy chairs, a cold empty fireplace, two horse and jockey paintings facing each other from opposite walls as though they'd been waiting centuries for this race that would never start.

I stood awkwardly in the middle of the room. My mother looked up at me. 'Would you like some tea?'

I smiled. 'No, thanks.'

She gestured toward a chair. 'Please sit down.'

I did and the fat cushion sank, leaving my arms on the rests almost at shoulder level. She moved silently in old blue shoes and perched on the hard edge of the chair opposite, waiting. Waiting to find out what was in the bulging brown envelope I'd brought. I placed it on my knee.

'Where's my father?'

'He's ill. He has to stay in bed.' She looked calm but determined.

I said, 'He's got to see this, Mum.'

Mum. Again. I watched for her reaction to the word. None. She reached out, her bony arm emerging from the sleeve of her beige cardigan, her wrinkled work-worn hand. I placed the envelope gently between her fingers. She opened it and drew out the papers. I settled slowly and watched as she read, her hand steady as she turned the pages, eyes set hard, the only sign of emotion the occasional flex of jaw muscles.

She put the papers back in the envelope and offered it to me. 'Why did you do it?'

'What?'

'This. After all this time?'

'It wasn't me. I found these in one of your boxes the other day, close to Alex Dunn's body.'

'Who wrote it?' Anger rising.

'That's what I'm trying to find out. That's why Father's got to see it.'

'No. It will kill him.'

'It'll kill him even quicker if the press get hold of it.'

She sat rigid, staring straight ahead, defying the welling tears to rise any higher. Determination to protect him, something that had served her all her life, was no longer going to be enough and she knew it. I edged forward in the chair and said quietly, 'Did Father tell Alex Dunn this?'

She shook her head, not looking at me.

'Are you sure?'

No answer. Tears winning now, glistening in her eyes, softening them, slipping out, seeking the widest wrinkle in her cheek. And I knew he must have told Dunn, and I realized she knew. And Dunn had told whoever was behind all this, maybe not intentionally, but he'd done it, betrayed my father, and condemned himself.

'Where is he?' I asked softly.

'Upstairs. In bed.'

I rose. 'I'll go up.'

'No.' She got to her feet. 'I'll take it. You wait. Please. Wait.'

She took the envelope from my hands and left the room. I sat down again, hearing her climb the creaking stairs, a door opening then dull voices punctuated by silence. And my mind drifted to the dark evenings when I'd lie in bed and hear those same voices rise from around the kitchen range, making me smile with delicious anticipation as I listened to them discuss plans for all the years ahead.

All the years.

The horses, the children - me and my brother and sister - the stud farm we'd build, the biggest in Newmarket. The champions we'd breed. The fun we'd have. All the years. All the dreams.

Then the world caved in.

Sitting in this strange house, I wished I had tears left for it. But they'd been used up a long time ago. That part of my heart was shriveled.

I became aware of my mother standing in the doorway. I hadn't heard her. 'He'll see you,' she said.

An audience bestowed by the mighty one, the withholder of happiness. I followed her up the stairs.

The room was gloomy, curtains drawn. The papers lay under a lamp on the bedside table. His gold-framed spectacles were on the top page, reflecting a coin of light onto an empty glass stained inside with a rim of white powder. The bed was high, wide. He had sunk into the middle of it, the horizontal position removing the superiority he'd always found in his height.

I went and stood by the bed, my mother behind me. He stared straight up at the dark ceiling, the gloom too deep to let me see the depth of his pallor, but his cheeks were hollow, his eyes dull. I tried to find some sorrow for him, but that had gone the same way as the tears.

'Hello, Father.'

His jaw clenched.

I waited. After a minute or more, he said to the ceiling, 'Who wrote that?'

I watched him. Demanding still. In a moment, it would be a command. 'Who wrote it?' There was grit enough in his voice. I didn't answer. He kept staring upwards. I heard my mother shuffle uncomfortably. I said to him, 'Look at me.'

He flinched noticeably though I'd spoken quietly. The jaw clenched again.

'Look at me,' I said.

All three of us waited. Just the sounds of our breathing. Gradually his jaw relaxed, and he turned his head on the pillow until our eyes met. A challenge from his strong son. It couldn't be declined. I hunkered down level with him and held his gaze. He never blinked. 'Who wrote that?' he repeated.

'You wrote it, Dad.'

Indignation flared in his face. I raised a finger to my lips to hush him. Surprise softened his features. 'You wrote it when you told Alex Dunn everything, just as surely as if you'd sat at the typewriter yourself.'

His head rolled back, breaking eye contact. 'He was the only person I ever told,' he said, voice shaky. 'It helped me…to tell.'

Look where it's got you now.

He closed his eyes, squeezed them tight shut. Mother moved forward and reached to take his hand, interlocking fingers with his. I looked up at her. She stared down at him, her eyes showing love and hurt, her jaw and mouth clamped with determination.

I stood and moved to the end of the bed where I could look at them both. I said, 'We might be able to stop this getting to the papers. I've got to find the person who wrote it and left it there. Whoever it was will call soon.'

My mother looked at me. I said, 'He'll call one of us.'

She said, 'What do you want me to do if he rings here?'

'Just listen to what he says. Write it down. Try to hear if there's anything in the background that might help us pinpoint where he's calling from. You know, like trains or heavy traffic.'

I watched her face as she accepted this new role, her brain making yet another adjustment in a lifetime of coping. 'Should I ask him anything?'

I half-smiled, trying to ease the tension. 'You can ask him who he is and why he's doing this, but I doubt you'll get an answer.'

She nodded thoughtfully and looked at my father whose eyes were closed again. I said, 'Dad, are you awake?'

At the sound of the word 'Dad', he seemed almost to stop breathing for a moment then, eyes closed, he nodded.

'You trusted Alex Dunn?'

Mother said, 'He was a very old friend.'

'So what would have made him betray you like that?'

She shook her head. My father frowned angrily. I said, 'Who did Dunn associate with? Somebody must have had a hold over him.'

Mother looked at Father, and he seemed to sense her gaze on him. He opened his eyes but looked at her as he answered. 'He did a lot of work for Capshaw, didn't he?'

Mother nodded as she reached again for his hand and squeezed it.

'Dad.' Slowly he brought his head round to look at me. 'What sort of work?'

'Just standard vet stuff as far as I know.'

'And what was he doing for you?'

Mother said, 'He was trying to find out what was wrong with Heraklion.'

'Did he say he knew of any other stallion suffering the same ailment?' I asked.

Father said, 'It baffled him. I'd never known him so annoyed or frustrated.'

I changed tack. 'Did he strike you as the type to commit suicide?' Looking at the ceiling again, he said, 'Alex could get pretty down when the horses weren't running for him. He gambled a bit.'

'So I've heard. But would he have killed himself?'

He shook his head quite vigorously. 'Not that way he wouldn't.'

'What way?' The police had been withholding the cause of death.

Father looked at me. 'One of the CID men told me he injected himself with prostaglandin.'

I flinched involuntarily. I knew prostaglandin was used regularly on mares to abort them, to clean out the uterus. God only knew what it would do to a human being.

The ridiculous scenario of a TV game show came to mind. 'We asked one hundred people their favourite method of committing suicide.' I'd bet injecting prostaglandin wouldn't be top choice. 'What sort of death would that have been?' I asked my father. He looked at Mother, probably wondering whether the conversation was getting too morbid. She responded by nodding encouragement. He stared upward again and said, 'It would have been agonizing, I'd have thought, but you'd be best asking an expert.' Mother said to me, 'Do you think Alex might have been killed?'

'It's a possibility.'

Father turned again to Mother, forlorn hope in his eyes. 'But maybe he did commit suicide. Maybe he wrote everything out, knowing we'd find it when we came back, before the police or anybody. That means nobody else would know about us.'

I felt a momentary anger as he excluded me from this potential get-out. But he was only following the habits of a lifetime. And anyway, I knew Dunn hadn't planted those papers, there were too many other things going on. My parents didn't know about all the peripheral stuff yet, it wasn't safe to tell them.

My father looked at me, animosity still in his eyes. 'You've brought this on us. Why couldn't you just have left Alex alone? What does it matter to you if he owed some bookie money?'

'It's nothing to do with that.'

'That's what the note said.'

My mother, too, was staring accusingly at me.

'I wasn't chasing Dunn for gambling debts,' I said. 'He was involved in something serious. Criminal.'

'Rubbish!' my father cried, then went into a coughing fit. Mother glared at me and fussed over him. I left quietly and waited downstairs. Ten minutes later, she came into the room. 'Is he all right?' I asked.

She nodded then sat down across from me, looking serious. She said, 'If Alex Dunn was involved with something criminal, is it possible those papers, that story, was meant to frighten you off?'

'It's probable.'

She clasped her fingers and moved uncomfortably. 'Well, couldn't you do what they want and not interfere anymore?'

I stared at her. She met my gaze. I said, 'Do you want these people, this person, to hold it over us for the rest of our lives?'

She shrugged, opened her palms. 'I just thought.'

'Mum, it won't work. We can't live that way.'

She lowered her eyes, stared at the floor.

I sat forward. 'The best I can do is promise that I'll keep a very low profile. I'll try and make them believe they've scared me off, try and convince them that it's worked.'

She looked at me again. 'But how will we know if they believe that?'

'I think that they won't call unless they decide I need another lesson. If the blackmail call doesn't come, it means they think I've dropped out.'

She knew from the look in my eyes I wouldn't change my mind. She said, 'Promise me you'll try hard?'

'To find them or to convince them I've given up?'

'Given up.'

'I'll try to convince them, but only to make it easier for me to find them. I'm not giving up.'

She watched me and I think I saw in her a hint of distorted pride, of realizing she had passed on to me much of her own iron will.

I stayed another half-hour or so, prodding gently for more information on Alex Dunn but learning little. He was an excellent vet and a terrible punter. He had never married and had no family that she knew of. But, said Mother, he was a nice man.

Well, he'd got in with the wrong people. The only link I had to Dunn now was the trainer, Capshaw. It might take a while to find out all I needed to about him, so it would be best if I was based not too far from Newmarket though I wouldn't want to be in the town itself. All part of lying low for as long as I could.

Mother came to see me out. I explained that I needed to be nearby for the next couple of weeks. She tilted her head to look up into my eyes, knowing what I was really asking, knowing it was the first favour I had asked since those dreadful days when what I'd begged for hadn't been in her power to grant.

'I'll speak to your father tonight. Perhaps you could call me tomorrow.' I nodded, smiling. Her neck was still arched and I felt a strong urge to kiss her gently on her upturned cheek. We stood by the door. I noticed how quiet the yard was. 'Where are the horses?' I asked.

'Gone,' she said flatly. 'We just can't cope for the moment. We've sent them to various people we know.'

People we know. No use for the word 'friends'.

She stayed at the door, watching me cast a long shadow in the beam of the security light as I walked to the car. That night I slept in a small hotel, closing my eyes with a strange mixture of fear and hope in my heart.

THIRTY-THREE

Next morning's *Sporting Life* told me William Capshaw had two runners at Ascot. Not all trainers appeared at the races when their horses ran, but Ascot was sufficiently prestigious for most to make an effort.

Even if Capshaw wasn't there, I'd get a chance to see Candy again. Sheikh Ahmad Saad had six entered at Ascot and his racing manager would be bound to be there. I wondered if Candy might just happen to bump into the same hard man I'd seen him with at Sandown.

If that had been coincidence and the tough guys were nothing to do with Candy, I couldn't risk talking to him. I didn't know who I could trust. The more I considered it, the more I convinced myself that the papers I'd found with Dunn had been meant as a silent warning. So long as I kept my nose out of things, no blackmail call would be needed. The day the call finally came would be the day I'd know I'd been rumbled.

It would be impossible for me to track Candy and Capshaw, so I arranged for Martin to meet me in the car park and to bring two cameras. Before getting heavily into booze, Caroline had been a photography buff, and Martin arrived with a couple of bags full of gear and began unloading them.

Bearing in mind my intention to keep a low profile, I was confident that few of the flat-racing community would recognize me, especially in 'civvies'. But I didn't want to bring attention to myself or to Martin.

I said, 'Martin, for God's sake! We're supposed to be moving around unobtrusively, taking a few discreet pictures. All we need is a camera each with a reasonable telephoto lens.'

'Okay, okay!' He spent a few minutes choosing and fitting lenses then gave me four rolls of film. 'If you need any more, give me a shout.'

'I won't. It's best if we don't speak to each other once we're through the gates.'

The plan was that we would take turns following Capshaw and Candy at what we hoped was a safe distance.

Capshaw had a runner in the first. I took up an early position by the parade-ring rails, watching the horses go round until owners and trainers filtered in. Capshaw was with two men and two women, smiling at them, fielding excited questions from all sides, stoking their enthusiasm and hope.

He was small and dapper in a well-tailored navy suit, white shirt and patterned tie. The tallest man in the party pointed to the ground and Capshaw smiled and bent over to fix his shoelace. As he straightened, he mouthed the words 'Good luck' and the party smiled and nodded, a slim dark-haired girl nervously patting his arm. I checked the racecard: the owner's name was K. Semple. I wondered which of them it was. I shot a few frames.

Their horse ran okay before fading to finish fourth. All seemed delighted. I tracked Capshaw as best I could, though he disappeared from time to time into places like the owners' and trainers' bar where I couldn't follow. The only sign all was not well with him came when he was alone. In company, he was animated and jolly. It was a good act. As soon as his companions turned away, Capshaw looked troubled.

Sheikh Ahmad Saad's horse won the fourth, and I moved toward the winner's enclosure to watch connections have their usual post-race discussion. Martin stood against the opposite rail and I saw him snap a few pictures then nodded to indicate that I'd take over.

The Sheikh's Racing Manager, Candy, tanned, fit and elegant, was among the entourage as usual. He too looked worried. The race they'd just won was hardly top class, but I'd have thought it would have produced a smile. Through the long lens, I scanned the rest of the party - mostly glum faces. The Sheikh himself had a smile of sorts, but grim and fixed, professional.

Here was an elite gathering on a fine afternoon at one of the world's biggest racecourses. Their horse had just won and their oil wells were pumping out more cash than they could spend - and all they could manage was an interesting variety of frowns.

I followed Candy for twenty minutes or so on the chance he'd run into the hard men who'd warned me off from Dunn's place. If Dunn had the clout to recruit those guys and he was as afraid of me as he'd claimed in the suicide note, why hadn't he sent them back to teach me a proper lesson? Or had they been the ones who'd doped me and tied me to the mare? The culprits must have known Dunn lay dead in that box. Could they also have killed him?

Even discounting the grim method of death, Dunn was an unlikely suicide candidate. Part of the nature of the compulsive gambler is the constant belief that something will turn up, that tomorrow will be the day fortunes change. Hopelessness tends to be a temporary condition.

Also, why kill himself at my father's place, and why with prostaglandin? I was certain Dunn would have had access to many more types of drugs that would have offered a more peaceful passing.

I recalled my first meeting with him and how shocked he'd looked when I'd mentioned Brian and the lab samples. He knew something crucial about one or both of those matters, and now he was dead. Did the burden of the knowledge make him kill himself, or was he murdered to keep him quiet?

All this was turning over in my mind while I followed Candy at what I hoped was a safe distance. He spoke to two of the trainers the Sheikh employed and various other dogsbodies, but the heavies didn't appear.

Martin and I swapped quarry again for the next race, then once again, for the last where Capshaw trained the winner. I went to the winner's enclosure to watch them coming in. Capshaw seemed relieved and I wondered if his owners had had a serious bet. They looked pleased enough. There were four of them around the sweating chestnut, patting and kissing the horse and posing for pictures while Capshaw spoke to the press.

I saw Martin in the corner, still snapping away.

Checking the racecard, I noticed that the winner was owned by Guterson's Gloves Ltd, and that the race had also been sponsored by them. It was always nice to win your own money. The company's name rang a bell with me, though it took me a few minutes to recall why: Guterson's had been the name on the boxes of rubber gloves stored in the locked cupboard in Dunn's bungalow.

The usual back scratching then; Guterson had a horse in training with Capshaw, Dunn is tied in with Capshaw, Dunn had to buy Guterson's gloves. Neat.

I stayed for the trophy presentation, which was made by Mr Bob Guterson to his own marketing manager at Guterson's Gloves. Guterson certainly had a grasp of monopolies.

When we met again in the car park, neither Martin nor I could claim to have photographed anything that looked crooked, but he said he'd get the films developed and I said I'd ask Mac to go through them to see if he could spot any dodgy characters.

I rang my mother. She said Father was no better but that I could stay in the spare room for a few weeks if I would try not to disturb him. I promised and hung up, unsure if this was a tiny repair in that long-shredded umbilical cord. I realized that the invitation was motivated by their terror of disclosure; it wasn't the way I'd have wanted it, but there was a bitter-sweetness I could almost taste.

I changed routes and headed north to pick up as much stuff as I could from the flat. If my stay in Newmarket turned out to be an extended one, I didn't want to be travelling back and forth.

I reached Shropshire just after eight. The yard was quiet. I hurried upstairs to empty my wardrobe and grab a few books and tapes. The light was flashing on my answerphone though, as always, I'd emptied it remotely that morning.

One message from a trainer, Ken McGilvary, offering me two rides at Exeter next day. I thought about it as I stuffed extra toiletries into a plastic bag. I hadn't ridden for a while and was missing it. I could do with a break from all the sneaking around and, more to the point, if I was seen to be riding again so soon, the people who wanted me out of the stallion case would be reassured that I'd given up and returned to normal life.

That decided it. I called Ken and accepted. He was confident about the chances of my first ride and advised me to have a bet. Jockeys aren't allowed to gamble, but many place bets through a third party. Personally, I avoid it. I find owners and trainers to be the worst tipsters in the land. They are optimists by nature and their default state is to favour their own horses.

I was at my parents' place for 10.30. My mother managed a strained smile as she led me along the hall toward the rear of the house, the sound of snoring from my father's room growing louder then fading as we passed. The big bed made the room seem small. Fresh flowers on a chest of drawers by the window scented the air. The patterned wallpaper was tobacco brown in the dim light, and this room gave the same impression as the others: that of steady decay.

But the sheets were clean, the quilt thick and the pillows deep. I laid my bags down by the bed. 'Thanks Mum.'

She nodded slightly, not convinced she'd done the right thing, but offered me tea and sandwiches. By the time I joined her in the long kitchen, they were on the table, though she couldn't quite bring herself to sit with me as I ate.

She asked if I had 'made any progress today'.

'A little. We certainly didn't take any steps backward.'

That short nod again. I was already becoming familiar with it. She excused herself then, saying that she must sit with my father a while. We said goodnight and I sat in silence, the sound of my chewing echoing in my head. I thought again of the old days when it was I who'd lain in bed while my parents sat in the kitchen. When it was I who'd relied on them. For everything.

They'd failed me.

Would I fail them now?

THIRTY-FOUR

Exeter Racecourse lies high on Haldon Hill where the weather was clear and sunny. I drove steadily down the main approach, weaving through the heavy pedestrian traffic, the usual herd of optimists moving confidently and excitedly toward the front lines to engage the bookies in battle.

When I entered the weighing room, I realized I hadn't smiled for weeks. It was so good to be among familiar faces, trusted people, friends. I had a strong desire right then never to leave these guys again. I wished we could all form some full-time travelling band of companions, going from course to course, sticking close together, never having to face the outside world.

But if I'd have told any of them how I felt, they'd have taken the piss for the rest of my life. I settled for talking to and laughing with as many of them as possible throughout the day. The horse McGilvary had said would win skated in by ten lengths. His other one fell when going well, dealing me a neat kick in the ribs as he scrambled up, but I was okay although I accepted a lift back in the ambulance.

I picked up a spare ride that finished third, and overall had a bloody good day until the cloud of gloom those papers had created settled on me again. I was sitting in the weighing room after the last, enjoying the banter as everyone packed up, thankful to be heading home still sound in the head, unbandaged and stitch-free. As I looked around, I wondered what they'd all think of me if this story got out.

A few of them were planning a drinking session at a local hotel. I'd been tempted but the creeping depression persuaded me to give it a miss despite plenty ribbing.

As I approached my car, I saw there was a bit of a party going on by the BMW parked beside mime. Two young men in light suits were wielding champagne bottles by the neck and singing tunelessly. I smiled. I hoped they had a sober driver stashed away somewhere.

They were sitting on the bonnet, backs to me as I opened my rear door and slung my kitbag inside. 'Beat the bookies?' I asked cheerfully. They both turned, smiling, holding their bottles toward me and moving in my direction remarkably quickly for drunks. They wore sunglasses. I recognized them too late. The darker one dropped his smile and his bottle and pushed me in through my half-open driver's door while the other guy climbed in the passenger side. I glanced desperately around the car park, but there was nobody nearby.

Dark Hair got in behind me. I heard my kitbag squeak on the upholstery as he pushed it across the seat. 'Drive,' he said.

I drove.

He gave simple directions till we were heading south. I'd planned to go north but I wasn't too despondent. At least this was something, a further step. Anything was better than blundering blindly looking for unfindable clues.

Anything, Eddie. Death?

Maybe not.

When we were travelling at speed, Dark Hair said, 'Should old acquaintance be forgot, Mister Malloy?'

'You've often been brought to mind,' I said.

'But not with sufficient nous on your part to want to avoid a resumption of that acquaintance.'

'You made such an impression on me,' I said, 'I just had to see you again.'

'Well, let's find out if we can consummate our relationship to your satisfaction this time. I'd hate to think you'd want to come back for more.'

At least that told me they didn't plan to kill me. I was scared, but wasn't for showing it. I said, 'I just can't get enough of such riveting company.'

'Riveting. Now there's a thought. We're not too far from a shipyard, actually.'

The thought of a hot rivet gun against my flesh was enough to silence me for a while. In less than an hour, we were on the North Devon coast. As the big orange sun began sinking, Dark Hair directed me through a series of winding single-track roads until I realized we were heading for the sea.

The further along the track I drove, the higher we climbed. The ocean lay far below as we drove across the grass, toward what could only be a cliff edge. I took heart from the fact that there were two other cars parked within sight of where we stopped. The people I assumed were their owners strolled in silhouette against the pinkish sky and sea, following their dogs.

I was told to switch off the engine. We sat in silence, watching the dog-walkers, my companions with growing impatience, me with the fervent wish the walkers would stay all night.

But they didn't. Within minutes of each other, they led their pets to the cars and drove away, the smell of their exhausts wafting through my half-opened window.

When the sound of the departing vehicles faded to silence the tension in the car increased. None of us spoke. After maybe fifteen minutes, the gulls broke from riding silently on the air currents over the cliffs and swept down on us crying for the show to begin.

Still the pair waited. The sun was huge, dropping gradually below the glassy horizon like an enormous orange coin into a wide slot. And I realized that what they'd been holding off for was dusk.

Dark Hair got out and opened my door while his friend sat next to me. With the door just halfway open, I'd already decided to kick out and slam it against Dark Hair's legs. Before I moved my foot an inch, the guy beside me hit me hard and fast on the point of my chin, and I felt my legs buckle and my eyes water as Dark Hair dragged me out.

They pulled me to my feet and half-dragged me to the cliff edge as I fought desperately to regain my senses. The blow had taken me by surprise. I'd been dazed often enough, concussed a few times, but somehow this was different. Falling from a horse at speed can be bone crunching, but that split second of warning is sufficient to prepare yourself mentally and physically for what's coming. Being hit in the face by a professional was another matter.

By the time we reached the edge, my brain had stopped rattling in my skull though my legs remained weak. Dark Hair gripped the back of my neck with his big left hand and pushed me forward.

The sea was calm. Low tide. Dusk and distance softened the rocks hundreds of feet below till they looked no more threatening than chocolates lying haphazardly in a box. The ozone-rich air rose in currents off the cliff face, sharpening my senses and my fear.

Dark Hair said, 'Ready? There'll be top points for artistic impression depending on the degree of difficulty.'

Smart answers didn't seem so clever any more. I thought of my mother and felt the strongest pang of regret that my plans to be a proper son again would never be realized.

Dark Hair said, 'Goodbye, Mister Malloy.' Then he pushed me over the edge.

I fought to keep my balance in what seemed an absurd slow-motion replay of those hundreds of cartoon characters windmilling wildly and pedalling furiously at fresh air, but there was no Hanna Barbera storyboard to keep me upright and I went over, head plunging downwards.

Then I stopped. I threw out my hands to prevent my nose hitting rock as I swung toward the cliff face. They had me by the ankles.

Suspended.

Suspended belief.

Renewed hope.

They lowered me slowly. My fingers scrabbled for a hold, a crack, in case they dropped me now. I felt damp vegetation, scratched it, releasing a rich smell. They held me there, panting. I saw the rocks way below. Nothing between them and my eyes. I closed them. Sweat prickled.

Then, very slowly, my tormentors hauled me up. They tried to make me stand but shock had triped my leg muscles. They laid me flat in the grass, and I went from staring at earth and sea to gazing lovingly at a darkening sky.

Dark Hair leaned over me, looked into my eyes. 'Stop following people. Stay out of this. Go back to riding horses for a living. Next time we'll drop you.'

Then they went away. I heard my car start up but didn't turn to watch them leave. I just lay there staring at the sky till it was black and sparkling with stars.

It was after midnight by the time I reached a garage. I called my mother and told her I'd been delayed with the lads, and she said she had been worried, which cheered me. My next call was to Johnny Westmead, a jock I'd spoken to that day at Exeter. He lived in Barnstaple, which, the kid in the garage assured me, was only half an hour away by car.

Sleepy as he was, Johnny agreed to come and pick me up and give me a bed for the night. I spun him a tale about picking up a girl at the races and bringing her to the cliff top, only to have her steal my car while I was dozing in the grass. He laughed; he'd get plenty of mileage out of it whenever my name came up.

Next morning I rang the police and reported my car stolen from Exeter races, that I'd left it there overnight when I'd gone for a drink. They told me it had been found abandoned on the slip road exit of Taunton Deane services on the M5, and that my keys and kitbag were in the possession of the Taunton police.

Johnny agreed to drive me there, and after completing a surprisingly small amount of paperwork, I was heading northeast for Newmarket. On the long journey, I had plenty to occupy my mind.

Whoever Dark Hair and his friend were working for was being extremely patient with me. Okay, last night had been scary, but that was all.

Was the cliffhanging episode really engineered by the same guy who'd had Brian Kincaid and Alex Dunn killed? If so, then why go easy on me?

More interestingly, why hadn't they used the much more potent threat of publication? Could it be that my father's hopeful guess had been right, and that Dunn had indeed kept the story to himself?

No, that didn't make sense, not if he'd been killed. In that case, the killer had laid the envelope out for me to find, knowing I was going to be there to meet Dunn. The killer must have known Dunn personally or he wouldn't have had that information.

Even if it had been suicide, Dunn knew I'd be the only one on the scene. If he'd never meant to expose the secret to anyone then why leave it for me, knowing I was already too well aware of everything in it?

Someone else had to know, and if it was the person controlling Dark Hair and partner, then why hadn't he simply used it? A phone call would have been all that was needed, rather than a trip to the Devon coast.

It made no sense.

Unless the person in charge specifically didn't want me hurt, in which case he or she must know me pretty well. The only lead I had on these guys, apart from my first meeting with them at Dunn's place, was seeing Dark Hair with Candy at Sandown. I'd like to have thought that Candy felt some bond with me, we'd been pretty good mates in his riding days. I knew him well and that was the trouble: I simply couldn't see him being involved in mayhem and murder.

As the noon radio news came on, I was ten miles along the M4. My mobile rang. It was Martin. 'Eddie! I need to see you! We're in bad trouble!'

He sounded panic-stricken. 'Martin, calm down. What's wrong?'

'Eddie! Eddie!' He broke down, sobbing.

'Martin! Listen, are you at home?'

Incoherent noises in reply.

'Hold on, Martin. I'll be with you soon.'

I had to assume he was at the stud. I reckoned I was less than an hour away.

I'd risked speeding on the motorway, which made it very frustrating having to slow down for the speed bumps on the driveway to the stud. But that caused me to roll quietly up to the cottage rather than arrive in a cloud of dust and burning rubber.

As I hurried toward the front step, I heard raised voices through the open door. Fiona first. 'It won't do you any good, you know that! You admitted it yourself!'

Then Martin. 'Look, fuck off and leave me alone!'

'They won't have to kill you, Martin, you're killing yourself!'

'Leave me alone, you bitch!'

Fiona began sobbing. 'Martin, please, for God's sake!' Her voice was softer, trying not to upset him further. She said, 'Tell Malloy. He'll help us. Tell him about Dunn. Let me tell him.'

'No. Tell him nothing. I'm out of this now. He can do it on his own. He can have the stud. And he can have you! And Caroline! He can have the whole fucking lot of you!'

I heard breaking glass, furniture moving, and then Martin came blundering out carrying a half-full bottle, almost knocking me over. He stank of whisky. He was clean-shaven for once, but a fresh bruise was rising on his right cheek and on his left jawbone was a crescent-shaped ridge of weeping blisters.

He stared at me, rage draining from his eyes as he realized I might have heard what he'd just said. Fiona appeared in the doorway, red-faced and sullen. When she saw us, she turned and went back in. Martin's hangdog expression drew the last of the anger from him and he sat on the step and swigged from the bottle.

I sat beside him. 'What's happened?'

He was washing the whisky around his mouth, staring at the sky. He swallowed it and said, 'Somebody took the pictures off me. And the cameras.'

'The pictures we shot at Ascot?'

He nodded.

'When?'

'Early this morning.' He drank again. 'He caught me as I went down to feed the horses.'

He swallowed a lump in his throat. A tear bulged at the corner of his left eye. I waited a few seconds before asking any more questions. Between swigs and tears and nervous swallows, Martin told me that a man with a gun had demanded the pictures and negatives he'd had developed yesterday. Then he'd taken Martin to the forge, made him fire it up, heated a horseshoe and branded him lightly on the jaw, threatening the full treatment if he continued 'following people around'. That was the same message I'd had from Dark Hair, but I bore no scars. Martin's description of the guy didn't match either of the heavies I'd chauffeured to the seaside.

Before leaving, the man had knocked him unconscious and locked him in the forge, which was in a small building well away from the main yard. Fiona only heard his shouts because she was out looking for him.

When he finished his story, he sat staring at the ground, his bottle two-thirds empty. 'Was that full when you started?' I asked.

He nodded. Still gazing at the ground, he said quietly, 'I'm finished, Eddie.'

I watched him.

'I'm scared,' he said, voice breaking.

I moved closer to him and put an arm around his shoulder, and he slumped against me and started crying, softly at first then the floodgates opened and Fiona came and helped me get him inside and into bed. He lay, eyes closed, gripping her hand as she dried his glistening cheeks. Gradually his breathing leveled out and I left them together and went to the kitchen.

Ten minutes later Fiona came in alone. She filled the kettle and washed two mugs. 'He's asleep,' she said calmly. I was revising my opinion of her. For all Martin's problems and booze now looked a serious one, she'd stood by him. He was nothing more than a child inside and here was she, twenty-five years younger, looking after him, carrying his baby.

She brought mugs of coffee to the table and, business-like, unfolded the *Racing Post*. There was a big colour photo of Alex Dunn above a story about the coroner's report whose verdict was suicide by self-administration of prostaglandin.

Fiona said, 'I'm sure Dunn came here about two weeks before Town Crier started firing blanks.'

'Go on.'

She smoothed the paper. 'He came here one day when Martin was out. I recognized him from this picture. He told me he was an RSPCA man come to check the horses.'

'And did he?'

She nodded.

'Did he say what he expected to find?'

'He said someone had reported that they weren't being fed properly.'

'And did he check them all?'

'Yes.'

She looked slightly doubtful. 'Did you go round with him?' I asked.

'Most of them.'

'What did he do?'

She shrugged. 'I don't know. Took a few tests, temperature, blood, that sort of thing.'

'Did he show you any ID?'

'He showed me a card or something, I think.'

'You certain it was him?' I indicated Dunn's picture.

'Almost. I think it was.'

'Apart from his looks, is there anything else you remember about him?'

'He was tall. Very tall and thin.'

'Did you tell Martin at the time?'

'I think I did but he was probably drunk. The man left saying everything was in order, so it didn't seem all that important.'

So, Dunn had been here and he'd had pretty much free access at my parents' place. Fiona found the list Martin had compiled of the other studs where we suspected one of their stallions was suffering from the same loss of fertility as Town Crier and my father's Heraklion. We had to try to find out if Dunn had visited those studs too. Fiona watched me pondering. I came close to asking her to help me further, but she had enough on her plate and it would only cause more friction with Martin, whose heart was no longer in it. I told her to look after him and not to worry. I said I'd make sure he was kept out of it in future and gave her my telephone numbers, making her promise to call me if she needed help.

She looked surprised when I kissed her goodbye.

THIRTY-FIVE

On my journey home, I wondered if my mother would agree to ring round the five studs posing as an RSPCA employee and saying something like, 'We've heard that a bogus vet is visiting studs, and wanted to warn you and to check with you in case he's actually been.'

It was worth a try.

Mother was in the kitchen mixing tuna and mayonnaise and chopping salad vegetables. A pungent mixture of smells filtered down the hall. She turned to look at me but couldn't quite manage a smile. 'You haven't shaved.'

'I know. Things were a bit hectic this morning.'

She sliced carrot lengthwise with smooth sweeps. 'When men reach a certain age they should never miss shaving. And they should always wear a tie.'

I smiled. 'And you think I've reached that age?'

'Yes, I do.'

'Okay.'

'Don't humour me.'

'I'm not. I mean it.'

We were quiet for a while, listening to the rhythm of the knife on the chopping board. 'How's Father?' I asked.

'Still unwell. Quite ill, I'm afraid.'

Sick of facing the world and his responsibilities, I thought. 'We need to talk later,' I said, 'all three of us.'

'We'll see.'

'It'll move us another step forward, Mum.'

She turned slowly to look at me. 'We'll see.'

I left her and lay for half an hour in a hot bath, noting the renewed colour in the old bruises on my ribs like a part-refilled artist's palette. Gazing at the steam-sheened brass taps, I turned over the new developments in my mind.

Our trailing of Candy and Capshaw at Ascot must have activated the visits from the heavy mob, but why had Martin been assaulted?

Because he'd been the one with the pictures? How had they known that? Why hadn't Dark Hair mentioned pictures to me when dangling me over that cliff?

Whatever the answers, at least we knew we were on the right track. Pity Martin had taken it so badly. Terror could be tough to deal with. I couldn't condemn him for wanting out.

The news of Dunn's RSPCA venture also added a very strong flavour. Again, there came that frustrating feeling of just having to shake everything up the right way for things to fall into place. I knew it wasn't far off.

That evening I ate alone again. My parents took their meals in Father's bedroom, and I realized I was still just a stranger in their house.

Next morning, after much canvassing by my mother, Father agreed to grant me another audience. I told them both about Dunn's deception in posing as an RSPCA man. Mother checked the diary and found that Heraklion's fertility had started failing a fortnight after one of Dunn's visits.

Most mares stay on at a stud after being covered, and are scanned within a few days of the mating to see if an egg has been fertilized.

Mother sat by the bed, the book open in her lap, and glanced at my father, his face pale in the curtained gloom. He wheezed breathing out, but there was some brightness in his eyes as he turned to me. 'Do you think Alex was doing something to those stallions?'

'It seems possible.' I was wary of condemning Dunn immediately, my father's friendship with him making me cautious. 'I think he was being forced into it somehow, possibly blackmailed.'

Father looked puzzled. 'Why? Who profits from knocking half a dozen small studs out of business?'

I shrugged. 'I don't think that's the objective. If these people had a grudge against the studs in particular, then why not just burn the buggers down?'

At the word 'buggers', my mother glanced up sharply at me as though I were still seven. I smiled but her expression didn't soften. Father said, 'Then why are they doing it, and who are they?'

'The sixty-four-thousand-dollar question,' I said. 'But if we can find the answer then we'll have the people who left those papers with Alex Dunn's body.' Father's mouth straightened to a thin line as he clenched his jaw. Mother reached for his hand again. All three of us spent the next twenty minutes discussing how Dunn could have 'got at' the stallions. If he'd been responsible for their fertility loss, how had he done it, why, and how could we cure them?

Father brooded throughout most of it, throwing in only the occasional remark, but Mother had been anxious to grasp the lifeline, to explore any option. But there were few and the room was soon silent again.

Father shifted uncomfortably and tried to clear his throat, which brought on a coughing fit. Mother propped him up on his pillows and he reached to squeeze her hand, the first time I'd noticed him initiate any affection. She knew he was going to speak. He looked at me and said, 'When I first met Alex Dunn, I remember he was very enthusiastic about chemical castration.'

Two words that came together like scissor blades cutting through all the supposition and speculation. My senses were suddenly sharp. He said, 'Alex was convinced that colts could be made much easier to handle when still in training by injecting chemicals on a regular basis.'

'Something temporary?' I asked.

He nodded. 'When they were finished racing and were ready for stud, the injections would be discontinued.'

I almost held my breath before asking, 'What was the chemical? Do you know?'

He shook his head slowly and I thought I saw just a trace of satisfaction in his eyes, a glimmer of spiteful pleasure that I was still going to have to work very hard to save this. But maybe it was the poor light.

We talked a while longer then Father glanced at Mother and closed his eyes, effectively dismissing me. She looked up and mouthed the words, 'He's tired.' I nodded. Before leaving, I said goodbye to him. He raised both eyebrows but didn't open his eyes nor speak.

I went to my room and found Martin's list of studs. When Mother came back, I explained what I needed, and she set to immediately, scanning the list as she picked up the phone. I felt like making a few calls too but was conscious of the risk of exposing myself, especially after the events of last night. How did they fit into the puzzle?

The more I thought about it, the more it bugged me. It made no sense. Why hadn't they simply threatened me with publishing the papers? I sat on the bed, Dunn's betting records spread out in front of me. I doodled lightly in pencil in the narrow margin of one of the printouts.

What had Dark Hair said to me? 'Stop following people. Stay out of this.' The message to Martin had been the same, albeit more forcefully delivered. Capshaw and Candy. Candy again cropping up with Dark Hair, his Sandown travelling companion.

Okay, assumption time. No hard evidence, so some speculation might prove worthwhile.

Candy sent the heavies after us. The first confrontation, at Dunn's place, had come with a friendly violence-free warning. The second was to scare the shit out of me but leave me unhurt. Martin hadn't had the protection of an old friendship to rely on, or maybe they had to frighten him more as they had no blackmail hold over him as they did me.

Could it be Candy was taking a similarly 'sympathetic' view with the papers, knowing what publication would do to my parents and me? Possibly, but that shouldn't have stopped him using them as a threat.

So did someone else have the papers? Were we up against two different groups? What was Candy's interest in Dunn's activities? Supposing he knew Dunn had been scuppering those stallions? Supposing he knew about Dunn dabbling in chemical castration? But what would that be to Candy? His boss had the top vets, the best of everything for his horses…something gnawed at my memory, something that hadn't rung true with me… Candy's party at Ascot the other day. How strained they'd all seemed, from the

Sheikh downwards. Candy, in particular, had looked under pressure. The same Candy who'd reacted just slightly oddly, just a little out of character, when I'd met him in Newmarket and told him about the stallion fertility problem.

The Sheikh.

What makes a fabulously rich, high-powered businessman unhappy?

A poorly performing business?

The Sheikh's racing empire was huge, probably the biggest in the world. What had started ten years ago as a hobby had developed into an obsession, some said, a desire to dominate racing the world over. The building blocks for that, the very foundations, were the Sheikh's luxurious studs, the largest of which was in Newmarket. He had most of the top stallions and many of the best mares. Although that didn't guarantee success, it went a long way toward seriously reducing the odds against failure.

His worst nightmare would have to be losing his stallions. Or the stallions losing their fertility. Maybe Alex Dunn's stallion-sabotage programme hadn't been confined to small studs.

No wonder Candy didn't want me blowing it wide open. If Martin Corish was petrified of breeders getting to know about Town Crier's infertility, how must the Sheikh feel if some of his stallions were also infertile?

I put down the pencil and sat back, trying to focus again, trying to pull away from the global implications and figure out the hows and whys. It was the equivalent of industrial sabotage in a multi-billion pound business. Who was behind it and what was the motive? Why mess around with a few insignificant stallions in tiny studs as well as the cream?

Was someone else involved? Had Dunn concentrated on the small studs? Was an accomplice still operating in the Sheikh's studs? If so, how? Security there must be tighter than Fort Knox.

I sighed and got to my feet. I had to slow things down, remind myself that all this had stemmed from a couple of assumptions. I was going to have to speak to Candy.

The door opened. Mother came in, still wearing her reading glasses and carrying the list of studs. She seemed quietly pleased. Of the seven calls she'd made, four studs told her that they'd had a visit from the potentially bogus RSPCA man in the previous six months. One couldn't recall what he looked like. The other three gave a good description of Alex Dunn.

'Excellent,' I said. 'Have you told Father?'

'He's asleep. I'll tell him later.'

I watched her. Outward calm. Inner turmoil. 'Is there anything else I can do?' she asked.

I smiled. 'No, thanks, Mum. You've done well.'

That slightly surprised look again then a trace of a smile before she turned to leave. Quietly I moved to the open door and watched her walk wearily along the hall. Her straight shoulders drooped now that she thought no one was watching and her feet dragged as she took a break from constantly bearing up for the sake of others. She seemed old and broken, and when she stopped and almost slumped against the wall, I resisted the urge to hurry toward her.

That decided it. I would contact Candy.

THIRTY-SIX

I phoned The Gulf Stud, where Candy had a house, which went with the job. He wasn't there. A secretary gave me his mobile number. It rang seven times then he answered and I concentrated acutely on his reaction as I said, 'Candy, Eddie Malloy.'

A moment's hesitation, then, 'Eddie, nice to hear from you! How are you?'

'Still full of health-giving ozone after yesterday's trip to the coast.'

Another moment's silence then his voice tightened noticeably. 'You, er, been taking a bit of a holiday?'

'You might say that. Just hanging around by the sea for a while.'

There was a long pause as we realized the stage we'd reached.

I said, 'Remember I told you I was working for that small stud on a stallion fertility problem?'

'Uhuh?'

'I think I found the answer.'

Another pause then he said, 'Have you told anyone else?'

'You're my first call.'

More silence. 'I think we should meet,' he said, 'but not in Newmarket.'

We met at a garage about fifteen miles from town. I followed Candy for a further three miles, speculating as I watched his head through the rear window whether Dark Hair and his friend were hiding in the back. He pulled off the road and down a slope into a long lay-by concealed by trees. I was relieved to see him get out of the car alone and walk toward me. He got in beside me and managed a grim smile.

I laid everything out.

'Well,' I asked, 'am I right?'

He stared at me, unsure if I was saviour or executioner, then nodded slowly and told me the story. All eight stallions which had retired to the Sheikh's Newmarket stud in the past eighteen months had completely lost fertility within weeks of taking up stud duties.

'Was Alex Dunn your vet at the time?'

Candy ran a hand through his thick chestnut hair. 'Alex Dunn's never set foot inside the place.'

'One of his deputies?'

Candy shook his head. 'We've checked every single person who's crossed the threshold in the past two years. All employees are thoroughly vetted as a matter of course. Every visitor has to go through a security point where a Polaroid is taken and logged on file. We've gone back on everyone right down to the newspaper delivery boys, put private investigators on to many of them. The budget for this just topped half a million and climbing.'

'How much are you paying to keep it out of the papers?'

'Nothing. That's one thing we've been terrified of. No more than half a dozen people know about the problem.'

'What about the private investigators?'

He shook his head again, shiny hair swinging. 'They were given a specific brief on each individual, that's all.'

'It was your boys who warned me off at Dunn's place and took me to the seaside yesterday?'

He made an apologetic face. ''Fraid so.'

'I wondered why they'd been so soft on me.'

'I told them not to hurt you.'

'You're too kind, considering I was on your side.'

He shrugged. 'Sorry, Eddie, we simply couldn't risk you stumbling on what had been happening at The Gulf.'

'Why the strong-arm stuff on Martin Corish, then? Was it just for the pictures?'

'What?' He looked baffled.

'You sent someone else to the Corish Stud yesterday to get those pictures we took at Ascot.'

'What pictures? I haven't a clue what you're talking about.'

I watched him closely, trying to figure out why he'd lie about it. I couldn't think of a reason. 'Do you know Martin Corish?'

'I know of him.'

I explained about our partnership. Candy said whoever called on Martin wasn't sent by him. That narrowed the field. Capshaw was in a one-horse race. I didn't dwell on it with Candy. I wanted time to assemble my thoughts.

He said, 'Can you keep this quiet, Eddie? It'll be worth a lot of money to you.'

'I'd rather find out who killed Brian Kincaid. And Alex Dunn.'

'I'm sure we can do that, in time.'

'How much time?'

'As long as it takes to find a cure for these stallions and mares.'

I sat forward. 'Mares?'

Candy rubbed his handsome face again, nodding slowly as he did so. 'Of the mares we've managed to get in foal, seventy-three percent have aborted within days of the pregnancy being confirmed.'

'Seventy-three percent?'

That weary nod again. 'They're still losing them. It's gone on right through the season.'

'Jesus, no wonder you look like shit!'

He let out a huge sigh. 'I've never felt so under pressure in my life, Eddie. Picked exactly the wrong time to saddle myself with a mortgage that would choke a Clydesdale. Bought a holiday home in Barbados just after New Year. Now the boss is looking around at us and all I can see in his eyes is my P45.'

'Spelt in Arabic?'

He managed another smile and I admired him for it. I knew I needn't ask about the quality of the veterinary care in trying to nail this. The Sheikh could afford the best in the world and that was what he'd bought. The horses had been given false names and taken in small groups to expert vets to avoid raising suspicion in the mind of any individual vet. No reason for the infertility had been found, let alone a possible antidote.

If the Arab stallions were suffering the same affliction as Town Crier and the others, I believed the clue to any antidote lay among Dunn's papers and lab samples, which had to be somewhere. Whoever was behind this wouldn't want to stop at eight of the Sheikh's stallions.

We talked about Dunn who, until now, hadn't entered Candy's equation. He'd concentrated solely on people who'd had access to The Gulf Stud. He accepted that there had to be a very strong chance that Dunn or his secret serum had to be involved, but the lack of motive troubled him.

'He had close links with Capshaw, didn't he?' I said.

'So?'

'Didn't the Sheikh take all his horses away from Capshaw?'

'That was three years ago.'

'Revenge is a dish best savoured cold, as they say, Candy.'

'Nah, he's not the type…Capshaw's not the type. He knew there was no malice in the horses being taken away.'

'What was behind it?'

He shrugged. 'Simple, the Sheikh was experimenting in having some of his horses trained in the Middle East. We'd seen improvement in the best we'd taken there and the Sheikh wanted to see what would happen by taking a full batch of horses of mixed ability at exactly the same time and preferably from the same stable. The idea was that they should, theoretically, show the same level of improvement.'

'And did they?'

'A large percentage did, quite a few.'

'And you don't believe Capshaw would have held a grudge?'

'I know him quite well, Eddie, he was philosophical. We never ruled out sending some horses back to him.'

'And did you?'

'Not so far.'

I looked at him. 'Maybe he ran out of patience?'

Candy sighed. 'Even if we assume he did, do you really think he'd go to all this trouble to stick one up the Sheikh, for the sake of twenty lost training fees? Also, believe me, Alex Dunn has not been near those horses. Thirdly, what about the mares? Was Dunn giving them some sort of serum, too? And if he was, why are ours still aborting after his death?'

I didn't have any answers. Candy looked even more tired and depressed. His brown eyes duller, as if leaking hope.

'Do you want my help on this?' I asked.

'What I want, what I need more than anything else, Eddie, is for you to keep it quiet. I'm running out of options but I know that the only thing keeping me in a job is the fact that this hasn't got out yet.'

'You've got my word on it.'

He nodded, almost managed a tired smile.

I said, 'Come on, the show ain't over till the fat lady sings.'

He looked at me. 'I think she's doing her final warm-up in the dressing room.'

We talked some more and agreed that it would be unwise for me to be seen at The Gulf Stud. We arranged to meet again next morning, and Candy promised to have a full brief with him listing everything they'd done so far.

I expanded on my theory that Dunn hadn't killed himself then asked Candy, 'Can you find out exactly what effect a syringeful of prostaglandin would have on a man? I mean, chapter and verse: how it would actually kill him, how long he'd take to die, that sort of stuff.'

'Okay.' He noted it in a small leather-bound book. 'I'll speak to one of the vets and see you here at noon tomorrow.' I nodded. As he turned to get out, I asked about his two henchmen and how much they knew.

'Very little. They don't ask questions.' He grinned.

'What's so funny?'

'Their names are Phil and Don. I call them the Heavenly Brothers.'

'Most amusing. They were a big hit with me.'

'Sorry, Eddie.' But the grin grew wider, and when he left, I even managed a smile myself.

THIRTY-SEVEN

I drove home at speed, boosted by renewed enthusiasm and relief at no longer having to face cracking this alone. All I needed was the link between Dunn and The Gulf Stud. I also felt considerably easier knowing Phil and Don wouldn't be paying me another visit.

Discovering Candy wasn't behind it all brought relief too, and a strong confidence boost. It had to be Capshaw or someone close to him. My only reservation now was Candy's insistence that Capshaw simply wasn't the type. Was the trainer being controlled in the same way Dunn had been?

One thing was certain: somebody connected to Capshaw had those blackmail papers. And they had to know I'd been doing the same as Martin at Ascot, so why no threat to publish? Maybe branding Martin was meant to scare me off too. And perhaps I'd be best pretending for the moment that I'd taken fright.

I called Charlie Harris, the racecourse photographer, who agreed to send me copies of all the pictures he'd taken at Ascot the day we'd been there. Then, still convinced that Dunn was a key figure, I spent the rest of the day and long into the night with his betting records. The bets were broken down between those placed 'live' on course by Dunn and those placed by phone. By the time I met Candy again next day, I had an extensive chart showing which courses Dunn had attended on which days over the past ten months.

Candy, informal for once in yellow polo shirt and cream trousers, stared at the hand-written columns covering a dozen pages. 'What's the point?' he asked.

'Those eight stallions. I need to see their racing records.'

'Why?'

'Because if you're convinced that security hasn't been breached at The Gulf by Dunn or an accomplice, then Dunn must have got at those stallions on the racecourse.'

'Impossible.'

'Why? Each of the stallions had to be in the racecourse stables. Dunn would have been one of the few people with legitimate access.'

'To do what? Every one of those stallions was tested for fertility before retirement and just afterwards. Every single one was satisfactory at the least. If anything was administered to them, it would have to have been after they'd finished racing.'

'But you've already said it was impossible for anyone to get at them once they'd entered the stud. You can't have it both ways, Candy. Now let me follow this hunch. Get me those racing records.'

He stared at me as though he wasn't sure he trusted my judgment.

I said, 'Come on, you've been negative for too long.'

His expression softened. 'Okay. Fair enough. You'll have them tomorrow.'

'Today. Ring me with them later.'

'No, it's not safe to talk on the phone.'

'Ring me from a call box.'

'I'll think about it. You'd better have a look at this first.' He opened his black briefcase and pulled out a grey laptop. He entered a password and sat the PC on my lap. 'When you're ready to start reading hit that button, but as soon as the text starts scrolling up you have to concentrate hard to take everything in. You can't return to anything you've missed because as each line moves up it's deleted. No copies can be printed and it's a real pain setting it up to run again. It's a complete record of what has happened and what steps we've taken.'

I nodded, bemused, then hit the start button and concentrated like a man with a DIY vasectomy kit.

Most of it was unabsorbable: dates, times and results of veterinary tests on horses with annoyingly similar Arab names, employee biographies including some fairly detailed sexual histories and one sudden death, monies paid out to various 'contractors', Phil and Don the most recent. And all the time, the words disappeared off the top of the screen as though some invisible harvester was scything them. After God knows how long I was left with a grey void.

Bug-eyed and brain fizzing, I asked Candy who was supposed to benefit from this blizzard of information.

'I told you, it's a complete record.'

'But what use is it?'

'It logs everything that's happened, everything we've done.'

'Oh, I must have missed that part, the bit about what you've done. If this is it, Candy, you've done nothing. You're no further forward. No wonder the old Sheikh's spitting sand. If you can't blind them with science, baffle them with bullshit. Is that the principle?'

He looked miffed. 'The principle is to keep the whole thing under wraps, and that's what we've achieved.'

I sighed and leaned back in my seat. 'My old mum found out more yesterday morning than you guys have in all the months this covers. You should have brought someone in ages ago, someone who knew what they were doing.'

'Eddie, it's too sensitive and you know it.'

He was getting huffy now, but I was angry that all this money had been spent on vets and tests and badly briefed private investigators. Angry that I was still pretty much where I'd been two days ago. I'd expected Candy to have some serious stuff offering good leads. He reached across and snapped the lid closed on the computer, then took it and stuffed it back into the case.

We sat in silence, giving each other time to cool off. Candy's window was open. I rolled mine down and the car sucked in a breeze that ruffled Candy's thick hair. He pushed it back into place and stared out at the trees.

One coldly reported fact that had scrolled past my eyes was the death of another vet. It stuck in my mind. I said, 'The vet who died, did they do a post mortem?'

'Heart attack so far as we know.'

'How old was he? What was his name again?'

'Simon Nish. He was thirty-four.'

'And he specialized in mares?'

'Uhuh. He was good.'

'But he didn't know what was making them abort?'

'No. It got him down badly.'

'Did he have a history of heart trouble?'

'Not that I know of. Why?'

'I don't know. It's young for a heart attack.'

'Not these days. I'm due about three myself.'

I looked across and smiled. Candy did too and that eased the tension. We talked some more about Simon Nish, who'd been found dead in bed at home just over two weeks ago. 'Definitely natural causes? No question of suicide?'

'Nope. Poor bugger probably died of exhaustion. He tested those mares to distraction, had his arm inside so many of them in was unusual to see him without a mare's arse attached to his shoulder.'

'And he had nothing to do with the stallions?'

'Nothing.'

'Never went near them?'

'What difference would it make if he did? He was trusted. He'd been with us for years.'

'I'm not slagging him off, Candy. I'm just trying to eliminate the possibility of him having been killed off as Dunn was.'

'He had absolutely no connection with Dunn.'

'Can you double check that?'

'I don't need to!'

'Candy, we're all on the same side here. Please just double-check it. Today if you can, and tell me tonight when you're confirming those stallion racing records.'

He bit his lip then nodded. Much more used to giving orders than obeying them, he was finding the adjustment tough. 'Did you get the details on the prostaglandin injection?' I asked.

He looked baffled.

'The thing that killed Dunn,' I said.

'Oh, yes. I spoke to one of our vets this morning.' He produced a black Dictaphone and pressed the rewind button then clicked to play, releasing the tinny voices. *Candy first: 'How would an injection of five ccs of prostaglandin affect a human being?'*

A slightly effeminate voice in which I could almost hear the flinch replied: 'Pretty grimly, I should think. Death would come from internal suffocation. First, you would feel sick, sweat heavily, the skin would turn very white as the shock effect hit the body. The chest, abdominal, and all other smooth muscle groups would contract, causing bronchial spasms then severe vomiting and diarrhea. As intense pressure built, the heart rate would increase rapidly and the system would quickly suffocate and cease functioning.'

'Painful.'

'Agonizing, I would guess.'

'How long before he'd die?'

'Three, maybe five, minutes.'

'Not the way you'd choose to go?'

'As the saying goes, I'll settle for being caught in bed with a young woman at the age of eighty-seven, shot by her jealous husband.'

Candy clicked it off. I looked at him. 'Still think Dunn wasn't deeply involved in this?' I asked.

'I'm coming round. We just need something more solid.'

'Call me as soon as you can with those racing records. That's the next step.'

He rang from a call box just before seven that evening, and I noted the information on the racecourse appearances of the eight infertile stallions. 'What about the dead vet, Simon Nish? Definitely no links with Dunn?'

'Absolutely none.'

We agreed to meet in the lay-by next morning at 8.15.

THIRTY-EIGHT

A thick mist rolled low over the flatlands. I drove through it, slowing automatically even though it reached only to the wheel-tops, making the car look like some air-cushioned vehicle in a sci-fi movie.

I was ten minutes early, but Candy was in the lay-by waiting. I got in his car and smiled. 'We can't keep meeting like this,' I said.

'You're cheery.'

'For good reason, my friend.'

He waited, anticipation in his eyes. I said, 'Your horses had a total of thirty-nine runs in the past eighteen months. Alex Dunn was at the course on every occasion.'

'In an official capacity?'

'I don't know, but he was definitely there.'

'But if he wasn't officiating, how would he have got access to the stables?'

'Come on, Candy, the security guys have known him for years. He'd walk into the stables without a question being asked.'

'Mmmm. I suppose that's possible. But I still think you're up against it statistically. The guy's job was on the racecourse, he must have been at the races more times than not. I'd have thought it would have been more unusual if he hadn't been there the thirty-nine times those horses ran.'

'But—'

'And, bear in mind that if we're now assuming those colts were got at before they were retired to stud, we're talking about investigating their different trainers, hundreds of stable staff, all the visitors to those yards including other vets. It's a fucking nightmare, Eddie!'

I was annoyed. I'd travelled here feeling very positive after working late and hard. I said, 'That doesn't mean you can ignore it. You can't just carry on building up reams of facts and figures, Candy. You need to take some action.'

'And how do we keep the damn thing out of the papers then?' He was almost shouting but it was end-of-the-tether stuff rather than anger at me. 'How do we work our way through, our *detailed* way through, all those people and not alert anybody?'

'That's why I'm saying, try it my way first. Believe me, Dunn is a very strong link, we've just got to build on it.'

'How?'

'We need to find out for sure if he visited the stables on each of those racedays. You know Peter McCarthy, Jockey Club Security. He'd be able to get the records checked. Every visitor should be logged.'

Candy looked nervous. He said, 'I can't risk making McCarthy suspicious.'

I thought for a minute then suggested he get one of the Sheikh's trainers to request the list. 'Tell him to tell Mac it's for an industrial tribunal hearing against a sacked lad or something. Ask for an additional few days outside those thirty-nine if you like, that'll help throw him off the scent if he does become suspicious.'

He looked at me as though I was crazy. 'Then the trainer would be suspicious!'

I sighed with frustration. 'Candy, this is the reason you've got nowhere on this so far. At some point you'll have to take a calculated risk.'

'It's not mine to take! How can I make you understand that?'

'Somebody has to bite the bullet. What about the Sheikh himself?'

'No way!'

'Why not? If nobody can make a proper decision without his approval then you're going to have to put it to him.'

He sat staring wide-eyed out of the window as the prospect sank home. 'Candy, if you don't, you'll be sitting here next year with maybe eighteen bloody stallions firing blanks and you no further forward. Believe me!'

He turned to me. 'Why don't *you* ask McCarthy? You know him. I'll make sure you get well paid if you can handle this side of things discreetly.'

'I told you before, I need to keep a low profile on this. I can't say why just now but I do. I'm willing to do anything you need behind the scenes, I'll direct the whole damned show if you want, but you're going to have to put a degree of trust in some people.'

He was shaking his head slowly. I said. 'Speak to the Sheikh. If you give him an honest summary of where you've got to, he will have to accept that something more needs to be done.'

Candy rested his elbow on the car window and chewed at his thumbnail. All that his expression told me was that he wanted the world to go away. I touched his arm. He turned slowly toward me, frowning, thumbnail still between his lips.

'Listen,' I said, 'you're fucked anyway, not to put too fine a point on it. Your boss won't tolerate this much longer, you admitted that yourself. The worst that can happen is that you bring things forward a month or two.'

I watched his eyes change. The frown faded and something of the old Candy came back with his smile. 'You're right, Eddie. What the hell? The job's not worth it anyway. I can do without it. I'll always work.'

'Of course you will, but don't admit defeat just yet. We can crack this if the Sheikh gives you a bit more of a free hand. When can you speak to him?'

'Tonight. I speak to him every night.'

'Good. Will you call me when you've talked?'

'Sure.'

I spent the rest of the day in my room trying to make a more detailed analysis of each horse's run, looking for a pattern. If my theory was right and Dunn was treating these horses in advance of their retirement to stud, then this chemical he was using had to be powerful stuff. I found one colt that went ten months between his last appearance on a racecourse and the announcement of his retirement. How the hell could Dunn's serum remain effective so long? And why were the horses showing up so positively in fertility tests well after Dunn must have got at them?

That night Candy rang. Sheikh Ahmad Saad had agreed to give him a much freer hand and had even volunteered to take a more active part himself. The Sheikh was a Jockey Club member and rather than having to ask McCarthy for that list of stable visitors, the Sheikh was going to request it himself via McCarthy's boss. No one would dream of asking the Sheikh for a reason, so confidentiality would be maintained.

Candy reckoned they'd have the list by tomorrow afternoon.

He had it before 11.30, and brought it with him for our daily meeting. I could tell by the satisfied look on his face as I sat beside him in the car that he'd come up with something. He handed me the list of stable visitors. On every one of the thirty-nine the name Alex Dunn appeared, gleaming in a broad yellow stroke of highlighting ink.

We smiled widely at each other and he reached over to shake my hand. 'Well done.'

'All in a day's work,' I said.

'What next?'

'That depends on your priorities. We need to find out what Dunn did to those colts, and we need to find out who was behind it.'

'How do you know he wasn't acting alone?'

'Well, what do you think? The guy couldn't even control his gambling habit. How's he supposed to plan something like this?'

I said. 'Capshaw has to be the next logical step. Dunn did a lot of work for him and as far as I know spent time at his place. He also spent plenty backing Capshaw's runners. That might have been part of the deal. Maybe Capshaw gave him information in exchange for damaging those horses.'

'You honestly think Dunn would try to destroy a multi-million pound business for the sake of a few tips from a trainer?'

'Maybe Capshaw put him up to it? I know you say he's not the vengeful type, but what else, who else might be involved on Capshaw's side?'

A big green van pulled into the lay-by and edged past to park fifty yards in front. We stopped talking and watched the driver's door. Nobody got out.

Candy said, 'If you don't think Dunn had the ability to organize this campaign then I'm telling you that Capshaw didn't either. I know him well. He's not up to it.'

I shrugged. 'Fine, so someone else is. But that still makes Capshaw the next link in the chain. It was after we followed him at Ascot that Martin was attacked and the pictures taken from him.

Now, if Capshaw or some of his cronies didn't set that up, who did? We need to find out more about him, more about his personal life, his history.' I made a mental note to chase Charlie Harris for those pictures.

'Okay, I'll get a man onto it this morning. Anything else we should be doing?'

'What about Dunn? This chemical castration idea he first had years ago, he must have discussed it with other vets, surely?'

'Maybe.'

'If we could find out the basis of it, the particular chemical he had in mind, it might help us solve the second problem more quickly. Even if we never catch the people behind this, at least with an antidote the stallions would be back to normal.'

'If only.'

We sat in silence for a while then I said, 'Bear in mind that if this is guy hates the Sheikh enough, he probably hasn't finished yet. He could already have someone else out there. If not, he'll want to recruit a replacement for Dunn.'

Candy nodded, looking grim.

I said, 'Put a man on Dunn's past too if you can. And maybe somebody could check with removal companies to see if any of them picked up stuff from his place out at Six Mile Bottom. It would be nice to know where all his lab kit and papers are now. That would cut through a hell of a lot of the crap.'

'Leave it with me.' Candy noted it in his little leather book then said, 'What are you doing for the rest of the day?'

'I'm going to bed to try and give my brain a rest. I haven't had a decent sleep for weeks. Then I'm going to go for a long sweaty run in the hope that a few more pieces get jogged into place. Can you give me a call this evening if there's anything to report on Capshaw and Dunn?'

'This evening? You're hopeful.'

'Let me know anyway, even if it's something that seems insignificant.'

'Okay.'

Back at the stud, I rang Charlie Harris and asked him to send those Ascot shots as soon as possible.

THIRTY-NINE

I put on my running gear. Leaving by the back door, I headed across the fields into the woods, building up a pace I knew I could maintain for miles.

And I started again to dissect the scraps of information in my mind. I had the niggling feeling that I'd overlooked something or misinterpreted it, so I mentally broke down the structure I'd built and tried to look again at each of the individual pieces. The steady rhythm of my feet on the forest floor seemed to help the process.

Most of my discussions with Candy had been centred on the conspiracy against the stallions and the commercial fallout. The deaths of Brian Kincaid and Alex Dunn had somehow faded into the background. My guess now was that Brian had simply been unlucky that I'd approached him about Town Crier.

Dunn had been his mentor to a large extent, and Brian would have been aware of Dunn's interest in chemical castration and sought his help to solve Town Crier's problem. Recalling Dunn's frightened reaction the day I confronted him at Newmarket, Brian's approach a few days before mine would have panicked him. If Dunn had blabbed about Brian to whoever was running this, the decision to kill him would have been taken quickly.

What effect would that have had on Dunn? I was assuming he had some affection for Brian and maybe at first believed the sauna death was an accident. What if he later came to a different conclusion? Would he have been horrified? Terrified? Would he have planned to go to the police? Was that why he disappeared so

173

suddenly? Was he removed from the equation, kept alive for as long as he was useful then killed off like Brian?

Toward the southern edge of the forest, shafts of sunlight through the tall trees sliced my moving shadow into fragments.

Brian Kincaid. Whoever was running things hadn't killed him personally. He had hired someone to do it. I'd been so blinkered about Tranter, I'd never given the matter any objective thought. As I did so now I realized how stupid I'd been. The fact that Brian had died in a sauna in the weighing room narrowed down the potential murderers dramatically.

The killer must have been well known on the racecourse. At Stratford at the very least, but more probably around other courses too. Jockeys and valets, trainers and racecourse officials, were the only ones entitled to use the weighing room area. The changing room itself was restricted to jockeys and their valets.

So, if it wasn't Tranter then it was another jockey, or a trainer, valet or official. A simple check through the newspapers or racecard for that day would tell me almost every one of the above who'd been at Stratford. Valets would be difficult, but if pushed I could probably come up with most of their names from memory.

Such a modern contraption as a shower was unheard of in my parents' house, and I had to settle for a cool bath before changing into jeans and a white T-shirt. I called Candy but got his answerphone. I left a message then drove into town to find a betting shop.

The manager agreed to dig through his file copies of *The Sporting Life* till he found the one from Stratford. I took it to the local library, photocopied the section I needed then returned it. I had no inclination to do any more work in that small cell I slept in at the stud, so I set off for the library again where I settled in the reading room to study the Stratford card from that day.

Working through the list of trainers and jockeys, I tried the simple method of rejecting those I considered incapable of murder. It didn't take long to go through the card without ticking even one suspect. I then tried going through again and awarding points in a sort of Man Most Likely To Murder game, nobody notched up more than three.

Next, I did racecourse officials, but apart from the two who scored very highly on boring people to death, I came up empty again. Valets were about the only ones whose names weren't published so, using pen and pad, I worked up a list from memory: six valets, all of whom I'd known for years. I'd have bet my life none would have killed a cat, never mind Brian Kincaid.

And yet somebody among all those I'd just discounted had murdered him. A stranger might gain access to the weighing room for a few minutes before being rumbled, but no way would he get to the sauna and, indeed, spend some time inside, as he must have done with Brian.

But...Brian would have gone in there after the last race. People would be packing up and heading home, rushing around. Maybe a stranger would have got further than usual at that time. The valets would be the guys to talk to. Their duties meant they were usually last to leave the weighing room. I scribbled a few more names and resolved to get contact numbers for them.

That too would have to be done through Candy, as I still couldn't risk putting my head above the parapet. Outside the library, I called him: answerphone. I tried Candy ten times over the next two hours without success and after hearing the start of his answerphone message yet again, I shouted in rage and frustration.

This reliance on others was really beginning to piss me off. I was finding it very tough to handle the fact that I couldn't simply ring up someone I wanted to ask a question of or jump in the car and go to the races.

Candy finally contacted me that evening with nothing new to report. Still annoyed at him, I complained that I hadn't been able to reach him all day and he got spiky, saying he had a business to run and couldn't sit waiting for me. It developed into a childish argument fuelled by my frustration. In the end, I apologized and explained why I was so wound up.

Candy said, 'Don't worry, I can get one of my guys to speak to all the valets that were at Stratford, see what they remember.'

'Which guy?'

'One of the investigators who's been working for me.'

'Racing man?'

'Well, no, but he knows his stuff.'

'Come on, Candy, valets are hardly going to be falling over themselves to tell him what they know. And not just valets, everyone else. Shit, you know how secretive racing people can be!'

Well, what else do you suggest? Why don't you go and do it?'

175

'I've told you, I can't fucking do it!' Bitter frustration again. I apologized immediately.

'Forget it, Eddie. I know you're under pressure.'

'I'm sorry, Candy. I'll tell you about it when this is all over.'

'Eddie, promise me it's nothing that will affect your confidentiality on this?'

'I promise. Don't worry, I promise.'

There was a long pause then Candy said quietly, 'You okay?'

'Yeah.' I didn't sound okay and I knew it. 'I'll call you tomorrow. '

I flipped the phone closed and laid it on the quilt, then sat rocking back and forth till I ended up elbows on knees, head in hands, almost crying with frustration in this big silent loveless house; feeling my life dry up, feeling this place and my parents sucking the life from my every pore, killing me slowly but just as surely as that terrible sauna had done to Brian Kincaid.

Unable to face the night here, I shoved a few things in an overnight bag and drove into Newmarket, booked a hotel, went on a pub-crawl, got as drunk as ten men and opened my eyes in the morning with a blank mind and a major headache.

Unable to stomach breakfast, I paid my bill and left to take a long walk up to the gallops to try to clear my head. It was one of those hangovers where your brain is two seconds behind everything else that's happening to you, and after an hour, I decided that the best place for me was bed.

Praying I wouldn't be stopped and breathalyzed, I drove to my parents' place. As I approached the stud, I became aware of a flashing blue light through the trees. When I was a hundred yards from the drive an ambulance pulled out from it and, light still flashing, accelerated away. I swung fast and hard into the drive, jumped out and ran, cursing my shaking hands as I tried to separate the front door key from the others.

I leaned on the bell with my shoulder as I fought to find the key. Finally inside, I bolted upstairs. My father's room was empty, the door open, bedcovers pulled back. If he was gone, Mother would be with him.

Within five minutes, I'd caught up with the ambulance. I trailed it to Cambridge Hospital.

FORTY

Almost certainly pneumonia, but they'd have to run a few tests before offering a prognosis. We settled in the waiting area. Mother looked as though she'd aged ten years. Distraught but silent she stared at the wall, deaf to words of comfort. After a while, I just sat in silence beside her, suffering an appalling thirst and a burning headache and a scorched conscience for not being there when I was needed. Ashamed too that I was sitting with my mother, at this time of the morning, unkempt and unshaven and stinking of booze.

But even at my lowest ebb, I couldn't find any real sorrow or sympathy for my father. It crossed my mind that he might die and that caused me no dismay, the opposite in fact, which did make me feel a twinge of coldness. But no guilt.

After more than two hours a doctor invited us into a small office and told us that Father would have to stay in hospital for a 'considerable period.'

'How long?' I asked.

'Six weeks, maybe more. He is very weak. His lungs are badly infected.'

'Will he die?' Mother asked. I looked at her to see if she was really prepared for the answer. She gazed at the young doctor with intense concentration.

'If he responds to treatment, he has an excellent chance of returning to full health.'

'Is there any reason he shouldn't respond to treatment?' she asked.

'Occasionally it happens.'

'When will we know?'

He smiled. 'Within a week or so.'

Mother straightened in her chair. 'I'd like to stay with him.'

'I'm afraid that would be difficult, certainly in the early stages. Your husband will be treated in ICU - sorry, the Intensive Care Unit. We simply don't have the staff to cope with twenty-four-hour visiting.'

I looked at Mother who was staring past him now, into the distance, the future, her eyes clouding with misery. I thanked the doctor and helped her out. Dazed, she leant heavily on me all the way to the car. I took her home, promising to bring her back as soon as she'd packed what she needed. I told her I'd find her a room in a hotel close to the hospital so that she could spend as much time with Father as they'd allow.

This financially rash promise brought to mind my last bank statement. Six or eight weeks of hotel bills. Whatever fee Candy was going to pay would have to be good.

My mother spoke little. She moved silently around the house looking at things, touching small ornaments, gazing through the window across the fields. It was as though she feared she'd never come home again. Eventually she wandered upstairs and I heard her go into my father's room. I knew then what I had to do.

After five minutes, I walked in to find her sitting in her usual chair, staring at the bed. I put my hand on her shoulder. She didn't acknowledge me. I said, 'Come on, Mum, I've made some tea. We have to talk.' I led her gently to the kitchen and sat her down at the big beech table.

I stirred sugar into her tea and pushed it across to her. She stared into the swirling liquid. 'Drink some,' I said. 'It'll help.'

She lifted the cup and sipped mechanically. After another silent minute, she looked at me and said, 'It's the pressure of this that's killing him.' We both knew what 'this' meant. And although she added nothing, it was implicit in her eyes that she thought I should somehow have done something to prevent it, to catch the people who might expose us, to make the future safe.

I said, 'I know, Mum. I have to find whoever's doing this.'

She nodded slowly, robotically, and sipped tea again. When we returned to the hospital, I'd ask that she be checked for shock. I drank some tea then said, 'Listen, the way we decided to do this, to lie low, make it look as if we'd pulled out - it's not going to work.'

She raised her tired eyes again to watch me almost like a disinterested observer.

I said, 'It's causing too many complications. It could drag on for months and months and I'm not sure Father can stand it that long. I think I'm going to have to go for these people, all out. That way we either stop them quickly or at least we get the painful part over with.' Her look changed to one I recognized, one that said, You don't understand, do you?

She spoke. 'It will never be over with, not if it gets out. People will never let it be over with. It would kill your father.'

I leaned toward her, wanting to take her hand, squeeze some reassurance into it. 'Mum, it's killing him now, slowly and painfully. The waiting's killing him. I'm sure I've got enough to go on now to crack this in a couple of weeks at the most.'

That was a lie but I could live with it. She said. 'Would we have to tell him?'

'If we didn't, and the news got out, could you live with it if he thought you'd...' deceived was the wrong word '...kept it from him?'

She gave the smallest of shrugs and her expression changed. She was trying to convey something with her eyes but I couldn't read it. She spelt it out. 'Maybe he would think you'd kept it from both of us.'

My heart sank. I said, 'Will there ever be a point in my life where you'll want him to see me in a fair light? Is it always going to be me that's to blame for everything that's gone wrong in this family?' She stared stony-faced at me, and I knew that so long as he was alive my father would be all that mattered to her. So I resolved then to do it with or without their approval, knowing that the whipping boy was on another hiding to nothing.

As I left, I saw that the Ascot pictures had come in the post. I picked up the thick envelope and took it with me.

I found a small hotel within a five-minute taxi ride of the hospital, booked my mother in, wrote the wide-eyed proprietor a cheque for a thousand pounds, and promised Mother I'd ring every night at the very least and try to make the visiting hours whenever I could.

I'd cleaned myself up before leaving the stud and although my hangover still simmered, the prospect of action started the adrenalin pumping again. I felt good. Nervous but good. I called Candy, got him first time.

'I'm coming out of the closet,' I said.

'Meaning?'

'You've got yourself another private dick.'

'No comment.'

I smiled. 'Candy, can you arrange an advance on my fee for this?'

'Sure. How much?'

'Five grand.'

'Is that the advance or the fee?'

'The advance.'

'You don't work cheap.'

'I don't think it'll make too much of a dent in the half a million you've already spent on this.'

'True. Very true.'

'Can you transfer it direct to my bank today? I'd like it to catch a cheque that's about to drop from a great height.'

'Give me your bank details.'

I called McCarthy next. 'Thought you'd died,' he said when he heard my voice.

'Felt like it when I woke up this morning.'

'Mister Booze?'

'That's the man.'

'Well, you should be sleeping it off so why are you calling me?'

'I'm back on the Brian Kincaid case.'

He sighed. 'Eddie, the case is that the police could find no evidence of suspicious circumstances.'

'On account of that evidence being reduced to a very fine grey ash.'

'Maybe, but what were they supposed to do next?'

'What I'm about to do, if you can give me a little help, Mac?'

'A little or a lot?'

'I need the names of all the valets working at Stratford that day, just by way of a double check.'

'Why?'

'Because I want to speak to them.'

'Why?'

'Because I think I might learn something,'

'You're in one of your determined moods again, aren't you?'

'Make a bulldog look meek.'

He promised to call me within a couple of hours. It took a bit longer, but by early evening I had eight names, six of whom I knew well. I reckoned at least four of the eight would be at Uttoxeter next day. I'd turn up at the track and see how they reacted to a few informal questions.

FORTY-ONE

I don't think I can remember going to Uttoxeter on a dry day. The rainclouds must see my car coming and hurry over to the course to guarantee the usual wet welcome. Today was no different, though trainers and owners travelling in the same direction would have little complaint about the weather. It had been a long dry summer of firm racing ground.

Most trainers preferred good or soft going before risking their horses. Galloping and jumping on jarring ground can damage a horse's legs.

As I pulled into the car park, I checked the back seat to make sure I'd brought my riding gear. I'd nothing booked but it paid to come prepared. There were still two hours before the first and most of the valets would be fairly relaxed. Their job is to look after a jockey's kit, make sure it's kept clean, that saddles, girths and stirrups are safe, that the correct amount of weight is loaded into the saddle 'cloths' if necessary.

They also act as friends, confessors, marriage guidance counselors, hairdressers, denture finders, bankers, and God knows what else. The camaraderie in the changing room can be as addictive as the most powerful drug. Many valets are ex-jockeys, hooked for life.

Half a dozen of them were already there making preparations. Two of them had been at Stratford. I filled three Styrofoam cups from the tea urn and went to join them in the corner.

We chatted for a while then I steered the conversation round to Brian Kincaid's death. They were happy to talk about that day at Stratford and answered my questions openly, but neither had seen anything they'd have called suspicious; no strangers hanging around, no odd behaviour from any of the other jocks. And neither could remember any particular racecourse official showing his face.

While we were talking, two of the other valets who'd been at Stratford turned up, and I managed to grab five minutes with each of them. But I learned nothing new. Before leaving I spoke to all four again, asking who had been last to leave the racecourse that day. Pete Crilly, who was my valet, said the only person still in the weighing room when he'd left had been Ken Rossington, also known as Oz.

I didn't know Rossington as well as the others. He'd been a valet for just over a year after arriving in Britain from Australia. He was a bit of a practical joker, always looking to create a laugh at someone's expense, but he seemed a nice enough guy. Crilly said Rossington told him on Monday he was having a few days off but that he was fairly sure he'd be at Bangor tomorrow.

Something about Rossington came to me. That day at Stratford when Brian had moved aside to let Tranter past, he'd stood on Rossington's foot and the valet had made a considerable song and dance of it. If Rossington had been that close, there was every chance he would have heard Brian say he was planning to use the sauna after racing.

I picked up a spare in the fifth that finished nowhere but jumped well enough for me to enjoy the ride round. The riding fee more than paid my expenses for the day, and the rain stayed off during the race only to resume as I drove home, wipers swishing at double speed.

Ten minutes from the yard, my mobile rang. It was Candy. He had the reports on both Capshaw and Dunn. 'Anything interesting?' I asked.

'Not really, unless you can see something I haven't spotted.'

'Are the reports actually in written form?'

'All neatly typed. Six pages on each.'

'I'll be at the yard shortly. Can you fax them to me?'

'Is that safe?'

'If you make sure you dial the right number it will be.'

'Okay, what is it?'

I told him.

The reports were hanging from the fax machine when I got to my flat, and I read while the kettle boiled. Candy had been right. Nothing was of any real interest, just gossip, mostly about Capshaw. Dunn seemed to have led a solitary life. His father had also been a compulsive gambler who had achieved 'the impossible' by quitting for good after a major win. Dunn hadn't been so lucky.

I called Candy.

'Well?' he asked.

'Dross.'

'I thought so. What next?'

'Good old-fashioned legwork.' I told him about Rossington the valet and that I was hoping to see him at Bangor. Then I talked again about my gut feeling that Capshaw was the key to the way forward. I'd been putting a scheme together in my mind over the last twenty-four hours. I told Candy what it was, and advised him to begin preparing for it. He said, 'You know how to make a bloke nervous, Eddie.'

'All in a good cause. Start practicing. And listen, I need you to look through some pictures of the people Capshaw was with at Ascot, see if you can identify any of them.'

'Fine, whenever you're ready.'

FORTY-TWO

I was at Bangor by noon and found Rossington already in the weighing room, spit-polishing a boot slipped over his arm.

'Hi,' I said.

'Hi, Eddie, how are you?'

'I'm okay. You?'

'Good fettle.' He swiped a shine into the long black boot with the red-banded top. 'Don't know why they don't make these buggers all the one colour, you know, life would be a damn sight easier for us guys.' He stopped polishing, leaned forward, his sandy-coloured fringe dropping into his eyes as he winked at me. 'Not that I'm complaining, Eddie, know what I mean?'

I wasn't quite sure I did but I let it go. 'Did you have a good break?' I asked. He looked puzzled. 'Somebody mentioned you were taking a few days off.' For a microsecond, I thought anger sparked in his eyes, though I couldn't be certain. He polished harder. 'Just caught up on my kip,' he said. 'Too many late nights, early mornings and long trips. To racecourses, I mean.'

I hadn't thought he meant anything else. Rossington seemed nervous. It was the first time I'd said more than hello or goodbye to him, and I didn't know whether he was always like this when the lads weren't around to be entertained or if he was hiding something.

I asked him about Stratford and Brian Kincaid. He polished faster, his voice flat as though making a conscious effort to keep it steady. And he wouldn't meet my eyes.

After a minute talking about Brian, he seemed to settle again, become calmer.

'Did you see him go into the sauna?' I asked.

'Can't say I did, I'm afraid.'

'Were you around quite late that day?'

'Not that I can remember, no later than usual.'

'Weren't you the last to leave?'

'No, definitely not. Pete Crilly was still there when I left, I'm sure he was.'

That wasn't what Pete had said. Rossington still wouldn't look at me. He knew something. I thanked him, and left to call Candy but got his answerphone. I hung around the weighing room for a while, saw Pete Crilly and briefly considered checking with him if he was sure Rossington was the last man left at Stratford.

But he'd been certain on Thursday and I didn't want him asking Rossington to confirm it. The Australian seemed nervous enough already.

Candy rang. I told him about Rossington and asked him to find out what he could about the guy, not forgetting he'd spent most of his life in Australia. 'That might take a while.' Candy said.

'I ain't doing anything else in the meantime.' I said.

'Okay.'

'What about our other cunning little plan, have you spoken to the boss?'

'He's given the go ahead.'

'Good, I thought he might. When do we start?'

'Monday. Windsor. I'm not looking forward to it.'

'Into every life a little rain must fall.'

'Except that this time every other bastard's going to be under cover watching me get wet.'

'Pack your shampoo. You can wash that lovely hair of yours.'

'Very funny, Eddie. It's not you who's going to be humiliated.'

'That makes a change, believe me. Call me if you learn anything, especially about Rossington. I'll be back in Cambridge this evening to see my father.'

'How is he?'

'No change. A very long-standing diagnosis.'

'Pardon?'

'Nothing. Maybe we can meet for breakfast tomorrow.'

'Call me this evening when you reach Cambridge, and we'll arrange a time.'

'Fine.'

Only twenty minutes remained of the visiting period when I reached the hospital, which didn't dismay me unduly. Father was sitting up, eyes closed but breathing on his own, albeit through lungs that sounded like decayed organ pipes. Mother was in her customary position by the bed, holding his thin jaundiced-looking hand. She looked more contented than when I'd last seen her. We nodded to each other and I gently placed the fruit I'd brought on the bedside cabinet.

I mouthed the words, 'How is he?' Mother nodded slowly and it was only when we got outside I learned there had been no change. She'd decided to treat this as positive news. I offered to take her to dinner but she said she'd rather go back to the hotel to be by the telephone. I took her there, and then returned to the stud to spend the night.

Candy thought it unwise for us to be seen having breakfast together. We met in our old reliable lay-by where he told me that the feelers were still out on Rossington, and that it might be midweek before he'd have any news on him.

It was a warm morning. We rolled the windows down and sat looking through the pictures Charlie Harris had sent me. Most of the shots had been taken either in the parade ring before each race or in the winner's enclosure afterwards. Capshaw's party in the last race featured in nineteen photos, a mixture from the same general pool in each.

Most of the pics were of the celebrations after the Guterson's Gloves-sponsored race that the company had won with its own horse, trained by Capshaw. Candy pointed to the smiling face of Bob Guterson. 'I've seen him around.'

'Bob Guterson. Owned the winner. Got three others in training with Capshaw.'

He nodded, scanned the others then stopped and held one up to the light. 'See the guy in the corner, grey hair, dark suit?'

The face was indistinct in the background, slightly out of focus. 'Uhuh?'

'I think that's Simeon Prior. What on earth would he be doing with that lot?'

'Who's Simeon Prior when he's at home?'

'He's the chairman of one of the biggest sales companies in Europe.'

'Sales?'

'Bloodstock sales. An outfit called Triplecrown.' He squinted closer. 'Could you get this one blown up?'

'Sure. Do you think there's any significance in Prior's being there?'

'They're simply not his type, Capshaw and this Guterson, a rubber-glove-maker.'

I looked again at the picture. 'Are you sure he is with them? He's standing well away from the main team.'

Candy shrugged. 'I don't know. It just seems odd. He seldom goes racing.'

'You know him well?'

'Not really, met him a couple of times, said hello.'

'I'll get an enlargement done.'

Candy flicked through three more and stopped at one in the parade ring. He smiled and pointed to an attractive blonde woman presenting what I assumed was the prize to the lad for the Best Turned Out Horse in the Guterson's Gloves race. 'Know who that is?' he asked.

She seemed vaguely familiar but I couldn't name her. 'Jean Kerman,' Candy said. 'Mean Jean.'

Kerman was the vicious gossip columnist who specialized in sports. She'd been the one Spindari had threatened us with. 'Is that her?' I asked in surprise.

'She's all right, isn't she?' Candy said. 'Doesn't look poisonous from here.'

'What the hell's she doing presenting the prize?'

'Maybe Mister Guterson had a giant Hooley to celebrate his sponsorship. They normally invite press and celebs, these corporate people.' Almost every race sponsor has a private box and makes a major day out of it, inviting business contacts and sometimes paying celebrities to mix with guests. The only reason for my suspicion was that Capshaw was in there somewhere. Everyone else in these pictures might well be completely innocent, but Capshaw was in deep.

It was getting hot in the car. We got out and walked to the end of the lay-by then back again. Candy wore an immaculate fawn suit, pale blue shirt and very expensive-looking shoes. Despite his year-round tan, he looked drawn.

'You're not looking forward to tomorrow, are you?' I asked.

'Not in the least.'

'It's for the best.'

'I know it is.'

'What's the plan?'

'Jidda runs in the first at Windsor. He cost us two point two million, bought on my advice. Wherever he finishes, the Sheikh is going to tell the press he feels he was badly advised, that he paid too much.'

'Even if he wins easily?'

'Yes. He'll do it another two or three times till they're in no doubt I'm not flavour of the month.'

'Then the word will spread that you're on your way out.'

He nodded.

'It'll be an interesting experiment in finding out who your friends are.'

'A very clinical summary, Eddie. I wonder if you'd be quite so nonchalant about it if you were the guinea pig?'

'Maybe not. I'm sorry, I didn't mean to make it sound like nothing at all, but everything will be put right once we catch these people. The Sheikh will tell the press then about the whole plot, won't he?'

'I don't know. I just hope he tells them enough to recover my reputation. What's left of it.'

'Don't worry.'

'One of the easiest used phrases in the English language, usually spoken by those who have no worries themselves.'

I looked across at him as we walked. His face was grim.

FORTY-THREE

By the end of the following week, everybody in racing knew Candy was for the chop. The racing media are too protective of their own to break a story like this, but one of the tabloids featured a paragraph about 'unrest', as they put it, between the Sheikh and his racing manager, confirming also that Candy had almost three years of a five-year contract to run.

Nothing happened that week to help us. Rossington, the Australian valet, came up cleaner than bones from an acid bath. Using Candy's private investigators to compile personal histories of suspects had quickly become a lazy habit. I gave Candy the names of all the racecourse officials and the other valets at Stratford that day, and asked for a report on each.

If they came through clean, I wondered how long I'd be able to resist setting Candy's investigators on my fellow jockeys. Brian's killer was seldom out of my mind now and unless I accepted that a stranger had somehow gained access to the weighing room, then it had to be someone who knew Brian.

I'd called Mac again and pressed him about Tranter's alibi with the Steward and the car crash. I wanted to be absolutely certain that he was out of the picture. Mac assured me he'd had word straight from the mouth of the Steward concerned. He could think of no reason why the man in question would simply have concocted that story.

I suggested Tranter might have had something on him. Mac said if he did then it hadn't affected the Steward's judgment three days ago when he'd stood Tranter down for what some had thought was a minor offence. Fair point.

That brought me full circle to the conclusion that someone in the weighing room that afternoon killed Brian Kincaid. My mind returned to how nervous Rossington had seemed when I first questioned him, and toward the end of what was probably the worst week of Candy's life I met him at the lay-by again and prodded him to get a double check done on the Australian. 'Why do you want another report? We've already done one?'

'A gut feeling. He was uncomfortable when I was questioning him.'

'Eddie, he didn't kill anybody. He has no history of crime or violence. He worked with sheep and horses in Australia. Came from Melbourne racetrack with good references.'

'Candy, he was nervous!'

'So maybe he's been smuggling fucking kangaroos or something! For Christ's sake, Eddie, gimme a break with these fucking personal profiles! They're costing more than the horses!'

I shut up for a while to let him cool down. Finally, he said, 'Sorry. I didn't mean to blow like that. It's been a bad week.'

'Yeah, my fault. I'm afraid I'm not the most sensitive guy in the world.'

'Leave Rossington with me, I'll ask them to have another look.'

'No, it's okay. Just get me the name and number of the guy who compiled that profile. Maybe he can tell me something or give me a few of his sources.'

'It would be best if I had him call you.'

'Fine, give him my mobile number.'

We walked in silence for a while. 'I'm going to see Capshaw tonight,' he said.

'Have you spoken to him?'

'Met him at Sandown yesterday.'

'Does he know what you have in mind?'

'I doubt it.'

We got back in the car. Candy sat rigid in the seat for a few seconds then leant forward, elbows on steering wheel, face in his hands.

I said, 'You'll be okay, Candy. You'll pull it off.'

He continued rubbing his eyes and temples, then his hands went down and he sat back, leaning against the headrest and triggering a long sigh. 'You think everybody finds this sort of stuff as easy as you do, Eddie. Why? Why do you think everybody sees things the same way as you, thinks the same way?'

'I don't.'

He turned to me. 'You do. You ought to listen to yourself sometime, watch yourself performing.'

Performing?

I smiled. 'You're performing pretty well yourself this morning, going all prima donna-ish on me. I'm not asking you to play King Lear. Just go to Capshaw's and be convincing, which means being nervous and hesitant and insecure, all the things you're feeling anyway. That's what he'll expect, not a command performance. 'Cos you look like a movie star it doesn't mean that's what everyone expects you to be.'

He sighed again. Then smiled.

'What time are you seeing him?' I asked.

'Seven-thirty.'

'I'll be in the royal box, cheering you on.'

The plan was for Candy to approach Capshaw and offer him a three-year contract to train ten of the Sheikh's horses. Candy would confess he'd fallen out of favour with the Sheikh and that he thought his employer was going to get rid of him soon, but that he still had the power to sign contracts that would have to be honoured or bought off for large amounts.

He'd say that, to take revenge on the Sheikh, he intended to approach five trainers offering this contract based on a fifty-fifty cut from the compensation money when the Sheikh subsequently cancelled. Capshaw was to be the first trainer on his list.

The purpose of the exercise was to flush out the lizards.

We reckoned that if they were still looking for a replacement for Alex Dunn, someone to carry on the sabotage at The Gulf Stud, then they would be sorely tempted to recruit Candy, an embittered member of staff with the power to do untold damage personally or else quietly put someone in place that could do it after he'd gone.

I wanted to see Candy as soon as I could after he left Capshaw's yard, but he was nervous about meeting twice in one day, especially if it meant coming to the lay-by again. He reluctantly agreed to drive to a derelict farm we both knew within two miles of my parents' stud. I reminded him to take his Dictaphone to Capshaw's.

I'd been waiting at the farm since 8.30, parked behind a half-ruined grey stone wall. I stood by the corner of it now, and as twilight fell on the empty fields, I watched the road junction half a mile away. By 9.45, I was getting worried about Candy. Maybe Capshaw had twigged the plan and called in the big guns. But how could he have known? There was no way.

The doubts niggled until I saw a car slow and turn down the track toward the farm, headlights bouncing wildly on the uneven ground. I waited until I was certain it was Candy before stepping out as he nosed along the weed-strewn drive and parked.

As Candy approached I noticed how much more relaxed he seemed. The stiffness and tension of this morning had gone from his limbs and he moved like the natural athlete he was. No frown either. He looked pretty pleased with himself.

I smiled. 'It went well, obviously.'

His white teeth flashed in the dusk. 'Hook and line. Sinker maybe tomorrow or the next day.'

'Brilliant.'

We leant on the bonnet of my car and he replayed the tape on his Dictaphone. At first Capshaw acted dumb about Candy's troubles with the Sheikh, though I got the impression his reaction was aimed at not embarrassing Candy. When he realized the whole subject was the reason for Candy's visit, he listened more and talked less. Until, of course, Candy offered him the horses; then he became very animated.

Capshaw cooled as the proposal was revealed. He seemed more interested in having the Sheikh's horses back than collecting a large compensation payment for breach of contract. I warmed to him for that.

But Candy played it smart and said that although the Sheikh might want out of some of the contracts, he did need to place horses with new trainers and there would be a chance, bearing in mind how well Capshaw had taken the Sheikh's previous clear-out of his stable, that the Sheikh would let him keep this batch for the full term.

Capshaw began asking about the horses Candy planned to give him, their breeding, cost at the sales, etc. Candy said he couldn't really give details at this stage but promised that, since Capshaw was the first he'd approached, he'd let him have his pick.

The trainer's enthusiasm increased a few notches then, and it was some time before he seemed to realize that maybe someone else might have an interest in this, at which point he started cooling off. He asked Candy if he could wait for an answer. It might be tomorrow or maybe in a couple of days. Candy said, of course, don't worry, no problem, and generally left Capshaw with the impression that there wasn't a high degree of urgency. But he did say he couldn't wait longer than a week. Capshaw promised him a call tomorrow.

Candy clicked the tape off and looked at me. 'What do you think?'

'I think that Mister William Capshaw is not the brightest guy in the world. He seemed far too open. I'd have thought he would have showed some suspicion at least. It only confirms to me that someone else is running things. I just wonder what hold they've got over him.'

'Me too.'

We never got to find out.

FORTY-FOUR

The call from Capshaw didn't come. When we heard early on Wednesday morning of his death, the sense of dejection, almost despair, was palpable. I thought Candy was going to quit on the spot. Candy got hold of a copy of the police report, which said Capshaw had received a call just before 10 on Tuesday night, and immediately told his wife he had to go out. He gave no reason but said he'd be home by midnight.

A police patrol found him dead under his car in the early hours of Wednesday, on a straight stretch down by Six Mile Bottom. It seemed he'd been changing a wheel when he'd been hit by a passing vehicle that hadn't stopped. The impact had shattered his pelvis, severed his spine and driven the jack out of its support, causing the car to collapse and crush Capshaw's skull.

The police had taken the unusual step of sparing Mrs Capshaw the ordeal of identifying the body, and had accepted the head lad's assurance that the corpse was indeed Capshaw's.

The police were seeking a dark blue vehicle that probably had bull bars fitted at the front, though they did not think it had been a jeep.

We'd gone through the report back at our derelict farm, standing in the sunshine leaning against Candy's car. He folded the papers and threw them in disgust through the open window onto the seat. He was angry too about Capshaw's death. He'd quite liked him.

'What now?' he asked.

'We find out who called Capshaw. Whoever it was must have arranged the rather convenient puncture and equally convenient hit and run.' Candy stared and I could see he was baffled by my certainty. I said, 'Between you seeing Capshaw and him getting that call, something happened. Whether he took cold feet and wanted out or Mister Big decided Capshaw had made a big mistake talking to you, who knows, but Capshaw had obviously served his purpose. Whoever the guy is, Capshaw was scared of him, scared enough to go dashing out as soon as he received the call.'

'So how do we find out who made it?'

'Why don't you ask your contact to get hold of the phone records? I'm sure the cops will have requested them already.'

Candy nodded thoughtfully then said, 'The guy's hardly going to be stupid enough to call from his own base.'

'Probably not, but who knows?'

'What if this Mister Big, as you call him, approaches me direct?'

'All the better, but I doubt it.'

We stood in silence for a while then Candy said, 'What if we can't trace the call?'

I shrugged. 'Rulers and pencils out and back to the drawing board.'

'Oh, fine! I feel I've been pinned to the drawing board this last week or so, and half my fucking life's been erased!'

'No point in giving up now then, is there? Let's get you sketched in again. We'll see if we can make a better job of you second time around.'

To his credit, he managed a smile.

The phone records showed the call to Capshaw came from a public telephone in Cambridge. Candy became disheartened. I told him we must press on and try to find out who killed Brian Kincaid at Stratford. The candidates were relatively few and that offered us the best chance of success.

The guy who'd compiled the profile on Ken Rossington called me at Candy's request, and we talked about his sources and what he'd found out. Rossington's persona in Australia - reserved, industrious, a private man - sounded quite different from the one he'd adopted when he'd stepped off the plane over a year ago. Unless Qantas had started dishing out personality changes along with the in-flight meals, then Rossington had transformed himself virtually overnight into the ebullient practical joker who now inhabited the weighing room.

I wondered where Rossington had been the day Alex Dunn died. I called McCarthy who came back fairly promptly with the information that Rossington had not been racing that day, so he could have been at my parents' stud injecting prostaglandin into Alex Dunn and tying me on to that mare.

Maybe a quiet spot of tailing Mr Rossington for a day or two might pay off. I pestered McCarthy again to find out where he would be next day. Mac was annoyed. 'What's this thing about Rossington, what are you up to now?'

'I'm trying to persuade the guy to admit he was the last man to see Brian Kincaid alive.'

Mac sighed. 'You know, Eddie, when you're an old man walking with a stick, you'll still be tottering around racecourses looking for the fictitious murderer of Kincaid.'

'I know. Tenacious, ain't I?'

'Tendentious, more like.'

'What does that mean?'

'It means partisan, biased, bloody stubborn.'

'I think I like tenacious better.'

Mac called me within five minutes with the news that Rossington would be at Worcester races next day. 'So will I, then,' I said. 'So will I.'

FORTY-FIVE

There's a small public car park just off the main road as you enter Worcester Racecourse. Most drive through it and over the track crossing to park in the grassy centre of the course. But it could be a bitch getting out and I needed to be close to Rossington when he left, so I got there early and found a space in the small car park.

I saw him a few times throughout the afternoon but did no more than say hello. I never strayed far from the weighing room. If the Aussie came out, I wanted to see where he was going. Sod's law was in operation that day and I was offered a ride in the last, which I had to refuse, as none of Rossington's jocks were in the race and there was every chance he'd leave before or during it.

He didn't, and was among the last to go. The horse I could have ridden got beaten half a length and Rossington hung around so long that there was no way I could safely tail him to the official car park to see which car was his. I left before him and got to my car, where I watched through binoculars until I saw him come walking bow-legged toward his, a green Nissan Estate. He slung two obviously heavy bags in then seemed to have some trouble opening his driver's door.

Eventually he came trundling out and I had to let him get onto the main road before following. Rossington lived near Bristol. If that was where he was headed I wouldn't lose him, we were only ten minutes from the M5 and a straight run south.

When we reached the motorway I tucked in a few vehicles behind on the inside lane, but the Aussie made life difficult by staying below sixty - the only person in racing who didn't drive everywhere at full tilt.

After twenty miles or so, he began varying his speed and I wondered if he'd sussed me. I dropped further behind, but ten minutes later the bastard pulled in on the hard shoulder, hazard lights flashing. I passed him on the outside of a truck so he wouldn't see my face.

I took the next exit and waited on the bridge for Rossington to come by. When he did, I rejoined and tucked in again. Five minutes later, he pulled the same stunt on the hard shoulder, and I thought it safest to give up. He was onto me.

I drove home with some degree of satisfaction. If Rossington was nervous of me, he might make a mistake or force someone else to make one. When I reached the flat, I made coffee and a sandwich and called Candy.

'Anything more on Capshaw?' I asked.

'Nothing.'

'How's old Sheikhy taking the setback?'

'Calm as ever on the surface but I think his patience is running out.'

'I'm not surprised.'

'And we've got another vet badly ill.'

'Who?'

'John Snell, the guy who took over from Simon.'

'Simon's the one found dead in bed?'

'That's right, Snell took over his duties. Now he's poorly too.'

'He's doing the mares now?'

'Uhuh, been doing loads of tests on the ones who lost foals.'

'Any findings?'

'Not a jot so far.'

'And what exactly is wrong with Snell?'

'They don't know. They're still doing tests on him too. He thinks it might be exhaustion, which they say could have been a contributory factor in Simon Nish's heart attack.'

'Can't you tell these guys to slow down a bit?'

'The vets? Eddie, everyone's the same here! It's not just them. We're all under pressure, we want this sorted out.'

'Okay, okay, but they're only horses, for God's sake! It's only a job even if it does pay well. Are *you* going to kill yourself for it, too?'

'Listen to who's talking. The scrapes you've been in!'

'But I do it for the love of it, not the money.'

'Ha, bloody ha.'

'Keep laughing, Candy. I'm planning to up the stakes now and you'd better get yourself in gear too. I'm beginning to think that whoever's behind all this might have sussed what we were trying to do through Capshaw.'

'Plant me in there, you mean?'

'Exactly. And if they do suspect that then they know we're closing in. Okay, we might not have them surrounded, but they'll realize we're on their heels. Also, Rossington's rattled, and if he is involved, I think we can expect some action soon.'

'If you're right then I think Rossington will be more worried about his own health than doing us any damage.'

'Maybe, but they've got to stop killing their own guys at some point.'

'And start killing us?'

'Start trying.'

Candy's man got me the names of three people in Australia who knew Ken Rossington. None of them was available to talk when I called, though one, Clive Torpen, promised me a call back later if I could 'stay awake long enough'

I don't know what time I dozed off but the trill of the telephone woke me. In a daze, I reached out and scooped up the receiver, trying to remember the name of the Aussie I was expecting a call from, but all I heard was a dial tone.

A phone still ringing somewhere.

Then a click and the sound of my fax machine working.

I rolled off the bed and went to the machine whose digital clock read one minute past midnight. The paper spooled out. No first-page identification, just heavy dark print in a large typeface like a newspaper headline. The words below were laid out in newspaper-style columns and the content was a reproduction of the document I'd found beside Alex Dunn's corpse. The headline read 'Shameful Secret of Top Jockey'.

FORTY-SIX

I didn't think they'd given it to the press. That was their ace and they wouldn't play it this soon. Also, whoever got the story would do the usual and ring me for my comments 'in the interests of fairness', which really meant in the interests of possibly getting some more salacious information. Still, thinking about it kept me awake, the light of the single lamp glowing on my scribbled notes on which I'd drawn boxes and arrows in the hope that some pattern would emerge to pull together damaged stallions, aborting mares and dead men.

At 2.10, my contact in Australia rang. Five minutes later, I told him how much I appreciated the call and how grateful I was he'd taken the trouble to tell me about Ken Rossington.

'No trouble, mate, anytime.'

Come morning I'd had no more than three hours of troubled sleep, and promised myself I'd catch up by having an early night tonight. Then, over breakfast, Charles Tunney, the trainer I rode for, reminded me of a dinner date we both had in London.

'Shit, that's not tonight, is it?'

'Afraid so.'

'I thought that was next month.'

'Afraid not.' He was smiling, his chubby cheeks red from an hour out walking the gallops, checking and planning. Six of our horses were due back in tomorrow and Charles, as optimistic as most other racing folk, was looking forward to a good season.

I told him I'd have to call off from this charity dinner but he reminded me that it was a 'three-line-whip' from Broga Cates who owned the property, the horses, and paid me a retainer to ride for the stable. Broga had 'bought' a table for this high-profile event at a cost of three grand. Charles and I were to be two of his nine guests.

After breakfast, I called Candy and told him what I'd discovered about Rossington, asking him to cancel any pending enquiries about the Aussie for fear of alerting him. Then I contacted McCarthy. I couldn't afford to tell him everything about Rossington; he'd have gone all official on me. But I said enough to convince him he should carry on co-operating with me over Rossington's past movements. I also arranged to take advantage of my trip to London by having a meeting there with Mac next morning.

At Euston station, the taxi rank was empty of cabs and full of people. We took the tube then walked the remaining few hundred yards to the Dorchester, skirting the edge of Hyde Park and its dog-walkers, roller-bladers and tourists.

It was a fine sunny evening and we smiled and chatted as we entered the pedestrian underpass to walk beneath Park Lane, at which point our smiles faded as we saw the ragged rows of homeless people already settled for the night in makeshift cardboard beds while chauffeur-driven limousines glided above their heads, carrying the lucky ones to their clubs and casinos and three-hundred-pound-a-night rooms.

My three-hundred-pound-a-head-dinner took some forcing down, and I couldn't quite bring myself to join in the applause as egos fuelled by liquor paid crazy prices for sports memorabilia. It was for charity, which made it palatable, but I wondered what charity would help those poor bastards sleeping in the basement of the world. Especially when winter came.

By 11, the tables had been cleared, the lights were low, the orchestra played in the background and alcohol had draped its usual soft curtains around each party, making them think they were the only ones who really mattered. Nonsense was talked, boasts made, libidos stoked, promises sworn - until finally I decided to have a few more drinks and stop being so bloody judgmental.

Charles had been away from the seat beside me for about twenty minutes when it was quietly filled by a woman in a black dress, a string of pearls and a sweet haze of perfume. Early- forties, blonde shoulder-length hair, pale pink lipstick on narrow lips, grey-blue eyes wrinkled pleasantly by her smile, biggish nose but not unattractive given her strong bone structure. Her breasts were too heavy for whatever wire support was pushing them up, making little wrinkles either side of the tight line of cleavage.

She smiled at me as if I should know her and I did. I recognized her from that picture at Ascot. 'Eddie?' She held out her hand. 'Jean Kerman.'

The newspaper columnist. The gorgon of the gossip pages, destroyer of reputations, specializing in sports personalities the way a forensic pathologist specializes in bodies - the difference being the medic has the good grace to wait till you're dead.

I took her hand. 'Nice to meet you at last,' she said.

'Likewise,' I lied.

A stalking waiter, eager to help seal what he obviously saw as a potential liaison, appeared and offered champagne. Kerman, without acknowledging the man himself, took two glasses and placed one in front of me. She drank half the other at a gulp. I left mine untouched.

We small-talked, but I was finding it tough to hide my wariness of her. I was tempted to ask if she shouldn't be moving around looking for someone to write about, but I had the uncomfortable feeling that was exactly what she had been doing.

She inched her chair closer and lit a cigarette, thin lips closing to a pencil line as she drew on it, then tilted her head to blow a stream of smoke from the corner of her mouth. Chin raised and eyes half-closed, she thought she was posing sexily, but the most striking part of the view was up her wide nostrils.

The band was doing some nice slow forties stuff and the floor was pretty full. Kerman stood up and asked if I wanted to dance. I didn't but nor did I want to embarrass her, so I got up and she led me onto the floor, turned and moved in so close her breast wrinkles washed backward like a wave. Her high heels brought her to my height and she pulled my head forward, raising her shoulder to nudge me nearer her neck.

'I never inspect ears on a first date,' I said.

She laughed, pulling back to look at me. I managed what I hoped was a reasonably pleasant expression with a hint of warning attached that I wasn't quite so keen on having sex on the dance floor of the Dorchester as she appeared to be.

She settled a bit then and we moved in a slow but rhythmic circle. She tried to ease her pelvis closer to me but her stomach got there first. Her perfume seemed muskier close up, her body warm. As the music came to an end, I was still trying to figure her out when she raised her chin, putting her mouth close to my ear. She said, 'You dance well. Did your mum teach you when you were a boy?' She drew back like a cobra and looked at me, eyes much colder now. Then she said, 'Or were you too busy going out for walks in the bracing Cumbrian air? Walks by the river. Or climbing trees? Maybe that was your favourite, Eddie, eh?' And I wondered if, in the relative darkness, she could see the colour draining from me. A smile glinted hard and steely on her face as she turned and walked away.

FORTY-SEVEN

I went out into the brightly lit busy streets and found a newspaper seller. Kerman's paper was called *The Examiner* and tomorrow's early edition was already on the stands. I scanned through quickly, knowing that if she'd run the story it would probably be over two full pages.

It wasn't there.

I leant against a lamppost, trying to breathe deeply, tension pulsing in my throat, realizing that the sense of relief I was feeling was false. It would be followed by another bout of fear, another steady winding of the anxiety spring as I waited for Friday's edition then Saturday's and so on.

The evening suit suddenly felt tight, the wing collar choking. I reached up to loosen it. Sweat broke through on my forehead as I stared at the sky.

It was after midnight when I reached the hotel, too late to call Mother and warn her. And what good would it do anyway? I'd goaded these people, tempted them to come out, and they had. They'd given the story to Kerman and she'd teased and goaded me and I knew she would publish the story soon. She had to, that was her job.

I spent another sleepless night, which led into the longest day of my life. The next morning I met Mac at Jockey Club HQ, Portman Square.

He looked at my face as we sat down in his office. A rich smell of coffee permeated the whole floor we were on and Mac ordered a pot. He said, 'I can't tell whether it was a good night or a bloody bad one, but you look like you've been up for most of it.'

'I was. One way or another.'

He smiled. 'One of those, eh?'

'No, not one of those.'

He kept smiling stupidly until the coffee came. I hadn't planned to tell him about Rossington, but Kerman had increased the pressure so much I was determined to get these people. I was going to suffer the consequences anyway, and if I could bring them down too it would help ease the pain.

I drank, savouring the long aftertaste, then said to Mac, 'Ken Rossington's not who he says he is.'

'He says he's Ken Rossington. His passport says he's Ken Rossington. His racecourse ID from Melbourne says he's Ken Rossington.'

'He's not.'

Mac settled behind the big desk in that comfortable way I'd now become familiar with. Before he knew me properly or trusted my judgment, he used to stiffen, sit straighter when I started setting out my theories. But experience had deflated the mild pomposity and quelled the doubts. We'd been through a few things together, arguing and falling out along the way, but always building respect for each other.

Slowly he drank his coffee. Lifting my cup and holding his gaze, I mimicked his action. We both smiled. 'Go on,' he said.

'The Ken Rossington who worked at Melbourne was at least three inches shorter than our man and maybe twenty pounds lighter. He was quiet, reserved, industrious and private. Our guy behaves like CoCo the Clown half the time. His hair and eye colouring are the same and he has the same general facial shape but they are two different men.'

Mac shrugged. 'Maybe they are. Maybe it was us that got them confused.'

I shook my head. 'Rossington's CV lays claim to everything his Melbourne counterpart has done.'

'Okay, who is our man?'

'I don't know.'

'Why is he impersonating Rossington?'

'I don't know.'

'Where is the real Rossington?'

'You've just completed the hat-trick. I don't know. The real Ken Rossington left Melbourne on March the twelfth last year, after the break-up of a long-term affair with a jockey.'

Mac sat forward. 'A jockey? A female jockey?'

'No, the type with the hanging genitalia.'

Mac looked shocked. 'A homosexual jockey?'

'I certainly hope so, or it must have been a touch unpleasant for him.'

He sat back again, slowly shaking his head.

'Why do you say "a homosexual jockey"?' I asked. 'Rossington was the other half, why don't you say, "a homosexual valet"?'

'I don't know. It just seems odd.'

'We're all human under those silks, you know.'

He nodded. 'Anyway, go on.'

'Rossington decided to make a new life for himself in England. He had dual nationality so didn't see a problem getting work in racing. The rumour is that an owner he knew out there, a guy who also had horses in England and France, promised to help him get started here.'

'Who was the owner?'

'I'm still waiting to find out. My man says he'll get back to me.'

'Well, when he does your problem is solved. If the owner knows Rossington well enough to offer him a job, then he'll be able to tell you if our man's an imposter.'

'Question is, how long can we afford to wait?'

Mac drummed on his thick blotting pad with a pen, finishing off with two pings on the edge of his coffee cup. 'Does this all lead to Kincaid?'

I nodded. 'And maybe Alex Dunn.'

He stared at me.

'And William Capshaw,' I said.

I watched him. When Mac felt matters had reached what he called a 'delicate' stage, he preferred to ask no more questions and hear no more theories. This was his boundary line. Beyond it lay formal obligations. His unblinking gaze told me we'd reached it.

'If you could just do me one favour?' I asked. 'I know you've got friends in Melbourne. Whoever Rossington really is, he does seem to know about horses and jockeys. Can you get hold of a photo of Rossington and send a few prints to Melbourne, see if anyone recognizes him?'

He made a note. 'Okay, I'll deal with it.' It looked like the potential implications were beginning to sink in. He agreed to do what he could on our usual understanding that if the shit hit the fan, he'd be free to claim he was nowhere in the room. I asked one more favour of him; to contact Ascot Racecourse and ask for a copy of Bob Guterson's guest list on the day he sponsored that race. He got me that by fax within minutes. It included the table plan for lunch. Kerman's name was there, seated between Guterson and Simeon Prior. There were nineteen more names on the list and Mac went through it with me, but of the few he knew none gave him any reason for suspicion though he raised the same point Candy had: that Simeon Prior, the chairman of Triplecrown Bloodstock, seemed out of place in that company.

Why then had Prior accepted Guterson's invitation?

I left and went straight home to wait by the phone. Kerman had to run the story next day, Friday. I sat waiting for her, waiting for the 'chance to comment'.

But the call never came, and the piece didn't appear on Friday or on Saturday. Sunday was their biggest circulation day; she had to print it then or risk losing it to a rival. Her informants wouldn't wait forever. She didn't, and I began to wonder what Jean Kerman's role was. Sitting on this must have been killing her.

Had she been invited to Ascot just so someone could plant the story about me in her mind? If so, how had they restrained her from running it? Had they fed her only the small part she'd teased me with? No, that wouldn't have been acceptable to her.

And why had she taken such a personal line with me? Why not simply ring me up and tell me she knew and that she would have to publish? I recalled that cold hard look in her eyes as she'd left me on the dance floor, that cruel glint almost of revenge.

Was she involved with them? Could Kerman be in on it somehow?

I rang Candy. Although I couldn't tell him why I wanted it, he agreed to put someone straight to work on finding every destructive racing piece Kerman worked on in the past five years.

'How many bodies can you spare?' I asked.

'How quickly do you want it?'

'Yesterday.'

'What's the big hurry?'

'I think the key to the next move might be in there among those stories.'

He sighed. 'Let me make some calls. I'll ring you back.'

'Candy…While you're at it, see what you can find out about Bob Guterson.'

FORTY-EIGHT

I travelled south and went to my parents' place to wait for Candy's call next day. I spent a miserable visiting hour at the hospital, my small talk ricocheting off the almost tangible barrier my father had erected round himself and my mother, resenting my presence, glorying in my discomfort, drawing every moment of my mother's attention toward himself.

I sat there, elbows on the edge of the bed, feeling like a trapped audience of one to a terrible soap opera that would never be turned off. And I took cold-hearted wicked comfort in the fact that when the Kerman story broke he would know some of the suffering I'd endured.

I dropped my mother at her hotel and drove away in a desolate mood. After re-establishing contact with her and moving into the house, I'd held such hopes for the future, such plans for repairing all the hurt. Now I wished earnestly that the pneumonia would kill him before all chance with her was gone.

My contact in Australia came through with the name of the owner who'd got Rossington the valet's job: Bob Guterson. Surprise, surprise.

Dunn, Capshaw, Rossington, Guterson...the links were steadily joining. Did Kerman fit in somewhere? Candy arrived with the cuttings and I told him about Guterson fixing up Rossington, or whoever he was, with the job. Candy already had some information on the guy. Guterson had sixteen horses in training in Europe and Australia; not a very big string to be so thinly spread, but understandable perhaps when Candy told me Guterson did business on both continents.

He'd been in racing as an owner less than three years, though his company had been supplying the veterinary industry with rubber gloves for quite a bit longer. Not a huge market, but one in which Guterson had a major share with large sales throughout Europe and Australia. The connection with Simeon Prior became clearer too: eighteen months ago, Guterson had bought a twenty percent share in Triplecrown Bloodstock, an investment that had seemed particularly poorly judged, as the company hadn't been performing well for some time. Nor had profits improved since Guterson bought in.

We kicked things around for a while without coming to any conclusions. I could see Candy was anxious to start going through the cuttings on Kerman's past victims. I made coffee, and we settled down at the big kitchen table and worked through the night sifting, sorting, discussing. Kerman had already laid bare most of the lives of her victims but we dissected them all at length, including our own memories of them, and Candy showed how sharp an eye for detail he had by recalling small facts and anecdotes.

We found three people of particular interest, all of them speared by Kerman within the last fourteen months. The first was Ben Campbell, who'd been the Sheikh's Racing Manager before Candy. Campbell had a heavy cocaine habit which was exposed by one of Kerman's 'reporters', who'd set the guy up.

The next to go was a man called James Summerville, a respected bloodstock journalist and agent who was heavily pro-Arab in his writing. Summerville supported Sheikh Ahmad's attempts to establish his own superior thoroughbred bloodlines, arguing that this was in essence the original intention behind thoroughbred breeding, which went back to the days of the Crusades.

Unfortunately, it was proved that while wearing his agent's hat he'd accepted bribes to help inflate the prices of horses he'd been entrusted to buy. Again, it looked like he'd been set up by a Kerman stooge.

The last one to go, and maybe the most significant to us, was a top vet who'd been based at the Equine Fertility Unit in Newmarket. His name was Stephen Spenser and he was the best man in his field. Kerman nailed him after discovering he'd conducted experiments on live ex-racehorses, two of which had died as a result of his research. Spenser had been struck off. Candy was certain he'd gone to America. He'd been one of the people Candy had considered trying to recruit when the stallion problem blew up. 'You think he could have cracked it?' I asked, sipping tepid coffee.

'He would have had a better chance than most,' Candy said, 'and I'd have used him if I could have traced him in the States.'

'And if he was that good, our friends might have known it and wanted him out of the picture before they started on those stallions.'

'Possibly,' Candy said absent-mindedly as he pulled the Ben Campbell page back under the lamp beam and stared at the picture, frowning. 'You know,' he said, 'I think Campbell was related somehow to Alex Dunn. Either related or his godson or something.'

'That would make sense. Dunn would probably have been very reluctant to damage Campbell's career. Whoever's behind this would realize that so he simply took Campbell out of the equation before involving Dunn.'

Candy sighed and shook his head. 'Shit, you could say all three of these affected our situation, directly or indirectly. You're talking about some pretty elaborate planning here.'

'Not to mention three killings. Somehow I think we're dealing with a slightly stronger motive than a simple dislike of the Sheikh and his empire.'

We still knew neither motive nor method, and were both getting too tired to think sensibly. We sat gazing at Campbell's smiling picture.

Candy sighed, and stretched and yawned, long and large as a hippo. Within seconds, I followed. We laughed gently then I stood up. 'You get the coffee. I'll get the fresh air.' And I went and opened the kitchen door to let in the cold night, to brace us. I stood on the step looking up at the black-blue sky and diamond-sharp stars.

Candy moved around behind me, fixing more coffee. 'We're close to something here, Eddie,' he said. I listened. 'Those three pieces point to Kerman doing more than her journalistic duty. She's working for somebody other than *The Examiner*.'

I smiled at the sky, knowing I couldn't tell him about her approach to me at the Dorchester, but feeling more and more certain she was in with these people. Because if she was, and we could bring her down with the rest of them, shame her, then there wouldn't be any *Examiner* story about the Malloy family. And maybe, just maybe, things would be all right again.

I turned to Candy as he poured hot water into a mug. 'I think it's time we got your personal profile man to work again. Let's see if the secrets of Jean Kerman's life can stand the test.'

FORTY-NINE

Next morning Candy rang The Gulf Stud to tell them he'd be there later in the afternoon. He came off the phone looking serious. 'What's up?'

'John Snell's back in hospital.'

'Who?'

'Snell, the vet who took over from Simon Nish, remember? He returned to work four days ago, now he's in hospital again, very ill, showing signs of heart failure.'

'You shouldn't have let him come back so soon. I thought they said it was exhaustion?'

'He wanted to. He seemed okay.' Candy slumped on a hard kitchen chair and rubbed his tired eyes. 'Jesus Christ! When are we going to get a break?'

Heart failure. That's what Dunn ultimately had died of, and so had Simon Nish. Now Snell.

I sat opposite Candy. 'Was he working on the mares?'

Candy nodded wearily.

I went to the phone and rang my mother at the hotel. She was surprised to hear from me so early in the day. 'Is anything wrong?' she asked.

'No, everything's all right. How's Father?'

She sighed quietly. 'Not much change.'

'Listen, Mum, did you have many mares abort this year in the early stages of pregnancy?'

She was quiet for a moment. 'Yes.'

'How many?'

'Quite a few.'

'More than usual?'

'Possibly three times as many. It was one of the reasons business was so bad.'

'Who treated all these mares?'

'Alex Dunn.'

I told her I'd call later and hung up. Candy watched me. 'What are you on to?' he asked.

'Your vets, Snell and the dead man, Simon Nish. Which brand of gloves did they use for examinations?'

He looked bewildered. 'Whatever we supplied them with at The Gulf, I suppose.'

I carried the phone to the table and handed him the receiver. 'Find out. Quickly.'

He dialed The Gulf Stud and asked the manager. Covering the mouthpiece, he said, 'Guterson's.'

'Tell him to stop using them immediately.'

He frowned at me.

'Go on!'

He told the manager to suspend all testing on mares, then slowly put down the phone and waited for an explanation.

'Just a hunch,' I said, 'a wild hunch. What makes mares abort?'

He shrugged. 'A number of factors.'

'What do vets use to clear out the uterus?'

'Prostaglandin.'

'What killed Alex Dunn?'

'Prostaglandin.'

'What would continued exposure of the skin surface to prostaglandin do to a man?'

'Kill him, I suppose, if he got enough of it. Or make him very ill.'

'Like John Snell and Simon Nish?'

He looked puzzled. 'I still don't get it.'

'Guterson's Gloves. What if they were impregnated with prostaglandin? It's a naturally occurring substance in mares, hence the reason that all the testing in the world wouldn't show up anything unusual. This way they get the mare and eventually the vet who's pulling on fifty gloves a day. What sort of prostaglandin dose does that add up to?'

He nodded silently, taking it in, then said, 'So why aren't mares aborting all over the country?'

'Because they're only impregnating selected batches. Dunn used Guterson's Gloves and he worked on my father's mares, which also showed a high abortion rate. I saw boxes of the gloves at his place and couldn't figure out at the time why they were under lock and key. He must have been trying them out on Father's mares.'

'What about the risk to himself?'

'Insufficient numbers, or more likely he'd have worn skin protection when using them.'

Candy shook his head and a smile slowly warmed his face as he gave me an admiring look. I was chuffed. Candy hurried to The Gulf Stud to arrange analysis of Guterson's Gloves.

He rang me within the hour, triumphant but angry. 'We've checked more than fifty gloves. Every single one is saturated with prostaglandin. Let's get that bastard Guterson!'

If I'd learned anything since that day five years ago when I'd been forced into amateur detective work, it was that cat skinning could indeed be done in several ways. I persuaded Candy it was pointless to go waving glove samples at the cops, asking for Guterson to be arrested. Although it seemed likely he was behind everything, we needed more evidence, especially about what we were now convinced were the killings of Kincaid, Dunn, Capshaw and Nish.

Also, it would have been nice to try to establish a motive for this madness. I thought it was time to pull in Jockey Club Security officially, and tried to persuade Candy we were close enough to cracking it to justify involving them. Maybe all I really wanted was an increased sense of personal safety. At the moment, it was Candy and me, and as the killings mounted, it was getting to feel more and more like we were defending the Alamo.

Candy put the blocks on me asking McCarthy. He was fearful things would drag on and that word about the Sheikh's stallions would get out. One thing we did agree on was that the man calling himself Rossington was the weak link in the chain. Strong circumstantial evidence pointed to him as Kincaid's killer, and if that was so, there was reason enough to assume he'd been involved in the deaths of Dunn and Capshaw.

I thought of Rossington's behaviour on the motorway, and concluded he'd known I was following him. The faxed mock-up of the newspaper article and Kerman's poorly veiled threat had come shortly after that. Rossington must have gone running straight back to tell them I'd been on his tail. I wondered how wise that had been from his viewpoint. Once I'd latched on to Dunn and Capshaw, they'd been killed. If the same policy was in force, then Rossington must be sleeping uneasily in his bed.

But who would they get to hit the hit man?

I called Candy. 'Have you still got those two heavies working for you, the ones who were using me as a yo-yo at the seaside?'

'They're available.'

'We need to pick up Rossington.'

'What do you mean, pick up?'

'For his own protection.' I explained my thinking but Candy was nervous. I said, 'Look, until we can prove Guterson's involved, and maybe Kerman, we need to keep Rossington alive. The guy is scared. If he's got any brains, he might welcome the chance of protection.'

Candy finally agreed to try to have Rossington picked up, by which time I was sure we'd know more about his real identity. Before hanging up I said, 'And, Candy, ask your guys to have a good look around Rossington's property for a blue vehicle with bull bars.'

FIFTY

There were still big gaps to be filled, like motive and Dunn's method.

The latter intrigued me. Whatever he'd done to the Sheikh's stallions, he'd done it in the racecourse stables, I was sure of that. It was the only time he'd had access to them. But whatever he'd treated them with had only been activated once they'd retired from racing. What the hell *had* he done, planted some sort of radio transmitter that could be switched on remotely?

I crossed my ankles, linked my hands behind my head and let everything I knew about Dunn run through my mind again. He'd been keen on experimenting with chemical castration, so we must assume he'd perfected something in that field that was undetectable. Then he'd had to test it, which he did on my father's stallion and on maybe half a dozen others, including Town Crier, in small studs around England.

But why? Why take that risk, the posing as an RSPCA man, the visits to different places? If the stuff needed road testing, he could easily have used it on my father's other three stallions. He'd buggered his business, so what difference would it have made to sterilize the other stallions? Whichever way I tilted it, I couldn't work it out.

I channeled my thoughts into filtering the hard facts. There were two definites: whatever he had used, he'd used it on Town Crier, and when he'd administered it, Fiona had been with him.

I rang the Corish Stud. Fiona answered. I asked how Martin was.

'Still drinking.'

'As much?'

'Almost, though he sleeps a lot now.' Her voice was flat, robotic.

'Are you all right?' I asked.

'Mmmm.'

I told her I wanted to come and see her to talk about Dunn's visit. She said she wasn't going anywhere.

By the time I reached the Corish Stud, the sun was low and insects buzzed among the trees. I stopped at the bungalow and watched the round figure of Fiona gathering washing from the line.

She told me Martin was asleep, passed out. She led the way to Town Crier's box. Standing in the gloom, the big horse seemed happy to see Fiona, but wary of my presence. I stood outside the box door. Fiona went in and rubbed his nose, clapped his neck, looking as if she was taking more comfort from it than the stallion was.

I said, 'Think hard about the day Alex Dunn came here, the tall guy posing as the RSPCA man. I need you to try and picture everything he did when he was checking Town Crier over.'

She looked vacantly at me for a while then shrugged. 'Just what you'd expect; he checked his coat and his teeth, his eyes, legs, feet, ears. He had me walk him round the box a couple of times. He took a blood sample.' She hesitated, frowned slightly. 'That did seem odd, seemed to take him longer than normal. Usually they whiz a syringe in under his neck and draw what they want. This seemed to take a few minutes and he worked on the other side of the horse, quite high up, for a sample.'

'What do you mean, the other side?'

'The side I couldn't see.'

'Were you holding him?'

'No. I suppose that was a bit strange too. He asked me to tie him up and stand by the door, saying he might get a bit fractious.'

'Quite high up, you said.'

She nodded, frowning again. Town Crier looked down at her as if to enquire what was wrong. She rubbed his nose. 'He seemed to be working under his mane.'

I moved into the box. 'Can you hold him, Fiona?' She gripped the halter. 'Which side?' I asked.

'Near side.'

I walked round, Town Crier's suspicious eyes following me, his muscles tensing. Fiona tightened her grip. I put both hands on his neck. He moved sideways. 'Whoah, boy. That's a good boy!' I said quietly, and kept up the horse talk as I ran my hands softly over every inch of his neck under his mane till, high up, just below the ridge where the hard hair starts growing, my middle finger came to rest on a small bump, a node the size of a pea.

I felt it, ran my index finger over it. It gave slightly, like a jelly capsule. We brought the horse out into what was left of the daylight and Fiona held the tuft of mane away. I could see no incision or damage to the hair around the bump, but that could easily have healed. I smiled and asked her to meet me back at the bungalow. By the time she returned, Candy was already on his way to check under the manes of the Sheikh's stallions.

I sat on the edge of the kitchen table, smiling stupidly. Fiona looked confused. I smiled wider, luxuriating in the feeling of having guessed correctly once again. It was a sensation I rarely experienced. Right on cue, at the height of my self-congratulation, the phone rang.

'Every fucking one of them! Exact same spot!'

'Yeehaaa!'

Fiona stared at me as though considering leaving quickly.

I said to Candy, 'Get them out and get them analyzed.'

'Already arranged! Results in under an hour!'

'You sound like an advert for Acme Pharmacies.'

'I feel like a glass of champagne.'

'Have one for me. I'll call you.'

Fiona stood open-mouthed. I smiled at her. 'You'd best close that before a fly gets in. Tomorrow I'm sending a vet to look at Town Crier. I'll let you know his name and I'll make sure he's carrying ID. If Martin sobers up sufficiently between now and then, tell him I think our problems are almost over.'

FIFTY-ONE

I left Wiltshire in the dusk and reached my parents' stud in darkness. My heart sang for most of the trip. The thought that my luck was running out kept entering my mind. I'd long ago learned the folly of tempting fate. But I prayed all the same, prayed that it would hold long enough to nail Kerman, to silence her, to save the secret.

Save the secret.

I didn't care about Guterson any more, or Rossington or Dunn or Capshaw. Or, to my shame, Brian Kincaid. I was obsessed with my own ends. At my parents' place, the phone was ringing as I turned the key in the lock. I ran inside. It was Candy. 'Can I come down there now?' he asked.

'Sure.'

'See you soon.'

It was almost midnight when he arrived, but Candy was bright-eyed, elated. He smelled of aftershave. 'You haven't shaved, at this time of night?' I asked.

He smiled, strong teeth white against the tan. 'Second shave of the day. Got to keep up appearances.'

'God save me from vanity!'

'He will.'

We sat down with a full teapot and two mugs, neither of us really wanting to risk a premature celebratory drink. Candy pulled a notepad from the pocket of his yellow polo shirt, and then dug in again to produce a small green capsule, which he rolled toward me.

I squeezed it between my fingers. It reminded me of a cod liver oil pill.

Candy said, 'Filled with a variant on methyl testosterone which Dunn must have concocted himself. They're still working on it, but the early verdict is that the chemical would lie dormant until set off by a surge of sexual activity, during which the increased testosterone levels play a dual part: they neutralize all traces of the drug in the system and they rapidly sterilize the sperm.'

'Hence the reason Dunn could pre-plant them in horses that were still racing, knowing they wouldn't take effect until the horse became sexually active.'

'Correct.'

'So yours were done in the racecourse stables as per the old list of visits, matey.' I smiled.

Candy returned it. 'You're a right bloody clever dick, aren't you?'

'Now all we need is the motive.'

'And the perpetrators.'

I nodded.

'Speaking of which,' Candy said, 'our boys picked Rossington up.'

'Where is he?'

'They're holding him at Dunn's old place at Six Mile Bottom.'

'Has he said anything?'

'They haven't asked him anything. We were sort of waiting for you.'

'Sort of?'

'Well, we were. I'm getting a wee bit nervous about it, to be honest. I think it's time we brought in the authorities.'

'The police?'

'Yes.'

'Not yet, Candy.'

'Why? We're in the clear.'

'You're in the clear. Your stallions will be operational again. But all we've got is one of the mugs. We need to get Guterson and whoever else is involved.'

He waved the suggestion away. 'Nah, the cops can do that.'

'The cops might fuck it up and I can't afford that!'

He looked surprised. 'Don't worry, Eddie. I'll make sure you're well paid.'

'I know you will, but it's not the money. You know I've got another interest in this that I can't tell you about. You can't dump everything just because your problems are solved!'

He lowered his eyes. 'Okay. I'm sorry. I forgot. What do you want to do with Rossington?'

'I'll go and see him tomorrow. Will those profiles on Guterson and Jean Kerman be ready?'

'I'll chase them in the morning.'

'Okay.'

'Right.' He got up. 'Brilliant. Well done, Eddie.'

'Save it till the fat lady's done an encore, Candy, I'm due a turn of bad luck.'

I walked with him to the door and watched him go out into the darkness. I lay in bed, luxuriating a while longer in the afterglow before settling down for what I hoped would be a rare peaceful night's rest.

In the middle of the night, the phone rang. Groggy with sleep, I didn't recognize McCarthy's voice at first. He had to introduce himself. 'I thought I'd best ring you straightaway. I've just been wakened by a call from Melbourne about your man Rossington.'

'Uhuh.' I was struggling to get my brain in gear.

'Remember, you gave me those pictures of him?'

'Yes, I remember.'

Mac told me what he'd learned and I extended the chain of early morning alarm calls by ringing Candy, though I gave him more time to come to his senses than Mac had given me.

'According to McCarthy's contacts in Melbourne, our man Rossington is a ghost. His real name is Paul Cantrell and his body was found on a road near Melbourne Airport in March last year in a hit and run incident very similar to the one in which Capshaw was killed. I've asked Mac to try to find out how positive the identification of Cantrell's corpse was. What would you like to bet that his face was badly disfigured?'

'You think the real Rossington was the hit and run victim?'

'A very convenient way to exchange identities. Cantrell was wanted by the police when he "died".'

'What for?'

'Armed robbery.'

'Shit!'

'Are your guys contactable at Dunn's place?'

'On mobile.'

'I think you'd best warn them Cantrell's a lot more dangerous than we thought.'

FIFTY-TWO

Exhaustion caught up with me and I slept late next morning, Candy's phone call rousing me at ten. 'Kerman and Guterson. We've got a connection by the look of things.'

'Uhuh?' I was still half-asleep.

'Should I bring the reports?'

'Sure, yeah, sure. I'll have a bath,' I said stupidly.

He arrived while I was still soaking and shouted through the letterbox. I wrapped a towel around me, let him in and told him to put the kettle on while I got dressed. He told me Rossington or Cantrell, whoever he was, was still securely locked up.

With my hair still wet, I sat at the table looking at the highlighted parts of the two reports Candy had brought.

Jean Kerman's maiden name was Prior. She was the daughter of Simeon Prior, the Triplecrown Chairman. Candy also had a breakdown on Triplecrown's business. They did everything from arranging matings to selling the subsequent foals, and in the past three years, turnover and profit had been on the slide.

When Bob Guterson acquired his 20 percent stake in Triplecrown, Simeon Prior had bought a 25 percent share in Guterson's Gloves.

I read it through again. 'Motive?' I said.

'Let me try this time,' Candy said, beaming. 'Triplecrown Bloodstock rose to prominence in the years when the Arabs were buying from them. They made millions. But now the Arabs are spending less and less as they build up their own breeding operation. Not only that, they're starting to do everything in-house and offer their facilities to other breeders. So Triplecrown hasn't lost only the Arabs' custom; all their other customers have the option of doing their business with the Arabs instead.'

I nodded, smiling. Candy went on, 'Simple solution for Triplecrown: smother the Arab operation at source by taking out the stallions.'

I applauded softly and Candy looked chuffed. 'Now prove it,' I said.

'Rossington will snitch to save his skin.'

'I doubt it. He's none to save. It's likely he's killed three men, at least. No plea-bargain there.'

Candy looked flustered. 'Okay, but he won't take the rap on his own. He'll take the others with him.'

I smiled. '"Take the rap?" You've been watching those old Edward G. Robinson films again, haven't you?'

'Well, you know what I mean.'

'I do, and you might be right, but we can't chance it and the police won't just take his word for it anyway. We'll need something more concrete, something that definitely incriminates Guterson and Prior.'

'Surely there's enough circumstantial evidence?'

'Where? All you've laid out is based on assumption, pure theory. There isn't a single piece of solid evidence linking Guterson, Prior or Kerman.' I said.

'It's obvious that Triplecrown would have the strongest of motives to—

'And what about Town Crier and Heraklion and the other half-dozen stallions at the smaller studs? Where's Triplecrown's interest there?'

He shrugged, confused. 'Red herrings. Decoys set up for exactly this type of situation, so they can use it in their defense. You know how well they've planned this, Eddie!'

'I know I'm only playing Devil's Advocate. You're probably right but how do we prove it?'

'We've got to get this guy Rossington, or whatever he's called, to talk.'

'But how?'

The phone rang. It was Martin. I was surprised. He sounded bright and sober. 'Fiona tells me we might be out of the woods,' he said.

'Not quite. We can see the edge of the trees.'

'How long do you reckon?'

'I don't know. Soon. A couple of days, maybe.'

'Anything I can do?'

The question provoked a sudden surge of anger in me. Martin had been unable to hack it when things got tough. Now here he was offering help because he thought it was almost over. I was tempted to concoct something dangerous and ask him to deal with it, but I resisted. 'If there's anything I can think of, I'll call you. It might be best if you stay off the booze for a day or two in case I do need you.'

He laughed. 'Sure. Keep me informed, eh?'

'Okay.' I returned to the table. Candy had been thinking. 'Maybe it *is* just Guterson. Maybe it was his stake in the company that made him set this up.'

'So how come Prior's daughter so effectively removes three of the possible stumbling blocks to the success of the whole thing in Campbell, Summerville and the EFU vet guy, what do you call him?'

'Spenser.'

'Yeah.'

Candy looked thoughtful. 'Good point.'

'I know, but having said that you can bet your boots Prior's kept his own hands lily white. Jean Kerman and Guterson will have done the high-level dirty work and Rossington the basics.' We sat around for an hour trying to figure some way to trap Guterson and the others. Martin's offer of help sparked an idea. I called him. He'd gone to the pub. I spoke to Fiona. 'Do you remember that guy Spindari, the one we had you make a phone call to when he was trying to blackmail us?'

'I remember.'

'Do you still have his phone number?'

'I'm not sure. I can probably find it.'

'Good, here's what I want you to do.'

Fiona called back within half an hour. 'He'll be here at two-thirty.'

'Fine. We'll see you then.'

FIFTY-THREE

When Candy and I walked into the office at the Corish Stud, the tall, dark and handsome Simon Spindari seemed to lose some of his Latin colour, not to mention his composure. He turned on Fiona. 'You little bitch! You said you had a good story for me!' Smiling, I said, 'We have, Simon, we have. Sit yourself down.' Glowering, he sat on the chair by the desk and swept the thick hair away from his eyes. 'Thanks, Fiona,' I said, and she left without looking at Spindari.

I explained that we knew everything about his blackmail attempt way back at the beginning, and he agreed to cooperate if we promised not to tell the police what he'd been doing. He admitted having 'investigated' a couple of other cases for Jean Kerman and said she still contacted him from time to time.

I told him what he had to do and watched as he made the call to Kerman, telling her he had a brilliant story for her about a guy named Paul Cantrell who was impersonating a certain man on British racecourses, and that if Kerman wanted the details she should meet Spindari in a pub in Newmarket and he'd take her to Cantrell.

'Incidentally,' he said, acting it out well. 'The guy he's impersonating is probably dead! How's that for an exclusive?' As I'd expected, Kerman didn't ask too many questions. She agreed the time and place, a popular pub on a country road not far from Dunn's place at 7 o'clock. Spindari arranged to meet her in the beer garden.

By 6.30 McCarthy, Candy and I were concealed in the woods behind the beer garden. Spindari sat at a white table sipping lager in the evening sunshine and reading a newspaper. At 6.50, a big blue BMW with smoked glass windows purred into the car park of the pub. Jean Kerman, wearing a tight black two-piece, got out of the back and walked toward Spindari's table. He saw her coming, smiled and reached into the pocket of his jeans as though to go and buy her a drink. Kerman shook her head and spoke animatedly.

Spindari pointed to the half-full lager glass and sat down again. Kerman turned to look at the car. The passenger door opened and a fat man in a dark grey suit hauled himself out and hurried forward. He was completely bald. Mac whispered, 'Guterson.' Candy and I smiled.

We crept backward through the trees to where our car was parked, and then headed for Dunn's place.

Within ten minutes of our arrival, we watched from inside the bungalow as the BMW slowed and pulled into the driveway. Each of us moved into position. I stood by the edge of the curtains at the side window, hidden, I hoped, from view.

Car doors clunked closed. 'Two heavies,' I warned everyone. In the corner, Phil and Don grinned. I watched Spindari, still smiling and playing the fool a bit, chatting to them as he approached the porch door. He knocked loudly. McCarthy was behind it and opened it almost immediately.

We could hear his voice along the hall and I could see reactions on some of the faces: bafflement, shock. I heard Mac say, 'Mister Guterson, how nice to see you again.' And I watched Guterson offer a very tentative hand. Mac shook it and stepped aside. 'And Mrs Kerman, always first on a hot story. Do come in.' Kerman turned and glared at Spindari.

The two heavies looked at each other, seeming unsure if they should be on red alert. All five filed in past Mac. 'This way,' he said, and led them right in among us in the living room. Kerman and Guterson looked around at me, Candy, Phil and Don, bewilderment giving way to anger then worry on both their faces.

Still smiling, Mac said, 'I think you both know Mister Malloy and Mister Loss. These other two gentlemen are from Cambridge CID.' Phil and Don smiled and nodded pleasantly. Kerman turned and looked at Guterson, whose face and head were reddening by the second. He reached up to loosen his gaudy tie.

Mac said, 'Now maybe your chaps and Mister Spindari could go into the kitchen and have a nice cup of tea. Would you both like one?' Kerman and Guterson shook their heads in unison.

'Coffee?' Mac offered pleasantly. He was better at this than I'd expected.

'No, thanks!' Kerman said bitterly.

Phil and Don walked forward. 'We'll show you where the kitchen is.' Guterson turned to his guys and nodded. They left. A smiling Spindari followed. They went to the kitchen and closed the door. A few moments later Phil and Don rejoined us. Mac said to Kerman and Guterson, 'There's one person you haven't met yet, if you'd like to come this way?' He moved along the hall toward the office, saying, 'Well, you have met him but not today.' Candy and I followed.

Mac turned the key and eased the door open. Kerman and Guterson moved into the doorway to look. I watched their faces go pale as Mac said, 'Mister Ken Rossington, alias Paul Cantrell.'

He closed and locked the door again before anyone could speak and we all returned to the living room. Kerman sat down on a chair, straight-backed, knees clamped, looking defiant, but Guterson slumped on the sofa, beaten and dejected.

Mac pulled some papers from his inside pocket. He looked at Guterson. 'Cantrell spent much of yesterday dictating this statement to our CID friends here.' Mac started reading everything Candy and I had put together, all the theories starting from Kerman's setting up of Ben Campbell, Summerville and Spenser through to the recruiting of Dunn and his methods of implanting the horses.

Every so often Kerman would splutter, 'Nonsense! Ridiculous!'

But when Mac started listing the dates that Dunn had visited the racecourse stables and implanted the Sheikh's horses, she seemed finally to give up, physically to deflate as though the weight of evidence had crushed the fight from her.

Shaking his head, Guterson said to no one in particular, 'Cantrell didn't know half of this. How the hell...?'

Kerman glared at him. 'He was obviously a damn sight smarter than you thought, you stupid bastard!'

Guterson was still shaking his head. 'But why? Why drop himself in it after what he's done?' He grunted then as he pushed himself to his feet, becoming more animated as the instinct for self-preservation took over. He went toward Phil and Don and said, 'Look, I don't know what else is in that statement but I was only acting as an agent for Simeon Prior. He's the main man. He thought the whole thing up.'

'Shut up!' Kerman yelled. 'Shut up, you silly bastard!' Guterson said, 'Ignore her, she's his daughter!'

Then began a long cursing argument, all of which was caught on tape along with everything else that had been said. Mac excused himself politely and went to call a police inspector he knew in Cambridge.

A proper one.

FIFTY-FOUR

The cops had to let Guterson's heavies go, as they'd done nothing. When Guterson, Kerman and Cantrell were being led out, Kerman turned to me, spite contorting her face. 'You'll regret this for the rest of your life, Malloy!'

I smiled. 'I don't think that even *The Examiner* will publish your stuff anymore, Mrs Kerman.'

'There'll be someone else, don't worry.'

And there was.

The Examiner made no announcement about the departure of Jean Kerman. It simply trumpeted the arrival of the most 'exciting voice in investigative journalism: Cynthia Clarke. Look out for her debut story on Wednesday which will shock the racing world'.

Cynthia Clarke rang me on Monday evening just after I'd returned from visiting my father, who seemed coldly determined now to stay in hospital as long as he could. He'd been moved to a new ward and had effectively trained Mother into this routine where she was with him for more than half the day, coming and going at his bidding.

Clarke was quiet-voiced, polite but unshakeable. She told me there was a story on file which she planned to run on Wednesday and she wanted to make sure I was aware of the contents, and to give me 'a chance to comment'.

She read it through to me and though I knew it word for word, my heart dropped a step closer to hell with every line she spoke. I told her that I thought that *The Examiner* was the last paper to be moralizing, bearing in mind the charges its previous columnist now faced. But Clarke was unmoved. 'It's news, I'm afraid, Mister Malloy. If we don't run it, someone else will. Now can I speak to your father?'

'He's very ill. If this story runs it could kill him.'

'Is he in hospital?'

My hopes rose for a moment. 'Yes.'

'Which one?'

'Will you put a hold on the story?'

'I can't, but I must give him the chance to comment.'

'He won't comment. Doesn't it make any difference to you that this might kill him?'

'I'm only doing a job, Mister Malloy.'

'I'd rather shovel shit!' I said, and banged the phone down, that familiar feeling of desolation engulfing me quickly. Filled with impotent rage, I drove at speed to the hospital to warn my mother.

We sat in the coffee lounge. She looked completely worn out. 'Is there anything we can do?' she asked weakly.

I shook my head. She bowed hers, accepting defeat for the first time in her life, then unexpectedly her hand reached across the tabletop for mine. Gently I clasped the warm, wrinkled skin, the fragile bones, and squeezed softly. Her head was down and a tear dripped silently into her lap.

I arranged to be with her at the hospital when the paper was due out on Wednesday. She warned Father about it, and suddenly he decided he'd discharge himself on Tuesday afternoon. He couldn't bear the thought of everyone at the hospital knowing.

First thing Wednesday I drove to a petrol station where nobody knew me and bought a copy of the newspaper. It was on the front page. I folded the paper and headed for the derelict farm Candy and I had used as a meeting place.

I got out of the car and went to lean against the ruined wall. The sun was beginning to warm the morning, but inside I was cold as I opened the paper. There was a smiling picture of me under a banner headline: Top Jockey 'Killed' His Brother.

"The father of top jump jockey Eddie Malloy believes Malloy killed his younger brother, Michael. When Malloy was just ten years old and living on a farm near Penrith, Cumbria, he was in charge of young Michael, six, when the child fell into a swollen river and was swept away.

Eddie Malloy, apparently unable to face his parents with the terrible news, returned home to tell them Michael had disappeared into the woods. It was two days before Malloy admitted to police and search parties what had happened.

Edward Malloy Snr. has always believed that had Eddie acted immediately to report his brother's fate, Michael could have been saved."

The story was continued on page three. Dry-mouthed and shaking, I turned to it with a picture in my mind of a million others doing the same thing.

"Malloy Snr.'s resentment of his eldest son led to the boy becoming an outcast. He was cruelly banished from his parents' house and sent to live with the horses in the stable block. For the next six years, the young Malloy's bed was among straw bales and his only companions were the horses he came to love and trust.

His mother, Constance, brought him meals three times a day in a regime that was almost prison-like. But there was to be no remission for the frightened ten-year-old. Malloy Snr. duped the local authorities into believing that his son was being educated at home.

But the only education Eddie found was in the racing books his mother smuggled out to him during the early period of his 'imprisonment', a privilege that stopped the moment his father found out about it.

The boy's misery ended on his sixteenth birthday when he was finally banished permanently from the farm and sent out to make his own way in the world.

But the years of living so close to horses served Malloy well, and maybe today he looks back with less resentment than some might expect. Within a week of being thrown out, he took a job with the late Peter Sample, a top trainer in Lambourn, and less than five years later he was champion National Hunt Jockey.

Eddie Malloy's parents now run a small stud in Newmarket where they've lived for…"

Clarke rambled on about my parents and how deep and damaging family rifts could be. Tell me about it, Cynthia. Tell the whole world about it. You just have.

I sat on the wall staring at the front-page headline, at the colour picture of me smiling and punching the air as I came in on Cragrock at Haydock, the first big race winner after my comeback.

There I was three years ago, jubilant, delirious.

Here I was now, ashamed, empty, desolate.

I stood staring into the distance. The sun was well up, drying the night's rain from the surrounding fields and raising a beautiful smell of freshness and newness. Away to my right, the road stretched straight and tempting toward the horizon, and I wished to God that I was in one of those old cowboy movies and could just get in the saddle and ride off to where nobody could ever find me.

Ride off to wherever our Michael was and tell him what I'd longed to tell him since that terrible day when I heard him shout and looked down through the thick branches of the tree I'd climbed, and sat there in horror, rooted as surely as the tree itself, unable to move as his fair head bobbed on the surface, as his little hands reached and scrabbled at the morning air. I could hear him crying in panic and confusion as he wondered what was happening to him and why his big brother wasn't there to help him, to save him, to pull him out.

Sometimes he'd come to me in dreams and tell me it was all right, tell me he'd died quickly and quietly after a few minutes in the water, tell me that he didn't blame me for what I'd done, tell me that heaven was a great place for kids, tell me that he loved me, tell me that someday he'd see me again.

And I'd tell him I was sorry.

'I'm sorry, Michael…'

An animal-like howl rose from my chest and burst from my throat, and my legs gave way as I slid slowly down the side of the wall to lie slumped and weeping uncontrollably by the front wheel of the car.

I don't know how long I lay there, but somehow I hauled myself up and drove, weak and shocked, to my parents' place, carrying the newspaper into the house as though it was the corpse of our Michael himself.

FIFTY-FIVE

The most heartening thing over the next week or so was the level of support everywhere from people I hardly knew. The warmth was unexpected and welcome. My parents didn't fare quite so well. There were a number of terrible phone calls and poisonous letters, and no matter how much they'd tried to prepare themselves, the shock was nightmarish.

My father never recovered from it. His health deteriorated steadily throughout the autumn. On the 2nd of December, he died in that prison-like room. My mother and I were there, and my sister Marie came back. She too had been scarred by what happened all those years ago. Her exile had been self-imposed.

Guterson, Simeon Prior and Cantrell are on remand, charged with the murders of Brian Kincaid, Alex Dunn and William Capshaw. Jean Kerman was released on substantial bail. Brian Kincaid's widow, Judy, made his funeral a true celebration of the life of a very good man. Afterwards, her concern for me showed in weekly telephone calls, and Judy has become as good a friend to me as Brian was.

Martin's been off the booze for over two months and tells me he can't wait for the birth of his baby. Candy's a changed man, too. Alive again, happy, looking forward to the new breeding season as I guess his stallions are.

Things are going well for me. Charles's horses are back to their best. I've ridden 67 winners for him so far.

My mother, at last, is showing signs of becoming her own person. Marie and I have stayed with her since Father died. On Christmas Eve, we travelled to Cumbria to visit our Michael's grave. In the early frost we stood in silence, facing the grey marble with my brother's name carved deep. My mother, standing between my sister and me, reached for our hands. A family again, what was left of us, but finally, I felt a sense of peace.

AN EXCERPT FROM RUNNING SCARED, BOOK 4 IN THE EDDIE MALLOY SERIES

ONE

Broga Cates...now there was a man. His first name was from old Anglo Saxon and it meant "terror". Up until he died, he was well named. After that, he became a pussycat.

Charles Tunney, a struggling racehorse trainer, had been at Eton with Broga. He introduced me to the big coffee-coloured character in the paddock at Aintree after I'd won a race.

'Eddie, this is Broga Cates. He's got more sense than money, unfortunately for me as I'm trying to persuade him to buy a horse.'

About six foot six, with a head of rich luxuriant black hair, Broga would have looked more at home on a rugby field than a racecourse. I shook hands and said, 'So Charles can't talk you into burning your cash on these animals?'

Broga smiled. 'My daddy told me many useful things, among them was this: "never buy anything that eats while you're asleep."'

I shrugged and turned to Charles. 'You can hardly argue with that?'

Charles said to Broga, 'You need to spend your money on something. No pockets in a shroud and all that.'

'I'm not planning to die anytime soon though Charlie.'

Well, he got that bit wrong.

Big as he was, probably pushing twenty-five stones plus, Broga fancied himself as a badminton player. When he heard I used to play the game at school, he invited me to his Cotswold mansion for a match. Charles was to referee it.

Broga rolled onto court wearing an orange T-shirt half the size of the net. But his belly wasn't sticking out, and his thighs in white shorts were muscular. Still, at twenty-nine I was fifteen years younger and close to fifteen stones lighter. And I was an athlete wasn't I, a supremely fit jockey?

'How much are we playing for?' I asked, cocky.

'You want to bet?'

'You bet I want to bet!'

'I will whup your skinny ass Malloy!'

'Well flash the cash, big man!'

I glanced at Charles and he was doing that kind of pursed-mouth, head-shaking, wide-eyed thing which was meant to warn me off. But I laughed.

'A hundred a game?' I offered.

'You're on Mister Malloy. Prepare to meet my boom.'

I smiled and served.

I'm sure he didn't move his feet. I was aware only of a graceful sway, a low dip, a soft scoop of his racket and the shuttle landing my side about a centimetre from the net.

It was like one of those times in a race where you cruise up confidently to some old chaser who looks to be struggling, only to find that your horse doesn't have what you thought it had.

I failed to win a point and on the last rise of his racket, as he was about to put me out of my misery, Broga grunted, gasped, dropped his racket, staggered back, his arms behind him seeking something solid, then hit the wooden floor. The force with which he landed sent vibrations across the boards to my feet.

Charles reached him first. He was already doing CPR by the time I got there.

His heart didn't work again until twenty-three minutes later when the paramedics jump-started it with a defibrillator.

Charles and I had kept his heart and lungs doing some kind of job using CPR. It saved his life and changed ours. Big time.

TWO

Broga was a Bajan, born in Barbados to an English father and a mother who described herself as Persian Irish. The Cates family went back a long way in Barbados; they'd owned plantations since the 17th century. Then they got into lots of businesses and ended up with more pies than they had fingers to stick in them.

Broga was bred to succeed. Educated at Eton and Oxford, he took over the family corporation on his thirtieth birthday, and blasted through it like a Caribbean hurricane. When four men huffed and puffed and hauled him into an ambulance that day, his worth on paper was north of three hundred million sterling.

He was in surgery that night and out of hospital in a week. The first thing he did was invite Charles and me to his Cotswold estate for what he called a 'thank you' dinner. It was close to the end of the season so I could afford a calorie blow out and Broga did us proud.

But he kept the big thank-you to last. When our cognac glasses were filled and the cigars produced, Broga said, 'Gentlemen, shall we retire to the bathroom?'

We laughed. Broga sat still and said, 'I'm serious. Come on!' He got up and shoved the cigar between his teeth so he could beckon us with a free hand. Charles and I slid our chairs away and followed him, not questioning this crazy man who'd been transformed by a brief death.

The bathroom wasn't much smaller than the badminton court. There were two shower areas, a sauna, steam room, a sunken bath and two other old-fashioned baths on legs. He led us to the sunken bath, tiled in sky-blue, yellow, and big enough for a swimming gala. 'Get in,' Broga said.

Charles and I looked at each other then at the big man. Charles said, 'No chance. We get in and you turn on the taps or blast some water through the floor or something.'

'I won't. I promise,' Broga said, holding out his right hand toward the steps.

I said, 'Should we take our drinks and cigars in?'

'Please do.' That big white-toothed smile.

I went first. Charles, shaking his head, followed and we sat on the second of the four tiered steps. Broga towered over us and, half-drunk, I was reminded of some old Frankie Howerd film about Roman senators and crazy parties.

'Close your eyes gentlemen.' Broga said.

We were too far in to question it. When Charles closed his, I closed mine.

We heard Broga's heels click, then footsteps returning. 'You can look when you want,' the big man said and as we opened our eyes, a waterfall of bank notes tumbled over us, each sharp-edged and new. The smell, the crispness, the sheer volume engulfed us, setting us laughing and dancing as they steadily filled till we waded knee-high, kicking them up in clouds, throwing up armfuls to open like fragmented parachutes and drift down on us.

When the deluge stopped, the six smiling girls who'd been emptying huge bags, the type builders use for rubble, threw the three empty bags in the air and joined us in laughter till the room echoed as though some mad orchestra had been let loose.

Broga helped us out. He looked happiest of all of us. 'If you haven't seen five million pounds in brand new tenners, you have now. I'm going to gather it all back up and you...' he turned to Charles, '...are going to take it and buy me a stable full of horses, and you Mister Malloy, are going to ride them all for me.'

Charles gazed up at him and said, 'I told you I'd nag you to death to buy a horse!'

So Broga gave Charles a free hand in setting us all up for next season. He started by purchasing two hundred acres of Shropshire countryside surrounding a failed holiday complex. That appealed to Broga. He said that once we were settled he might resurrect the holiday side and build luxury cabins.

In the meantime, he converted a barn overlooking the stableyard, into a block of apartments for Charles's staff. I got first pick and chose The Penthouse, as Broga called it, giving me views over ancient woodland as well as into the heart of the yard below. The sounds and smells of racehorses were only an open window away.

Charles lived in the old manor house at the south side of the quadrangle of stableblocks. At night, when the horses were quiet, the sounds of Mahler's music, of laughter and often the clink of whiskey glasses could be heard. I learned to treasure those days and evenings of that first summer. I'd be thirty soon and was becoming conscious of time moving faster, of life getting away from me.

Racing had taught me the dangers of complacency, of tempting fate. But a couple of drinks with Charles as twilight blanketed us on a still and scented evening in the garden, would lead me to dwell on the belief that things had finally turned for me. For me, for him, for all of us lucky enough to be in that blessed place at that blessed time. Maybe my troubles were over.

Will I ever learn?

THREE

I knelt on the Worcester turf watching consciousness return to one of my old friends, Bill Keating. He'd hit the ground a few seconds after I had fallen at the fence farthest from the grandstands. As I rose, cursing, to watch my mount gallop away, Bill pulled his horse up on the way to the next jump. As he slowed the big gelding to walking pace, he slid off and lay still. I ran to him.

The ambulance, which always follows us in a race, had passed, only the roof in view through its dust wake as it tracked the galloping pack turning for home. They'd slowed when I fell but I'd risen quickly and waved them on.

As I crouched over Bill, everyone's focus would be on the finish of the race, but the Stewards would want to know why Bill had pulled up a horse travelling well, especially as it had started a short-priced favourite.

He stared at me. I eased his goggles off. Still he struggled to recognize me, to work out what was happening. 'Bill. Bill. It's Eddie.'

I saw my reflection in his pupils on this bright late September day. I undid his helmet strap. 'Eddie,' he said, 'what happened?'

'You fell off. You looked like you were pulling him up then you just slid off and hit the ground like a sack of spuds.'

'Fuck. Get me up.'

'Lie there for now. The medics will be here in a couple of minutes.'

'No! Get me up, Eddie, get me up!' He tried to turn on his front and push himself onto hands and knees, his blue and white checked silks smeared with dirt.

'Lie there, you daft bugger! This has been going on for too long. You need to get some help!'

He reached for me, looking desperate. 'Just this once, Eddie, please! Please! I won't ask again.'

I helped him to his feet. He swayed, eyes closing again. I grabbed his arms. 'I'm okay, honest, I'm okay.'

'You're not okay. What's wrong? You're the colour of boiled shit and have been for weeks. Blakey told me he found you staring at your car keys yesterday. Then you asked him what they were for. Tell me what's wrong with you.'

'I'll tell you, Eddie. I will. I just need you to stick up for me in the Stewards' Room.'

'Lie for you, you mean.'

He put his hands on my shoulders as though trying to get my full attention, but he had much of his weight on them and I had to brace to stop from being pushed back. He was like a drunk, but he held my gaze with his brown eyes. 'I'd do it for you, Eddie.'

I knew he would. 'Okay mate.' I said.

He smiled, that familiar four-tooth gap in the centre of his much battered mouth, and I softened. In his face, I saw my own in ten years' time. And I saw Bill's life. His two decades of riding steeplechasers, mostly moderate ones, setting out with the same dreams of stardom we all had, then, with each dragging season, with every poor-jumping slowcoach plodding through cold mud and freezing rain, those stars drift further and further away until they're beyond reach.

And you quit.

Or you stay. You stay because all the excitement you've known, every burst of adrenaline, has come from riding horses over jumps. The men who have surrounded you each day in changing rooms up and down the country, are the closest and most understanding of friends. You've never needed to explain your life to them because it is their life too, all consuming. What is there left when you can no longer ride?

Whatever was wrong with Bill Keating, my bond with him was strong. He'd mentored me as a kid and he'd revelled in my success. As I had galloped on through my early career, my stars still within reach, there had been no envy, no regrets from Bill, just warmth and congratulations.

With my arm around his waist and his over my shoulder, we started the long walk to the weighing room. As we crouched to go under the rail onto the ambulance track, I grabbed a small rock and used it to scar the right lens of Bill's goggles.

In the Stewards' Room, I told the officials I'd seen a large clod of earth fly up from the hooves of the group Bill was following. I said it had hit Bill in the face. Bill produced his scratched goggles and said there'd been a big stone in the clump of turf. Our final joint lie was telling them Bill hadn't lost consciousness. If you're knocked out in a fall, you get an automatic suspension. Bill had recently divorced and could ill afford the loss of a few riding fees.

So I covered up for Bill Keating. After racing, I walked with him to his old Fiat. It was an effort for him to hoist his kitbag onto the seat. 'Bill, you look like death warmed up. Why don't you come back with me? You can sleep at my place?'

Leaning on the wing of his car, Bill reached out and squeezed my arm. 'Thanks Eddie. Amy's eight today. I promised I'd be there for her party tonight.'

'Then, I'll drive you to Lambourn.'

He smiled wearily, 'I'll be fine, honest. I'll stop if I need to but once I'm sat down, I'll feel better.'

'Look, do you want me to arrange for a doctor to see you privately? I'm owed a few favours. It'll be no names no pack drill, I promise.'

He looked at me for a while and I realized he knew what was wrong with him. 'I'll think about it, Eddie. Thanks. And thanks for today. I know who my friends are.'

Bill pulled away through the car park dust into the late afternoon, and I never saw him alive again. His birthday girl, daughter Amy, found him dead that night in the stall of a horsebox.

Thank you for buying Blood Ties. If you enjoyed it, we'd be grateful if you'd write a review of the book online.

We plan to publish a new title every three months. If you'd like to be notified when each is released, please visit our website – pitmacbooks.com, or follow us on twitter - @pitmacbooks.

Best wishes
Richard and Joe

Printed in Great Britain
by Amazon